PRAISE FOR THE DUMPL

PUMPKIN

★ "With her signature blend of humor, sensitivity, and panache, Murphy has crafted a sensational narrative that is bursting with life and is anything but a drag. Murphy's best-selling Dumplin' series grows bigger and better with every installment." —ALA *Booklist* (**starred review**)

★ "Winning." —Shelf Awareness (**starred review**)

"Full of inspiration, fabulousness, and romance. Enticing as homemade pumpkin pie. Bon appétit!"—*Kirkus Reviews*

"Tackling heavy topics with humor, this novel touches on the importance of staying true to yourself even (and especially) when it's hard." —*SLJ*

"Leaves readers cheering for Waylon, his Clover City cohort, and any kids taking a chance to be their full selves right now." —*BCCB*

"A celebration of individuality and self-expression." —*The Horn Book Magazine*

PUDDIN'

"I am wildly in love with *Puddin'*." —Becky Albertalli, award-winning author of *Simon vs. the Homo Sapiens Agenda*

★ "Murphy's plot brims with unlikely friendships, irresistible romance, fabulous fat acceptance, and a kick-ass ending. Buoying." —*Kirkus Reviews* (**starred review**)

DUMPLIN'

★ "Splendid." —ALA *Booklist* (**starred review**)

★ "Harmonious, humorous, and thought-provoking." —*Publishers Weekly* (**starred review**)

Also by Julie Murphy

Side Effects May Vary

Ramona Blue

Dumplin'

Puddin'

Faith: Taking Flight

Faith: Greater Heights

Dear Sweet Pea

PUMPKIN

JULIE MURPHY

Balzer + Bray
An Imprint of HarperCollins*Publishers*

For Alessandra. My friend, my editor, and a true queen. Meow.

Balzer + Bray is an imprint of HarperCollins Publishers.

Pumpkin
Copyright © 2021 by Julie Murphy
All rights reserved. Printed in the United States of America.
No part of this book may be used or reproduced in any manner
whatsoever without written permission except in the case of
brief quotations embodied in critical articles and reviews. For
information address HarperCollins Children's Books, a division of
HarperCollins Publishers, 195 Broadway, New York, NY 10007.
www.epicreads.com

Library of Congress Control Number: 2020952898
ISBN 978-0-06-288046-8

Typography by Aurora Parlagreco
22 23 24 25 26   PC/LSCH   10 9 8 7 6 5 4 3 2 1
❖
First paperback edition, 2022

People who used to make fun are now fans. I had the last laugh.
—Divine

Listen, drag doesn't change who you are,
it actually reveals who you are.
—RuPaul

It's hard to be a diamond in a rhinestone world.
—Dolly Parton

ONE

Ten years from now, when someone asks me how to survive life as a fat gay kid in a small West Texas town, I will tell them to become best friends with the school nurse. I learned from a very young age that the best way to brave the mean streets of Clover City was to endear myself to as many adults as humanly possible. Sure, being made fun of behind my back doesn't exactly fill me with joy, but if being teacher's pet saves me from merciless lunchroom politics, swirlies, black eyes, and boys chock-full of toxic masculinity, I'll gladly do my time.

"Ms. Laverne!" I call with a fresh cafeteria churro in my fist. "It was shirts and skins day again," I mutter just loudly enough for her to hear. "The shirts don't fit and I resent that showing skin is my only other option." I mean, honestly, if I'm going to show skin in gym class, it will be because I want to and have deemed the gym class worthy of my skin. Not because it's my only option during our basketball unit. Frankly, the fact that I've lasted through all four years of high school without having to once don a shirt or strip to skins is a testament to my resolve and inventiveness. That's the kind of thing colleges should be looking for in prospective students.

The nurse's office is empty as far as I can see, the curtain around the cot drawn shut. I creep closer, careful not to let my gym shoes squeak against the linoleum. Knowing Ms. Laverne, she's taking a little afternoon siesta—and with only two months left in the school year, who could blame her?

I yank the curtain back and say, "Wakey, wakey!"

Ms. Laverne, who stands with her back to me, shrieks and twirls around, her gloved hands holding a jar of ointment and a wooden applicator.

The churro falls from my hands and hits the floor as I let out a gasp. Sitting right there on the cot without an ever-loving shirt on is Tucker Watson. He's got the kind of farmer's tan that I should find totally gross, leaving lines around his arms and neck so that his skin transitions from white to whiter. His medium-brown hair is freshly cut, and it's the kind of hair that really needs an extra inch or two to adequately express itself. When he's past due for a trip to the barber, you can see wild waves start to take shape. With eyes more gray than blue and full lips that only seem to smirk or slightly frown, he might seem a bit on the boyish side if it weren't for his tall, muscular frame. Not that I've noticed.

"Um, wow. I am so sorry. I thought that—you wanna know what? I'm going to wait in the hallway." And die. I'm going to go out into the hallway and die and then I'm going to tear open the floor with a jackhammer and dig my own grave. I'll spend my afterlife haunting the halls of Clover City High and warning all the other quietly gay boys that straight boys won't love them back and that there is probably a whole great, wide world out there to discover full of perfectly suitable bachelors and dream careers. But I will never know, because I am dead. I am dead in the hallways of CCHS.

"Yes, Waylon," says Ms. Laverne. "Why don't you go ahead and wait out in the hallway for me? I'm nearly done with Tucker."

Tucker smirks, because of course, and the way his two bottom teeth gap a little makes my guts rumble. To Tucker, I'm just Waylon, the same kid he's gone to school with since we were hugging our respective moms' legs as they dropped us off for our first day of kindergarten and the same guy he ditched mid–group project sophomore year. I try not to travel outside of my own very small social circle, and group projects are a perfect reminder of why I shouldn't ever bother.

I wait out in the hall, and surprisingly, I do not die. A few minutes later, Ms. Laverne opens the door, and Tucker and I do an awkward tango as he tries to exit and I try to enter.

"Excuse me," I grumble, my voice way deeper than it normally is.

"Sorry," he grunts without bothering to make eye contact with me.

I don't even try to respond before Ms. Laverne shuts the door, because if I open my mouth, I might hiss at him.

Ms. Laverne, a Black woman around the age of my grammy with soft brown walnut-shaped eyes and the most perfect Cupid's bow I've ever seen, plops down on the cot. I take her chair, twirling in a circle, like I'm some kind of office chair figure skater. (I can find the glamour in anything. My twin sister, Clementine, swears it's a gift.)

Shaking her head, Ms. Laverne says, "You really did drop that piping-hot churro on my floor, didn't you?"

I sigh. "And Gloria said it was their last one. Life is a series of tragedies."

She lies back and crosses her ankles, her feet clad in bright white orthopedic shoes as they dangle off the edge. God, those things look comfortable. Why do all shoes that are basically pillows for your feet always have to be ugly? Is it some sort of sick universal law? Today Ms. Laverne's hair is a wavy dark-brown bob with a few golden highlights. My first favorite thing about Ms. Laverne is her willingness to give me safe harbor. My second favorite thing about Ms. Laverne is her rotating collection of wigs.

"Shirts and skins in PE class, huh?" asks Ms. Laverne.

I nod.

"Life really is a series of tragedies," she confirms.

TWO

Clem and I are twins who have been raised with one universal truth: when you're a twin, nothing is entirely your own. And for our sixteenth birthday, my parents demonstrated this by giving us every teenager's dream gift: a car.

Of course, our parents would see no problem in giving us one single car. To share. The truck—or Beulah, as we have lovingly named her—is a cobalt-blue single-cab hand-me-down that was once Dad's work truck. Since Clem barely passed the driving test—and in a rather traumatic fashion—she only drives when she absolutely has to. So I am her eternal designated driver. Still, this clunker of a vehicle is 50 percent hers, which is why I'm sitting in the parking lot waiting for my sister, who is waiting for her girlfriend.

Yeah, you heard that right. My twin sister is a lover of the ladies. Our parents basically hit the queer lottery.

"Clem!" I shout out the driver's side window. "Clementine!"

She twirls around at the front of the parking lot, her mouth set into a deep pout. Two long orange braids lie down the front of her shoulders over her striped ringer T-shirt, and bright red glasses frame her soft blue eyes. Mom always jokes that no one actually knows the real texture of Clem's hair because she's been wearing it in braids every day since we were kids. Straight out of the shower and into two braids. When I've prodded her about cutting them off, she gets weirdly defensive and begins to pet them, like they're the source of everything that makes her Clementine. My twin is only a few inches shorter than me, which means she towers over her girlfriend, Hannah.

Just behind Clem, Hannah saunters out of the school entrance, flocked by her posse of oddball friends, and waves a quick goodbye to them. Even though Hannah's general response to people seems to be that she's allergic, she takes Clem's hand, and her whole expression gets a massive glow up. Hannah is a small person with big energy. I can't imagine she's taller than five three, but honestly anything shorter than five nine and I lose my ability to discern height. You're either shorter than me or much shorter than me. Unless you're Tucker Watson, in which case you are slightly taller than me.

Hannah and Clem have been dating since last summer. They met only four days after Hannah's then girlfriend, Courtney, broke up with her. Since Hannah is Clem's first real girlfriend, I was scared she would be nothing more than a rebound for Hannah, but turns out I was wrong. Wouldn't be the first time. If Clem dresses like she could be a kid on a playdate, Hannah looks more like an extra in *Mad Max*. They make an odd duo at times, but watching them together is like watching two people who have gone their whole lives speaking a language only they can understand. Plus, Hannah isn't as tough as she looks. Clem once confessed to me that she was named after a character from *General Hospital*, so I feel like having a daytime soap opera name means you have to have at least a slightly ooey-gooey center.

"Come on, come on, come on, come on," I mutter to myself, tapping my thumb against the wheel. I timed today perfectly. If we run by and check on Grammy like Mom asked and make it home by four thirty, I should have just enough time to rewatch every episode of this season of *Fiercest of Them All* before tonight's live finale. There are maybe three things I take seriously in this world, and *Fiercest of Them All* is right up there after my grammy and my post–high school master plan.

Fiercest of Them All is in its sixteenth season and was basically Drag Queen 101 when I was a ten-year-old boy at the library pretending to do research on photosynthesis while I was actually watching YouTube clips of this mythical art of drag I never even knew existed. Honestly, I think some people in this town would have been less disturbed if they'd caught me looking at porn rather than grown men in dresses. Not that anyone should have been surprised. I've always been the kind of gay that announces itself and asks for a wide berth. *Flamboyant*, as Grammy says.

It was in that library that I gobbled up the history of drag and all the ways it's woven into queer history, especially Black queer history, which is definitely not something I had any luck finding reading materials on within a five-hundred-mile radius. Thank Goddess for the internet.

As for *Fiercest of Them All*, it wasn't until I was in middle school that I figured out how to watch episodes from sort of sketchy websites. (I'd like to think that the drag gods would forgive me for my early and ill-informed pirating days.) Around that same time, all the things about me that signified to other people that I was definitely not straight grew bigger and took deeper roots.

Some people are obviously queer, and others . . . aren't. I just so happen to fulfill some of the broader stereotypes surrounding gay guys. Mom once admitted that when I was younger, she and my dad thought it might be a phase. Maybe just my grandmother rubbing off on me. It's true that her love for glamour, themes, and drama was contagious, but I never did grow out of it, so by the start of high school, watching *Fiercest of Them All* on the family TV was suddenly the least shocking thing about me. And sometimes, Mom and Dad even sat down to watch an episode, which in real time was annoying, because I was constantly having to explain context and how the show worked. Now, though, with only a few months left at home, it's easy to feel nostalgic for their old-people quirks.

I honk—with love—as Clem pulls Hannah through the parking lot. My sister gives me a hmph as she slides in next to me with Hannah in the passenger seat.

"Sorry to make you wait, Waylon," says Hannah in a voice that honestly doesn't sound that sorry, if we're splitting hairs. She bites on her lip ring, a recent addition and birthday gift from Clem. Not my style, but it complements Hannah's whole look, which is combat boots and shaggy bangs. Some people say the eyes are the windows to the soul, and if that's the case, Hannah's thick, wavy bangs are the curtains. Of course, there's the matter of her teeth too. A little oversized and a little gapped. Hannah's been getting shit about them for years, but what those losers don't know is that some people become supermodels thanks to their quirky teeth, so if you ask me, Hannah's teeth are a major future asset.

"He barely waited," chimes in Clem. "We got out of school like eight minutes ago."

"Listen," I say as I shift the truck into drive. "It's not my fault our parents have done us the inhumane disservice of not including DVR in their cable package."

Clem groans. "It doesn't even matter. This season is a done deal. Ruby Slippers has it in the bag."

I let out a hiss as the truck rumbles out of the parking lot and into downtown Clover City. "Don't you speak that evil in my Beulah."

"*Our* Beulah. *Our* truck," she reminds me.

"Mimi Mee is the one true queen of season sixteen and I will accept nothing less."

"They'll never crown a fat queen," Clem says. "At least not anytime soon," she adds gently.

Hannah lets out a here-we-go-again sigh.

"It's not that I don't think they should," Clem continues. "But how many plus-size queens have we seen make it all the way to the finals season after season only to be shut down again and again? Honestly, I think we should stop watching altogether after this season. Go on strike."

I roll my eyes. "Yeah, that's going to make a real statement. Two kids from Clover City refusing to watch literally one of the biggest television shows in the world is going to make a real dent."

Outside my window, Clover City ripples by in a blur as we make our way through downtown, past the weathered gazebos in the main square, and beyond the civic center. I'm not supposed to love this place. For as much as I love the fat queens on *Fiercest of Them All*, the small-town queens always hold a special place in my heart too. It's a reminder that incredible things happen in all kinds of places, even Clover City. This is the kind of place gay teenage boys like me are supposed to dream of escaping. But my relationship with my hometown is much more complicated than that. Yeah, I think about the wider world out there and what it might have for me, but there's also some comfort in walking into a room and feeling like the most refined, smartest person there. Even though Clover City feels like one big joke sometimes, it's my joke. My charming joke of a town that thrives on beauty pageants and dance teams and a football team that couldn't figure out how to win a game if the other team had forfeited, but underneath it all, it's more than that small-town stereotype. It's a shithole. But it's my little shithole.

As we pull into Grammy's driveway, Clem reaches over Hannah and opens the door before the truck is even in park.

Grammy lives in a house with her two best friends and fellow widows, Bernadette and Cleo. If it's true what they say and that in our old age, we revert to our youth, Grammy's in her party-girl college years. The three of them are always driving out to New Mexico for the casinos and getting into trouble—sometimes even requiring bail. Basically, they're everything I aspire to be.

I hope I live to be old and wrinkly with Clem, getting into as much trouble as humanly possible. Maybe I want to kill her more often than not lately, but the idea of riding into the sunset with her by my side is one hell of a way to go out if you ask me. (Assuming we both outlive our spouses, of course. Though I would be lying if I said I didn't fantasize about being the town's famous black widow, who wipes his tears away with piles of cash and furs. Just kidding. Murder is bad or something.)

Bernadette, an older Black woman with medium-brown skin who famously has a mole behind her ear in roughly the shape of Texas (seriously—she and it were in *Texas Monthly*), sits on the front porch in her rocking chair. "Darlinda! Your little chickadees are here and they brought that delightfully grumpy girl!"

"I'm not that grumpy," murmurs Hannah as we get out of the truck.

I glance over the hood of the car at her. "Seriously?"

Clem catches her hand. "It's endearing."

"You're grumpy," Hannah retorts as she takes Clem's hand. "Hi, Ms. Bernadette!" she calls in an extra-cheery voice.

"Really proving us all wrong," I say.

The Hen House (as Grammy refers to it) is a basic brick ranch-style house, the kind that defines the nicer, older neighborhoods of Clover City. Except there's nothing basic about this house. When Grammy, Cleo, and Bernadette bought this place, they decided it would finally be the house of their dreams, unfettered by their husbands or the needs of their families. Much to their neighbors' dismay, they painted the brick light pink and added yellow trim, as if the pink wouldn't catch enough looks. If you think the outside of the house slows cars, you should see the inside.

Grammy, tall, white, busty, and broad, pushes the screen door open and beckons us inside. She stands framed by the doorway with her white hair tucked into a leopard-print bonnet, her hot-pink coveralls rolled up to her knees, and her shiny red toenails peeking out of her leopard-print kitten-heel slides. "Y'all come take a look at this faucet for me, would ya?"

Grammy dresses for every occasion of her life, whether she's wearing an elaborate sundress to pick up her prescription, a teal faux-fur coat for bingo, or even a battery-powered cocktail dress on Christmas Eve with actual string lights. The woman loves a theme, so of course she would find her faucet is leaking and don her hot-pink coveralls before even putting in a call to her grandkids.

Inside, we each take our shoes off and leave them in the entryway. (The Hen House might be a bachelorette house, but these women are no slobs.)

Grammy takes turns hugging us all, including Hannah,

whom she has a soft spot for. *Takes a real fierce sort of person to pull off that much black. Chic, but edgy.*

When Grammy hugs me, I hug her back, letting our embrace linger for a minute. Her perfume—the one she's worn for as long as I can remember—is crisp and floral but not overpowering. Everyone ought to have their own personal scent. Which is why I've been wearing two spritzes of Bleu de Chanel every day since she first bought it for me on my thirteenth birthday.

"Oooh, Pumpkin," she says.

Pumpkin is more than a term of endearment. Orange hair and orange freckles set off by the pale white of our complexion. Grammy has called me Pumpkin since the day I was born. Clem's a ginger too, of course, but with a name like Clementine, she didn't need a nickname.

"We've got to make it fast today, Gram," I tell her as I pull away. "We're doing a marathon of *Fiercest of Them All.*"

Gram pinches my cheek. "You've got to teach me how to watch that on the streamer TV software y'all got me for Christmas. But first, let's get this kitchen sink looked at. Come on, Hannah," she says, taking Hannah's hand. "You and I will have some rhubarb pie while these two have a look-see at my sink."

Clem laughs. "She gets pie and I get to crawl under your sink. What kind of treatment is that for your only granddaughter?"

Gram snorts. "Perks of being family."

Clementine gingerly takes the pink toolbox from the kitchen table and plops down on the ground, pulling me down with her. The toolbox was a Christmas gift from Dad. I remember him coughing into his fist as he said, "Now, I know a toolbox need not be pink for a woman to use it, but—"

"But it certainly is fabulous," Gram finished.

Clem and I are well trained on basic household fixes. Dad owns a pavement striping company, but he's been known to pick up handy jobs, especially when we were younger and he was first starting out, so we spent a lot of summer days at Camp Dad while he jumped from job to job.

"Check the washer. It could be cracked," I tell Clem, shining my cell phone light under the sink as I shimmy beneath the counter.

She grunts, wiping her hand on her jean shorts. "Nope, that's not it."

My brain wanders as Clem fidgets with the pipes and sink undercarriage. It's not that I don't know my way around a basic kitchen sink and it's not like my sister is some kind of stereotype of a lesbian, but she's got a brain for technical stuff. A mechanic's brain is what Dad calls it.

Heck, she'll probably be the smartest person at Austin Community College. We were both wait-listed at University of Texas, but convinced our parents to let us move to Austin to attend ACC until we're accepted to UT.

Even if it's only a few hours away, Austin is like a world away in terms of culture and has plenty of space for me to blossom into Waylon Stage Three. Waylon Stage One was Waylon before I came out of the closet. The entire history of me until that moment. Stage Two is my life in Clover City out of the closet, which hasn't been unbearable, but is not exactly full of memories worth remembering. I try to dress in unassuming clothing and keep to myself at school, which sometimes works. Stage Three, though . . . that's the big reveal. My butterfly moment. Austin will be the perfect arena. And Clem will be right there with me. The idea of us not going to the same school was never on the table. It wasn't even a discussion. Besides, Clem can barely drive. She wouldn't get very far without me.

"Hand me that wrench, Waylon."

I sit up too soon and hit my head on the frame of the cabinet. "Shit," I whisper as I rub my forehead.

Grammy chuckles. "You're lucky Cleo's sunning herself in the backyard. She'd have a bar of soap between your teeth faster than you could say Judas."

I retrieve the wrench and hand it off to Clem.

"Check the faucet, will ya?" she asks.

I hop up and peer out the window over the sink to the backyard, where Cleo is laid out on a lounge chair in an old-fashioned-looking black swimsuit with daisies lining the straps. She holds a big foil shield, like the kind you put in the window of your car, and is using it to reflect the sun onto her face.

"How does that white lady not have skin cancer?" asks Hannah.

Grammy takes a sip of her tea. "Cleo's been oiling up with Crisco since we were girls and she's already outlived two husbands and a boyfriend. She thinks she's gonna live forever. There's no telling her."

I turn the faucet on. "No leak," I confirm. Holding a hand out, I yank Clem up onto her feet. "That was fast."

"Which means we've got time for pie," says Clem as she plops down next to Hannah.

I let out a guttural groan and check the time on my phone.

Grammy takes my hand and pulls me down beside her. "Come on now, Pumpkin. Just a quick bite." She tugs on the collar of my polo. "I swear, with these clothes your mother buys, she's got you lookin' like a damn insurance adjuster."

I roll my eyes and yank my hand free of hers. When I let loose, my mash-up of a southern Valley Girl voice and animated gestures might be a dead giveaway if your only barometer of a gay guy is how femme he is. But at school I do my best to keep a low profile, and that means steering clear of most social circles and wearing all the oversized polos and cargo shorts my mom showers me with on Christmas and birthdays. *Handsome and sensible*, as she puts it.

Clem's mouth is already full of rhubarb and pie crust. "Oh, God, yeah. That's the good stuff."

"One slice," I say.

Clem reaches for the pie server. "That was the appetizer slice. This is my real slice."

"And then home," I tell her.

She winks. "Sure thing, *Pumpkin*."

THREE

We make it home a few minutes before the marathon begins, and even though Clem knows I'm annoyed that our detour took longer than expected, she doesn't acknowledge it. She and Hannah disappear for chunks of time every once in a while, which definitely translates to making out in Clementine's room before Mom and Dad get home. Dad's got an overnight job, so he won't be home until morning, and Mom, who does all of his admin stuff, is probably helping him make sure he's got his crew and equipment all lined up.

After a quick bathroom break, I pound on Clementine's closed door. "Clem! Mom's home!"

I have to hold in my laughter as I listen to the two of them curse and tumble over each other. Clem races to the door and swings it open, straightening her T-shirt.

"JK," I say.

Clem shoves me gently. "What the hell, Waylon?"

"Not cool," Hannah says from where she sits on the edge of the bed, smoothing her bangs back down.

I roll my eyes. "Think of it like a fire drill."

After the three of us heat up frozen taquitos for dinner, Mimi, my favorite queen, sits for her episode-five interview after nearly being kicked off the show.

This was the first challenge that didn't rely on Mimi's strengths (design/sewing and comedy) and instead was dependent on her dance skills. "Listen," says Mimi in masculine street clothes. "I got into drag to play to my strengths. Design and comedy? Those are my currencies. People will forgive you for just about anything—including being fat— if you can make them laugh. But dancing—something plenty of fat people are great at, by the way—well, when you see me fumbling around on that stage, it reminds you that I'm fat and that's a sin America won't forgive me for unless I can make a pretty dress or tell a clever joke. During the dance number I was no worse than Sasha or Belle. My runway was fierce. Definitely better than either of theirs. So you tell me why I was up for elimination and they weren't."

Even though I've seen this particular moment countless times, thanks to reruns and fan recaps, it still hits me right in the gut. There are times when I feel like I can't be me. I can't simply exist. I have to offer something in exchange. Something that absolves me of being fat and gay and even worse—both of those things at once.

I know it sounds dramatic. Especially since my family seems very okay with me and Clem. But I can't help but think it'd be easier to love me if I was at least thin like my sister or ripped like Tucker. That might make up the deficit somehow.

"Are you okay?" Hannah asks in a low voice while Clementine is in the kitchen heating up some queso.

I open my mouth to talk and then realize a few slow tears are rolling down my cheek. "Oh, yeah. Me? I'm good. I'm fine."

Hannah eyes me suspiciously. "When Bianca Blanco won a couple years ago, I got that tingly feeling behind my eyes. I kind of still do."

Hannah is Afro-Dominican, and Bianca was a Dominican queen who spoke a mixture of Spanish and English and had a signature phrase that caught on all over the internet. Two years ago, she was the first Dominican queen to win ever after a couple of near misses during previous seasons, and she became infamous for her catchphrase, *Don't you wishy you could be this fishy?*

According to Clem, Hannah's grandma got so into the show that season that she made a Dominican feast for the season finale and invited all their neighbors.

My phone vibrates in my pocket.

Lucas: I'm working until 1am if you want to swing by.

My cold, dead heart flutters as I type back.

We'll see. Dad is working all night, so maybe.

Lucas: Really want to see you. Maybe we can talk too.

Talk? Ha! Lucas. Oh, Lucas. Lucas is my highly problematic and slightly older (literally by a few months) booty call. Is it still a booty call if you've never gone all the way? I guess he's more like my Very Handsy Make-Out/Sometimes More Call.

I would say it's complicated, but it's not. What it is:

two horny boys who like to make out in the stockroom of a gas station. We met last summer when I got a flat tire down the road and he let me hang out inside the gas station where he works until Dad could bring me a spare. We ate ice cream and flirted. I wasn't sure if he was gay, but I found myself stopping at the gas station for Mr. Freezee's soft serve ice cream every afternoon until Lucas made the first move, and we've been making out in the back room ever since. Lucas is charming and polite in that perfectly southern way, and if I'm being honest, he's everything I dreamed of when I was a little boy and imagined someone sweeping me off my feet. But even though he is all of those things, he can't be any of those things *for me*.

Maybe it would be more complicated if Lucas was interested in kissing me and holding my hand in well-lit places, but he isn't ready for that. Lucas is very much in the closet, and he's the kind of guy no one in Clover City assumes is gay. Yeah, it's not easy for guys like me who are sort of like every nineties stereotype of gay, despite my efforts to be more subdued. But guys like Lucas can really throw people off, because if big, strapping Lucas, who is a total Clover City golden boy in his beat-up Wranglers and muscle shirt, can be gay without anyone suspecting it, then—GASP—anyone can be queer.

And even though I sometimes wonder if the reason Lucas and I aren't publicly out together is because he's embarrassed of me, I know that Lucas being out is a decision only he can make. Regardless of where I stand in the equation. Once you come out of the closet, there's no going back in.

The freaking closet door disappears, and you're left totally unprotected in the middle of the world at the mercy of everyone else's goodwill, hoping the people you've known your whole life really are decent and kind and that all that unconditional-love Bible stuff people spew is the real deal. That's what coming out in a small town is. I would never jeopardize that for someone else. Never.

Small-town gay life doesn't have to be a drag. It can be great in some ways, and it helps that I've not done anything like try to star in the school's production of *Oklahoma!* Clem and I have been lucky, especially with our parents, but I've heard whispers about other kids in town. Everything from getting kicked out of their homes to being sent to Bible Bootcamp. (A real place with actual Yelp reviews, by the way. *Five stars! Would send my once-homosexual kid back again!*) Clem and I might have made it through life so far without any major bumps or bruises, but I know that we're both just one unfortunate moment away from someone seeing us do something like hold hands with someone or even a moment of us "acting gay" before one of us is in actual danger.

As the commercials begin after last week's episode, I stand up. "Okay, last call for bathroom breaks! This finale is live with zero commercials. Look alive, people!"

Clementine races to the bathroom.

"I'll take my chances," says Hannah.

I situate myself in Mom's knitting armchair and can't help but squeal with excitement.

Hannah laughs. "Have you ever even been to a real drag show?" she asks.

I flap a hand in her direction. "Um, out here? Yeah, right." I know that drag queens come from all types of places, but sometimes it feels impossible to imagine here.

She clicks her tongue. "You'd be surprised."

I start to ask her what she means, but the theme music begins to play as Carmelo Santiago in full drag takes the stage of the live recording in some huge theater all the way out in Hollywood. "Hello, and welcome to the sixteenth season finale of *Fiercest of Them All*. I'm your host, Carmelo Santiago, and tonight's the night we crown our queen. Isn't that right, ladies?"

The lush, red curtain behind Carmelo lifts to display every single one of the eliminated queens from this season, each one of them decked out in their best signature drag. There's a wide array, including Marjorie Simpson, who specializes in fandom drag, Betty Deadly, who's known for her spooky goth look, Sheyoncé, who's an infamous Beyoncé impersonator from Vegas, and Angela Dolittle, known for being crowned Miss Southern Belle from New Orleans.

For the next fifty-five minutes, I watch as Carmelo interviews the eliminated queens, takes audience questions, and announces lesser titles like Miss Congeniality. The top three queens—Cinderhella, Ruby Slippers, and Mimi Mee—each lip-synch to a song of their choosing, and it's quickly clear that Ruby and Mimi are the top contenders.

The two queens hold hands as Cinderhella is eliminated, and I find myself reaching for Clem's hand. She doesn't flinch when I squeeze.

"Mimi, Mimi, Mimi, Mimi," I chant under my breath.

"America, your newest reigning queen is . . ." Carmelo pauses dramatically, everyone in the audience and at home hanging on her every word. "The incomparable, the beautiful Ruby Slippers!"

"Turn it off!" I snap. It's the same thing Dad does when the Texas Rangers lose a game. "Turn off the damn television." Watching your fave lose is one thing. Watching their opponent win is actual torture. I don't need to see Ruby's tearful acceptance. I don't need to hear about how they were just a gay boy in Chicago, searching for acceptance. We're all searching, Ruby!

Clementine fumbles as she hunts for the remote. The music on the television crescendos as Ruby is crowned and Hannah marches right over to the TV and unplugs it from the wall.

I cross my arms over my chest. "There was a button on the side."

"Whatever. It's off." She goes back over to the couch to take Clem's hand. "Walk me home?"

Clem looks to me and I nod. I'd rather be alone anyway.

Hannah's normally furrowed brow softens. "Sorry about Mimi, Waylon."

My truck rumbles along the dark road at the edge of town, the sky above milky with clouds. After Clementine left with Hannah, Mom texted to say she'd be working late and not to wait up, so it was just me on a Friday night and

23

barely ten o'clock. Suddenly being alone didn't sound so great.

After I park on the side of the gas station, I walk in and the door chimes as I enter. Lucas glances up from the couple of guys he's ringing up. "Fountain drinks are half off," he calls.

"Thanks," I barely respond.

I circle around the back aisles, eyeing the display of gummy worms as he thumbs through the cigarettes, looking for the exact package the guys at the counter are requesting.

"No, man," says one of them. "The green carton."

Lucas looks up again, watching me in the security mirror, and I can't help but smile.

I nod to the back-room door and he gives me a quick head tilt as confirmation.

In the back room, I maneuver through boxes of stock and hop up onto the desk, trying to fix myself in the perfect, most seductive yet natural pose I can manage. *Oh, who me? Yes. I always sit perfectly perched with half an ass cheek in the air.* Maybe that's not hot, though. I square myself on the desk and hold my hands in my lap. Yeah, no. Back to perching.

Lucas steps through the doorway with a big goofy grin on his face as he pushes his floppy blond hair back. He's got this huge forehead that seems to tell you everything he's thinking at all times. Every worry and relief is always written right there for me to see. "I was hoping you could make it tonight."

He moves through the boxes in three easy strides and cups my face in his hands, pulling me to him gently but with force. Our lips collide, and I can still taste the spearmint gum he chewed in the hopes that I would come by and the waxy lip balm he keeps in the little tin under the cash register alongside the keys to the Camry he bought off his older sister when she upgraded to a minivan.

Lucas, Lucas, Lucas, Lucas. Sometimes I wonder what would have happened if we'd known each other better in high school before he graduated last year. It's this impossible, fantasy-like alternate reality. We could have been this unlikely pair turned high school sweethearts. Maybe we'd even be popular—a novelty! Girls would love us, because straight chicks adore a gay guy and they really love two. Maybe other guys wouldn't be threatened by us. Maybe they'd accept us. Lucas seemed to be one of them, after all. We would have each other. We'd be together. In public.

Lucas pulls my shirt over my head and I begin to unbutton his and then immediately stop myself. The stockroom feels private and safe, but in reality, anyone could walk right in.

I don't really like the whole metaphor of baseball bases and physical intimacy. Mainly because I don't really care about baseball and also, has anyone in the history of teenagers ever agreed on what bases are what? I guess in the world of gay teenage boys, I'd have to say first base is making out or heavy petting (a term I've only ever heard Grammy use), second base is mouth or hands below the belt, and, well, third base is . . . below-the-belt action. By that barometer,

Lucas and I have made it to second base, but the idea of doing anything more than making out when a customer or Lucas's dad, who owns the gas station, could easily wander back here freaks me out no matter how many times he tells me it's okay.

"Ruby Slippers won," I breathe into his lips.

"I don't care about boys in dresses right now," he says. "I care about you out of this shirt." He nibbles at my earlobe softly.

My hands are unbuttoning the rest of his shirt before I can remind myself of all the reasons this is a bad idea.

I hate hiding. Everyone in this town knows I'm gay—for better or worse—and there's something supremely unfair about the fact that I have to hide this when I still have to deal with a handful of dumb pricks hurling homophobic insults in my direction and Bible thumpers who want to pray my gay away. If I'm going to have to put up with all of that, shouldn't I at least have this? And shouldn't it be for everyone to see?

After we fool around for a bit and no one barges in on us, Lucas settles in next to me on the desk as we watch the TV wired to the security cameras out front.

"How's class been?" I ask.

"Almost over, but I'm thinking I'm gonna sign up for summer classes too. The sooner I finish my basics at Clover City Community College, the faster I can transfer, ya know? Who knows? Maybe you'll see me in Austin one day."

"That'd be something." Lucas had high hopes for a

football scholarship, but the offers never came. It's the same sad story of most of the male population of Clover City. But I kind of like the thought of Lucas in Austin. With me.

After a few more minutes of watching the security cameras, Lucas clears his throat. "I . . . actually—are we exclusive?" he asks, dropping a very serious question out of nowhere.

"Excuse me?" I can't tell if this is his way of telling me he only wants to make out with me or that he wants to also make out with other people.

"It's just something I've been wondering is all."

Yes, yes, yes, yes, I nearly scream, but I'm not in the business of being overly eager and I definitely don't want to sound desperate. "Um, not that I'm aware of."

On the monitor, a woman walks in and waits at the counter.

"Hang on," says Lucas. "I'll be right back."

Once he's gone, I quickly grab my phone and shoot off a text to Clem.

911! I need a pep talk.

On the monitor, Lucas stands with his back to the woman as he types her numbers onto her lotto tickets. He looks up to the camera—to me—and rolls his eyes, letting out a short sigh that blows the hair off his forehead.

"Clem, Clem, Clem, come on!" I mumble.

My phone lights up with her face. "Okay," I say into the phone. "I don't have time to explain. But I need a pep talk. Quick."

"Wait—what's—" she sputters. "Okay. Waylon Russell

Brewer. You are a gift to humankind. God or whoever's in charge made you and mwah! Chef kiss! Perfection! You deserve to have good things and good people. You have more vision and culture in your pinkie than most people have in their whole bodies. Ten years from now—"

"I gotta go," I say. Lucas has disappeared from the monitor. "But that was good. Your pep talk game is at an all-time high."

"Wait," she says. "I love you. My life is better because I share it with you. Twin love for life."

"I love you too," I whisper back into the phone and hang up, my whole chest glowing with optimism.

Lucas pushes the stockroom door open and I shove my phone back in my pocket. He wipes his hands down the front of his jeans, and I can see that he's as nervous as I am.

I inhale sharply, shuddering as I exhale.

"Were you talking to someone?" he asks.

"Nope, just, uh, humming to myself."

He stands between my knees and presses his palms against my thighs. "Waylon?"

"Lucas?"

"I think I'm ready to . . . tell people."

I hook my arms around the back of his neck. "Are you sure?" I try to keep my voice perfectly even and measured. This is all his decision, and I don't want to sway him one way or the other.

He pulls my arms down and takes a step back, his whole face lighting up. "I never thought I'd feel like this."

"Yeah?" Hope bubbles in my chest and I feel like I might

burst. I'd told myself over and over for the last few months that this was only physical. Nothing more, but somewhere along the way, it became more, and now—

"I met someone." He sighs, like a hulking weight has been lifted. "His name is Rashid. He works in the library at school and he makes me so happy. Just talking to him about stupid stuff like our allergies flaring up and our favorite TV shows and weird things our moms say . . ." The words roll right out of him and he claps his broad hand over his smiling lips as he takes a step back. "I haven't even asked him out yet. Isn't that shit wild?"

"But you . . ." I force myself to recalibrate, blinking over and over again, because I will not cry. I refuse to cry. Definitely not for this piece of shit. "Good for you, Lucas."

Realization settles on his face. "You're not upset, are you?"

I stand and wave a hand in his general direction. Breathe in. Breathe out. "Um, no. I'm fine. Completely fine. So fine."

"So fine?" He dodges my path to the door. "We said this was just physical, Waylon. From the very beginning. And you just told me to my face we weren't exclusive. Just now."

"I. Am. Fine," I say through gritted teeth as I shove him out of my way.

He loses his footing and stumbles backward into a pile of empty boxes. "We can talk about this," he tells me.

I stomp out of the stockroom and pray to God he's watching me on the security monitor, because if the best thing he's ever had in his life is about to walk right out the door, I hope he's there to see me go.

Anger rolls through me in fresh waves until I slam my car door shut behind me. Then, and only then, is it safe. The tears come in a quick surge, and once they start, they don't stop. Sobs rack my whole body as I pull out of the parking lot and leave Lucas right where I found him, in a grimy gas station on the outskirts of town.

FOUR

At home, I don't even knock on Clem's door. "Clem?" I ask, fully prepared to free-fall onto her bed, so she can tell me all the ways Lucas is an asshole and how I deserve better and blah-blah-blah feel-good bullshit.

But her room is empty. The clock on her nightstand reads 12:48 a.m. She should've been home by now. Ugh. I don't have enough emotional energy to process this breakup—is this even a breakup?—and worry about Clementine's well-being.

I plop down on her bed and fidget with her laptop, looking for the perfect song to properly wallow in this very particular sorrow. I settle on Lizzo's "Truth Hurts," and I swear to God I'm about to push her laptop to the side when an email alert from the University of Georgia pops up in the corner of her screen.

Subject Line: Re: First Year Bulldog Camp Dorm Request

I click. It's a reflex. I can't control it.

Dear Clementine,

Yes, if you decide to attend First Year Bulldog Camp, we would likely be able to fulfill your dorm request. Though the final say would be up to your camp adviser. I believe you would be with Julia. This is her second year doing Bulldog Camp and I think you two will really hit it off. Testing out your dorm is a great idea. I actually stayed in Hawthorne for my first two years of undergrad and loved it. My roommate was even in my wedding!

I know you have yet to commit to UG, but as a reminder, our extended deadline is right around the corner in a few weeks. Please don't hesitate if you have any more questions.

-Paulina

Paulina Fernandez
Admissions Adviser
University of Georgia
Athens, Georgia

I snap the laptop shut like it's a can of worms.

What. The. Fuck. I scrub my hands through my curls, like that might somehow erase everything I just saw. Clem can't be going to Georgia. Georgia? Why Athens, Georgia? If she's going to leave me, she might as well make it worth it. Everyone knows cities in the south named after European cities are total duds. You don't see people lining up to go to Paris, Texas, do you?

I go back to my own room and take a few deep breaths.

Clem and I aren't just twins. We're best friends. But we have boundaries too. Text messages. Emails. Those are things we don't go tromping through, so even though I am aching with confusion and hurt feelings, I'm not about to get caught snooping through her emails.

After marking the email as unread, I settle into my own bed, and it hits me harder. Forget snooping through emails! Clem is about to betray me in the biggest way. She's abandoning me. On top of that, she's not even offering me the decency of a warning.

My twin—the person who I am so closely synced with that when I lose my keys she always knows where I left them—is considering leaving me. And worse than that: she kept it a secret. Does Hannah know? Our parents? Grammy? Surely Grammy would have told me. If Clem is considering her dorm prospects, then this is more than her feeling out her options.

An alert buzzes on my phone, jarring me back to the present. I grab my phone and swipe to find an Instagram post from @FiercestOfThemAllOfficial. The image is of a crown on a red velvet pedestal, and below that, the caption reads: *Season 16's queen has been crowned, but the search for Season 17's queen begins now! Click the link in our bio and send in your audition video today. Who knows? You might just be the Fiercest of Them All!* 👑

I read the caption again and again until I've memorized it. *You might just be the Fiercest of Them All.*

Double dumped in one night. Lucas wasn't worried about coming out. He just didn't want to come out with me. Hearing it, really piecing it together in my head and seeing the dots connect, cuts deep. But Clem. That hurts me in a way no boy could ever. If she really is going to Georgia, I get the message loud and clear. The life I dreamed up for us isn't enough. She wants something bigger and better. Without me.

Fine. Let her have it. She can go. She can leave me. She can be anyone she wants to be. And so can I.

It doesn't take me long to find the Merle Norman makeup starter kit Grammy bought Clem for her fifteenth birthday. The mauve leather case was tucked under her bed, collecting dust in between a shoebox full of failed drawings Hannah ripped out of her sketch pad and Clementine secretly kept and a chest of old dance shoes and recital costumes.

This moment feels almost inevitable. I always knew I would try drag, at least once. I just didn't expect it to be today.

I sit down at my desk and use the old makeup mirror Mom keeps under the sink in the hallway bathroom. The bulbs around the mirror are burned out, so I take the lampshade off my desk light and use that to illuminate my face and highlight every little spot and blemish. Talk about a damn reckoning. Who needs extreme sports when makeup mirrors exist? Is this why we all hate ourselves? Instagram and harsh lighting?

Poking through the makeup kit, I find a few things I recognize from merely existing in a house with two women. Powder. Lipstick. Blush. Mascara—which looks terrifying, by the way. Who in their right mind would put that pointy-looking brush stick thing so close to their eyes?

I've definitely dabbled with things like lipstick and have found myself scrolling through pages and pages of time-lapse makeup tutorials, so I have an *idea* of how makeup works in a theoretical sense. I understand things like the fact that drag queens glue down their brows with a glue stick and repaint their brows on top. And I can see all the ways contouring can give you the illusion of cheekbones and a jawline. But I've never actually tried any of those things myself. It turns out that application is not as easy as the internet makes it out to be.

Thankfully, I shaved this morning, so my face is smooth at the very least. I start with foundation, and what I'm working with is not nearly as effective as what I've seen queens use on TV and online. I don't have any sponges or brushes, so I use what the Lord gave me and apply it with my fingers. I do the same with blush, and decide that more is more. I'm going for drag. Not Monday morning real estate agent at the office.

Outside my room, the floorboards creak as Mom knocks on my door. "Waylon? Darling?"

I gasp, and begin to choke. Is it possible to swallow your Adam's apple?

"Waylon?"

"I'm fine!" I rasp out.

My mother has caught me in a fair amount of unfortunate circumstances. Crusty socks. Crusty boxers. Crusty sheets. (I have since learned how to do my own laundry, thank you very much.) Scandalous videos on sketchy web-sites. The list goes on. And it's not like she doesn't know I'm gay, but makeup is a whole new level of queer that my mother, who has only left Texas enough times to count on one hand, might find . . . alarming.

"Are you sure?"

"Yes?" I call back in a deep voice. "Yes!" I try again in my normal voice.

She chortles. "I'm heading to bed, baby."

"Okay, good night!"

"How'd Mimi do?" she asks.

My pounding heart slows. It doesn't matter what it is. If we are interested, so is Mom. (Bless her for download-ing Pokémon Go the summer Clem and I were absolutely consumed by that addictive little game.) "Ruby took the crown!"

"Ah, well, maybe Mimi will make the Hall of Fame season?"

"All-Stars, Mom! It's called All-Stars."

"Ahh, yes. That's right. Well, good night, baby. Your sister already asleep?"

I could rat on that jerk and get her in real trouble. But then I'd probably have to account for this half face of makeup. "Yes, ma'am!" I say.

"Love you, baby! Night!"

She pads down the hallway to her and Dad's room, and once I hear the door close behind her, I exhale.

I continue on, tracing some version of eyebrows,

covering my lids in sparkly green eye shadow, lining my lips, filling them in with an orangey-red lipstick. Lastly, I attempt mascara. There's lots of eye watering and blinking, but eventually I get some color on my nearly translucent lashes, which are actually sort of long. Because I'm feeling exceptionally brave, I scoot to the edge of my chair and try my hand at the eyelash curler I found at the bottom of the makeup kit.

A sharp pinch tugs at my eyelid. "Ow! Shit!"

I detangle myself from the curler and try once more. I feel actual fear as the metal closes around my lashes, but when I feel nothing, I press a little harder.

When I'm done with both eyes, I see that in the case of eyelash curlers, the pain is worth the gain. Tilting my chin down, I bat my lashes a few times. *Damn, girl.*

My makeup isn't great. It's a little too everyday, but like drunk-girl everyday, so it's all a bit smudged. But still, there's something different about me. I've transformed into someone else. Someone who wasn't dumped and abandoned. Someone who might even have a few secrets of their own. Every time I glance in the mirror, I feel a fluttering in my chest.

I stand and open the bottom drawer of my dresser, where I keep swimsuits and discarded Halloween costumes. I've got a feather boa from the year I went as Hulk Hogan, and then there's the black wig from the year I went as Tina from *Bob's Burgers.* (Mimi Mee once said that Halloween is a drag queen testing ground.)

There's a tickle of excitement in my fingers as I open my closet and reach for my Waylon Stage Three Wardrobe. Like my life, my clothing is clearly divided into phases, and for years, I've been stocking up on clothing that I'll wear after high school when Clem and I are living our truth in Austin. Sometimes when I'm feeling brave, I'll bust out a piece or two for a night at home or dinner at Grammy's, but for the most part, this half of my closet remains untouched. A shrine to the person who I will soon become. Leggings, skinny jeans, dramatic robes, capes, Elton John–style sunglasses, and an incredible shoe collection. I either bought it with my own money earned working for Dad over the summer or it was passed down from Grammy. One day, I'll wear it all, and I'll wear it with intention.

For tonight, I reach for a hot-pink embroidered silk robe and use my Hulk Hogan feather boa to fashion a collar to hide my wisps of chest hair.

At my desk, I sit down and open my laptop, turning on the camera. It takes some effort to tug the wig over my orange curls. The black really doesn't suit me, but it's all I have to work with for now. I try a few different poses, pouting my lips and squinting a bit as I prop a hand under my chin.

"Yes, honey," I say to myself. "Darling," I drawl.

I hit the red record button, and for a moment the wind is sucked right out of me, like I've just been hit square in the chest with a dodgeball—a reality I'm all too familiar with. I gasp a little, but then force my pulse to slow as I clear my throat.

Everyone wants to leave me? I'll show them what they're missing.

I wave into the camera, my fingers fanning up and down. I really should have painted my nails, but that doesn't matter. No one will notice my nails if I give them plenty of other things to notice.

"Good evening, y'all. I'm Pumpkin, but you can call me Miss Patch."

FIVE

"Incoming!" Clem warns as she slams her body down onto my bed.

"Nope," I moan and bury my face into my pillow.

My face! Shit, shit, shit.

"It's almost noon," she says. "Mom told me to tell you that if you want to sleep this late, you can start working overnights with Dad."

"Well, then go, so I can get out of bed. I require privacy."

She groans. "Guys are gross, you know that?"

"I'm not telling you to go because of that," I say. Though, honestly, it's always best to give me a few minutes to collect myself and Clem knows that. It's biology, okay?

But that's not the issue this morning. The issue is my face. I slept hard last night after trying to scrub my face with a bar of soap and warm water. (I keep thinking about getting into skin care, but it just hasn't happened yet, so sue me.) I ended up making more of a mess than I started with and went to bed looking like a melted clown. Judging by the crusty sensation around my eyes and mouth, I don't look much better now than I did last night.

Clem rips the pillow from my hands. "What are you hiding from me? Did you get a face tatt—ooooh," she finishes as she sees my clown mug. "Are those . . . is that . . . lipstick? On your chin? . . . and your ear?"

I reach past her for my phone and open the reverse camera to examine the damage. Lipstick smeared down my chin and mascara and eyeshadow blended into a storm around and under my eyes. The blush and foundation, though, have managed to mysteriously evaporate when, in reality, I'm sure they've sunk deep into my pores, where they'll live forever. Or until I figure out how to suck the dirt from and shrink my pores.

I look to my pillow, Clem still holding it clutched to her chest. *Ohhhh* there's my blush and foundation. Or at least some of it. Note to self: be sure to wash pillowcase myself.

"Your lipstick, actually," I finally say.

"Oh," she says, her voice an octave too high. "I didn't know you were into makeup."

"I'm not," I say quickly. "I could be. Or maybe I am. I don't know. Jury's out."

She nods. "Fair. So you were just chilling in my room?"

"I was looking for you," I tell her. "And for your information, I totally covered for you when Mom came home."

"Thanks," she says with a sigh.

I reach under my bed and grab my laptop. "I did a thing last night and if I show you, you can't make fun of me."

"Waylon, I would never make fun of you."

"That's bullshit and you know it."

She nods, conceding. "Okay, but I would never make fun of you for something that was actually important."

She gasps. "Is this why you called for an emergency pep talk?"

My stomach turns at the memory of sitting in the back room, waiting for Lucas to return. "Not quite," I say as I open up the video and hit play.

I wait for her to say something, but she watches in silence.

On-screen, after introducing myself, I lip-synch to Lizzo's "Good as Hell," Robyn's "Dancing On My Own," and "Lady Marmalade" from *Moulin Rouge*. At the time, I felt my selection showed range. Thankfully, the middle-of-the-night blaring music coming from my room is nothing new for my parents. Between each song, I tell funny stories about myself. The first and only time I wore a skirt in public (outside of Halloween), which happened to be at school in eighth grade because Clem got in trouble the previous day for wearing a skirt that was shorter than her fingertips even though the cheerleaders routinely wore their uniforms to school, which were much shorter. And besides, my sister has very long arms and shouldn't be punished for our father's genetic makeup. There was nothing in the boy's dress code about skirts and definitely nothing about hemlines. Of course, I was tormented for weeks, and I think this was probably the first time that I promised myself if I could just survive high school, there'd be a better version of my life waiting on the other side.

The second story is my coming-out story, and how I'd

dreamed of the moment the way some people dream of their wedding day. In the end, though, the whole family kind of shrugged and said they knew all along while Clem stole the show (without warning me) and dropped the bomb that she was gay too. My third and final story was a recounting of last night and how my disappointment over the results of *Fiercest of Them All* had turned into a very specific kind of motivation that had spurred me on to create this very video.

"And that's why I'm here in this wig and lipstick," I said. "Eat your heart out, y'all. Miss Pumpkin Patch is here to slay the day and my fat ass won't take no for an answer. Your season seventeen queen has arrived. Game fucking on."

Clem sits beside me, her jaw unhinged. "That. Was. FIERCE." She turns to me and grips my shoulder. "You never told me you wanted to do drag, Waylon!"

I shrug. "It didn't even feel like drag. It's like I was showcasing a very specific part of myself, ya know?"

She gasps. "Waylon, what if they actually cast you?"

I scoff. "Never gonna happen. I've never even performed. I probably won't even send it in."

She jumps up to her feet, standing on my mattress as she towers over me. "What are you talking about? You have to send it in!"

"Clem. Come on. The people who try out for these shows are pros. They're actual performers. This was just for fun."

She crosses her arms over her chest before plopping back

down and nuzzling against my shoulder. "You know, Hannah says the Hideaway has a few drag nights."

I shake my head. "I'm good." The Hideaway is the scary former biker bar outside of town that could barely stay in business, so for three nights a week they have what they call Rainbow Nights, and it's definitely not a church outreach event dedicated to celebrating the promise of God's love like Mrs. Michalchuk, my former Sunday school teacher, had thought it was.

"You know—" I start, intent on asking her about my discovery. By the time I fell asleep last night, I'd convinced myself that the email was no big deal. Just Clem testing the waters to see if she could even get in and how far she could take it before backing out. The same thing happened with swim team in tenth grade. She joined, quickly became the best on the team, and won the district championship in the hundred-meter butterfly. When the time came to pick it back up again the following year, she skipped out and said she'd already proven to herself she could do it and that was enough. Clem is a joiner. She likes to join every club and team and group there is. To her, life is a buffet, and everything from mock trial to astronomy club to the soccer team is on the menu.

She reaches out and rubs the light stubble on my chin. "Isn't it so weird that we have body hair? I swear to God, one day we were eleven years old and hairless and then BOOM! Pubes and facial hair!" She jumps up. "Okay, I promised Hannah's grandma I'd come over today and force Hannah to organize her room. It's the only way she'd let her out of the house this weekend."

"That sounds miserable," I groan.

"I didn't say I'd be doing the cleaning," she points out. "Just watching."

"Kinky."

SIX

I like to think of my life in moments. In scenes. Like the moment I came out to my family in ninth grade over Christmas break. I could see it exactly in my head before it even happened. My mom would cry and my dad would clear his throat (the closest thing to crying I've ever seen him do), and they'd both tell me that they'd love me the way I was no matter what. It would be a moment in time when their hopes and dreams for me would change. I'd never marry a girl in a puffy white wedding dress, and maybe some people in town would think differently of us. It would take adjusting. It would take time. It would be difficult, but I would prevail and maybe one day Mom and I would walk in a Pride parade and we'd hold hands, our eyes glistening as we remembered all the obstacles we overcame.

I know that, in reality, coming out is not an easy thing for most people, but imagining this slice of my life as a dramatic highlight reel gave me the courage to follow through with it and maybe even got me a little excited about it too? Is that so bad? To love a bit of drama?

But what happened instead the morning I came out was about as eventful as announcing I had an anatomy quiz.

I chose a Saturday morning on a day when Dad didn't have a job scheduled. I waited for Mom to be completely done making breakfast. In fact, I even let her finish her breakfast first. We had bacon, waffles, and scrambled eggs.

I hadn't given Clem much of a warning, only that I wanted to do it sooner rather than later.

"You two want to help me take care of dishes, so your mother can relax a bit?" asked Dad.

"Sure," said Clem as she began to scrape everyone's leftovers into one big pile for the trash. The plates were Mom's favorite, a plastic Christmas hand-me-down set that would most definitely not survive a trip through the dishwasher, so this would be a hand-wash-and-dry effort.

"Wait, wait," I said. "I have an announcement." In the background, *Elf* played quietly on the television. It was the part where all the North Pole creatures looked like Claymation and the narwhal pokes up through the frozen lake and says, "Bye, Buddy. I hope you find your dad."

Okay, so maybe this wasn't exactly how I had imagined, but there would be no perfect time.

"Mother, Father," I said, in my most formal-sounding voice.

Mom looked to Dad and tugged on his wrist, pulling him back into the chair beside her.

"I need to tell you something, and it's something I've lived with for a very long time." This was my moment. This was my Ursula from *The Little Mermaid* "Poor Unfortunate

Souls" solo. (. . . *and don't underestimate the importance of body language*.) I'd rehearsed it over and over again, and there was more to it—much more—but suddenly I just wanted to get to the point, so I did. "I'm gay."

Mom didn't skip a beat. "Sounds good, baby!"

Dad nodded and gave me a thumbs-up. Not even two thumbs-up!

"I'll never marry a woman," I said, like it was a threat.

Dad chuckled. "I think we'd be pretty horrified if you did, son."

"Me too," peeped Clem. "I am too."

Mom smiled at her with a laugh, and then her whole expression went from relaxed and cheerful to shock and confusion as she realized what Clem was saying.

Tears began to roll down Clem's cheeks and she touched her hands to her face, like she might be able to hide away now that she'd said it out loud.

Mom reached for her wrists and pulled her hands away. "Oh, baby," she cooed. "My darling girl." And then Mom began to cry too. "It'll be okay."

"Your mother's right." Dad cleared his throat, his eyes glistening. Was that a tear? Was that a damn tear? "Wooo, you caught us by surprise there."

Clem wriggled with discomfort. Even though she was having the moment I'd craved for so long, it was hard to be mad at her right then. She'd seen me cannonball out of the closet, and the moment she saw that the water was just fine, she had to join me too. Besides, if I know my sister, I know she's precise and thoughtful and economical. Why have two coming-outs when you only need one.

I leaned over and pulled her into my arms. "Trying to steal my spotlight, sis?"

She laughed through her tears and poked me in the side, tickling me. "I could never. Your spotlight is so bright, I'd burn."

So I guess all that explains why, over the weekend, I had plenty of chances to confront Clem, but none of them felt like the *right* moment.

By Monday morning, the idea of Clem on the other side of the country is festering inside of me and every possible reason why she would think about doing this without me turns me into a hulking rage monster. She's jealous of me. She's tired of living in my shadow. She wants to be her own person. She's ashamed of me. It all roars inside me.

At school, Clem and I set out on separate paths. Her to Macro Econ and me to Business Math before we reunite for second-period choir.

I wave to Mrs. Bradley, our school secretary, her iconic red lips grinning as she waves back to me. Her daughter, Callie, leans on the counter with her boyfriend's arm draped over her shoulder. Callie's boyfriend, Mitch, is a total bear—burly and a little rough around the edges. Definitely my straight doppelgänger sans red hair. The two are the ultimate odd couple and I've got to be honest: I was sort of shocked to see them pair up. Mitch always seemed like the kind of guy who girls wouldn't appreciate until after they'd lived through some awful college boyfriends first. But seeing the two of them together gets me a little soft in the feelings. Somebody wants a fat guy, and even if Callie isn't my flavor, that's just generally good news for fat guys.

I let out a heavy sigh.

"You hear that, man?" says Patrick Thomas as he elbows one of his sophomore lackeys. "Waylon is swooning for you."

"Oh, no, Patrick," I say, my voice as high-pitched as it will go as I skate right past them both. "That was my deep sigh of regret as I realized the only legacy our senior class is leaving this school will be you. Repeating senior year over and over again. Like a ghost, but without all the hot ethereal vibes."

He and his friends stare back at me, dumbfounded.

"Ta-ta, boys."

"I don't even know if I have to retake any classes yet," I hear Patrick say.

Life after senior year might be one giant question mark, but at least it will never include seeing Patrick Thomas on the daily. Patrick has spent the last twelve years of his life circling every weirdo on campus, but especially the fat kids. He's constantly poking and prodding at them. I'd like to think there's some reason why he hates fat people so much. Maybe he lives in fear of being fat himself or maybe an older brother at home terrorizes him. But the truth is: I don't care. Bad shit happens to plenty of people who still manage to treat others like human beings, so Patrick gets no breaks from me.

I take the stairs at the end of the hall to Mr. Higgins's

classroom and I settle into the only remaining seat on the front row next to Alex Wu and in front of Tucker Watson. Great. Stupendous, even.

If sandwiches were made of humans, this would be a highly uncomfortable human sandwich.

Alex Wu is one half of the only openly gay male/male couple at CCHS. He's into gaming and skateboarding and he's so thin that skinny jeans are loose on him.

As I sit down, he looks over his shoulder and gives me a nod.

Oh, and he was my first kiss. Did I mention he's cute? Very cute. But Alex is very much off the market. He's basically married to his longtime boyfriend and my own self-proclaimed frenemy, Kyle Meeks. I love Kyle, but more than that, I love to hate Kyle.

"All right," says Mr. Higgins as he lowers the lights. "Settle down. Eyes and ears up front for announcements." He's the kind of teacher who was definitely taunted in high school and enjoys his power now just a little bit too much. I mean, the guy is wearing a sweater vest and a turtleneck. At the same time. That's a whole new level of nerdy white guy I didn't know existed.

A spunky intro plays with graphics zooming across the TV suspended in the corner of the room until the screen cuts to Millie Michalchuk behind the desk of the school newsroom. Millie and her boyfriend resurrected the once-defunct school news program by using it as a vehicle for morning announcements, which I am a huge fan of, because this Millie chick is sunshine. She used to do the morning announcements from the intercom in the attendance office, but someone at this school woke up and gave her the spotlight she deserves, though based on the snickering at the back of the classroom, not everyone agrees.

I roll my eyes and mutter, "Let a fat girl live."

Behind me, Tucker Watson loudly shushes me.

I repeat: he *shushes* me.

And that's it. That's Tucker Watson's third strike against me.

I whirl around in my seat and say, "Excuse you. Rude."

His mouth forms a soft O, like he's shocked I would ever talk back to him.

And somehow, despite all the ways he's been a total dick in the past, I'm still slightly disappointed by this confirmation of his dick-ishness.

"Mr. Brewer," warns Mr. Higgins, and I turn back around, still snarling.

Strike one: sophomore year. Tucker and I are paired up for a class project in Texas Government. We make a plan to meet twice outside of school to prepare. The first time is at my house. It goes fine. Great, actually. And I might even have had a very slight harmless crush. Our second meeting is at his place, but when I show up, he doesn't answer. I see the blinds move while I wait outside. I swear a few kids walking by even laugh at me. When I confront him the next day, he tells me he forgot and that we should finish the project separately.

Strike two: junior year. First day. World Literature.

We're seated at the same table. Tucker asks for a seat reassignment. In front of the whole class.

There are some people at this school who I've never even shared a class with, but by some awful twist of fate, Tucker and I have shared at least one class a semester. Thankfully, besides our run-in at Ms. Laverne's office, we've managed to stay out of each other's way, but him shushing me gets me riled up all over again.

"Prom court nominations will be tallied this Friday and announced on Monday morning," sweet, sweet Millie continues. At least she can't hear the jokers in the back of my classroom from the safety of her little studio on the other side of the building.

Mr. Higgins zaps the TV off and immediately starts droning on about business loan interest rates.

After class I follow close on Alex's heels and make small talk about his weekend just to avoid having to face Tucker and his stupid jawline.

"It's only fair that I get the solo at graduation, ya know?" Alex says, for what I'm guessing is not the first time.

"Huh?" I nod as we turn the corner into the choir room. "Oh, yeah. Totally."

Kyle is lounging on the risers, with his legs crossed at the ankle, a reminder that in this room, he is a king.

Clem sits with her chin perched on her knees, laughing at something Kyle's said. Kyle is a total golden boy. Brown hair parted down the side and even the occasional sweater vest. I'm not entirely sure which schools are even

Ivy League, but he's definitely got the look. Very white guy at a Saturday morning brunch with the tennis team. Very punchable.

"There she is!" Kyle says. "Do you prefer Pumpkin or Miss Patch?"

My stomach drops. I look to Clem, the only living human who saw my audition video.

She grimaces and holds her arms up. This morning, she even let me pin her two braids around the crown of her head for a Heidi moment, so I'm finding it a little hard to maintain my anger as I admire my work. "I was just so proud of you."

I have two choices: One, I could dig into Clem and let her know that I feel personally violated that she would share that video with anyone. Or two, I can play it off and act like it's no big deal. I quickly decide that option two will elicit the lesser reaction from Kyle.

"Babe, what are you even talking about?" Alex asks Kyle as he curls in next to him on the risers. Some people might say that's a lot of PDA for two high school dudes in a tiny Texas town, but this room—the choir room—is a little microscopic queer-kid haven in a kingdom built for cis-het white good ol' boys.

I slump onto Ms. Jennings's chair behind her music stand and turn to Alex. "I slapped together a silly little audition video for *Fiercest of Them All*. Not a big deal, honestly. And really it was just a joke."

Kyle smiles in that glittering, charismatic way that reminds me he is such a politician. "Didn't seem like much of a joke to me. I mean, can you imagine what an inspiration it would be for the younger members of Prism?"

I grin and bite back whatever sarcastic remark is trying to claw its way free. "Wow, Kyle. I hadn't even thought about that."

Clem nods, like *wow, Kyle is such a genius. Wow, Kyle, what a big genius brain you have.*

"That makes the club sound like a charity case," says Corey, the quiet ninth grader who usually stands on the riser below me. Their curly blue hair is vivid against their light-brown complexion and they wear a shirt that says I EAT GENDER NORMS FOR BREAKFAST. "But you really should come some time, Waylon. For some of my friends, you're like one of the first gay people they heard about in town."

I think I was supposed to find that touching, and I do, really. But suddenly, I feel very old, like I'm one step away from referring to Corey as a *youth*.

Kyle clutches his chest and looks at Corey like a proud papa. "Corey's taking the reins next year."

I look past Kyle and smile at Corey. "Congratulations."

Ms. Jennings breezes through the door of her classroom, and I don't use the word *breeze* lightly. Somehow the goddesses of the universe have gifted us with this woman due to the fact that her wife (You heard that right! A gay teacher! In Clover City!) signed a deal with the city a few years back to do some kind of revitalization project that's supposed to drag us into the twenty-first century twenty-something years later.

Ms. Jennings, a tall Black woman, with her natural hair always playfully styled into two pom-poms on the top of her head, is a little bit chic and a little bit eccentric. Her patron saints are Lauryn Hill and Tori Amos, and her room is decorated in concert posters from shows she's actually been to, including some for a thing called Lilith Fair that she swears was her own personal awakening. Sure, she's a little stuck in the nineties/aughts, but it's charming in a relic-of-the-past kind of way.

"Ah," she says, her voice melodic. "Waylon, my dear, thank you for keeping my seat warm."

She gives me a soft pat on the back, and something about the way she talks and moves and touches me makes me want to scream PLEASE BE MY MOM! Even though I have a perfectly fine mom. A great mom, in fact! But instead of any of that, I clear my throat and scoot out of her seat.

I've never actually told Ms. Jennings how awesome I think she is, because what's the fun in truly sharing your feelings with adult humans? And maybe the thought of graduating and not seeing her every day makes my throat clam up in a gross way. Anyway. Moving on.

I take my place on the last row with Kyle, the other baritone. Except I'm not *just* a baritone. I'm a tenor too, but Kyle doesn't have the range and his baritone is too weak to carry. So one day, back during sophomore year, Ms. Jennings discreetly pulled me aside after class and asked if I wouldn't mind spreading my talents to the baritone section, since we lost a few seniors. I, very smugly, have treasured that day for the last two years of my life.

"So," he says while Ms. Jennings takes attendance. "Did you send your video in?"

I scoff. "Uh, no. Really, it was a joke."

With all the fake sincerity in the world, Kyle touches my arm. "Waylon, you could really make it. Can you imagine? A kid from Clover City on one of the biggest drag shows in the world?"

"I'm not a drag queen," I tell him. "That show is for, like, professionals. I was annoyed by who won and wanted to make my own little video. I was messing around."

"Don't sell yourself short," he says. "You know what I think? I think you're really brave for putting yourself out there like that. You know, I used to be . . . bigger too, and it's not easy for people like us."

"Um, okay."

Ah, yes. How could I forget? During the summer between eighth grade and freshman year, Kyle lost seventy pounds working out day in and day out at Motion, the circuit gym for middle-aged women . . . and Kyle, apparently. He was such a success that the owner of Motion bought a billboard to display his before-and-after pictures. Most kids would have been mortified, but stupid, genuine Kyle treated it like a victory lap and used it as his platform to win student body vice president for three years in a row now.

"Just think about it," he tells me earnestly. "Have a little faith in yourself, because I sure do."

Alex turns around and squeezes Kyle's hand briefly as Ms. Jennings calls for our attention.

We get it! You're both very happy!

We cycle through warm-ups and our graduation performance songs, and right before the bell rings, Kyle raises
his hand beside me. "Um, yes, Ms. Jennings, could I make
an announcement?"

She gives him an indulgent smile and nods.

"I want to remind everyone that we have a Prism meeting here in this room after school. I've signed up the club
to help with prom decorations this year, so we'll talk about
our plan of attack and also, a reminder that prom court
nominations close later this week."

"Thank you, Kyle," says Ms. Jennings. She holds a finger up, and right on cue, the bell rings. "Class dismissed."

The single greatest joy of my senior year is off-campus
lunch, which is why my foot is on the pedal, hauling to
Harpy's with Clem and Hannah in tow. I'd hoped that
maybe Hannah would ditch and now would be the time to
talk to Clem about her big plans, but I'm not about to have
Serious Sibling Discourse with a third party in the mix.

Harpy's is a Clover City staple and also the location of
many of mine and Clem's childhood birthday parties. It's
not even particularly good (honestly, their secret sauce is
just mustard), but I still feel a fierce loyalty to their curly
fries and will always choose this place over whatever new
chain has set up shop.

Lydia, longtime Harpy's employee and the grumpiest
woman alive, sits perched on a stool behind the cash register.

"Hello, sunshine," I say.

"Number three extra pickles hold the onion?" she asks without looking up.

"Music to my ears," I tell her.

And I swear her lips twitch into an almost smile.

I pay and then Hannah and Clem place their order, which has turned out to be an intricate feast of sides they like to share since Clem convinced Hannah to become a vegetarian. I score the highly coveted circle booth in the far corner of the restaurant as Lydia slowly evaporates.

Hannah waits for our food while Clem gets our drinks from the soda fountains. When they finally both sit down, I let out a long-held groan.

"I'm going to kill you," I tell Clem, half joking and half serious.

"What'd she do this time?" asks Hannah as she chomps down on an onion ring.

"Oh, she knows."

My sweet golden-retriever sister shrugs.

"Tell her," I say. "Tell Hannah what you did."

She side-eyes me and turns to Hannah. "I . . . uh . . . the video I showed you—"

"Oh, so she's seen the video now too." Of course Clem showed that video to every living being she came into contact with. "I'm so glad I could provide entertainment for you and your friends."

"It was good!" Clem says. "We share a cloud! It was there! And besides, when Kyle saw it, I was already watching it on my phone. It's not like I went out of my way to show him."

My nostrils flare and I shake my head. "Whatever." I can't get over this betrayal, and the fact that it's not more of a big deal ratchets my anger up a whole notch.

Clem clears her throat. "So, either of you want to go to the Prism meeting with me after school?"

Hannah and I both groan in unison.

"I have a thing," Hannah says as she pushes up her sleeves to reach over the onion rings for the cheesy tots.

"Oh, come on!" Clem says. My sister isn't bothered by large groups or strangers or organized activities that might make her look dumb. But she's usually pretty good about not expecting the same of me. Groups and gatherings make me feel emotionally claustrophobic. I was a little freaked out when she started dating Hannah over the summer, like suddenly they would be so social together, and I would either be stuck home alone or left being their third wheel at a party. But luckily, Hannah's tolerance for socializing is even lower than mine.

"Babe," says Hannah as she checks a text on her phone. "You know organized groups aren't really my thing."

I shake my head. "And you know I'm just a bad gay."

"There's no wrong way to be gay," Clem righteously declares.

"Well, then file me under Hannah's reason," I tell her, my mouth stuffed with fries just as Kyle and Alex walk in followed by Tucker and a few of his friends, who all skip the long line by scooting in with some cheerleaders to place their orders. I slither down in the bench as much as I can, hoping that I can hide from all three of them.

"Besides," Hannah says. "I really do have a thing. My 'lita texted a second ago to say she needs me to help her pick up patio chairs she bought from someone on Facebook."

Clem turns to her. "Grandma Camile has a Facebook?"

Hannah sighs. "She got a hand-me-down iPhone from my cousin Paul last month and now she can't be stopped. He just dropped off the phone and left me with her. Do you know how long it took me to explain Face ID to her? Now that she knows how to use it, though, she's everywhere. She even started her own Facebook group called DRC of CC Y'ALL, for other Dominicans in Clover City. She has exactly nine members, and five of them are moderators. She even wrote down the name of her group for her cashier at the grocery store the other day. When the cashier explained that she was Puerto Rican, 'Lita told her she could be an honorary Dominican."

"Would it be weird if I tried to get our grandmas to date?" I ask. "At the very least, can I be her friend on Facebook?"

Hannah takes a swig of soda. "It's not all sunshine and friend requests. Last week, she called me during class to tell me she got a message from a random person saying that the government was monitoring her Facebook page and that she needed to send in her social security number to verify her identity."

"Oh my God," Clem gasps. "Do they have like child lock on phones but for grandparents?"

"Is it bad that I don't know my social security number by heart?" I ask.

"You don't even know your cell phone number." Clem throws herself against the back of the booth. "I guess I'll just go to Prism by myself."

Prism is the only school-sanctioned queer club, started by—you guessed it!—Kyle Meeks. And, for the record, I don't think I'm actually a bad gay, but I've never been good at being . . . political the way Kyle and the other members are. The group has done really awesome things, like a gender-neutral bathroom in the attendance office and fighting to remove gender-specific dress codes for school dances, but some days I feel like I'm barely getting by in Clover City and maybe there isn't always safety in numbers. Maybe numbers put a bigger target on our back? I'm *this* close to graduating. I'd rather not become any more of a target than I already am. (And trust me. Femme-leaning fat, gay ginger guys already stand out plenty, even when they're wearing basic-ass clothes their mom bought them at Sam's Club.) Especially if Clem is about to leave me here to survive on my own.

Okay, maybe I also really can't stand Kyle Meeks and everything he does, and maybe disliking him so much also makes me feel like a colossal jerk. I don't know. Jury's still out.

"Room for two more?" asks Kyle, as if summoned by our conversation. He slides in next to me, followed by Alex.

"I guess so," I say as Clem says, "Of course!"

I slide to the center point of the U-shaped booth seat. *Great. Now I'm trapped.*

"Nice and cozy," says Alex.

"So cozy," Hannah deadpans, and I could kiss her cute little unimpressed face.

Kyle says longingly as he looks at all of our trays and then back to his grilled-chicken salad, "I was bad over the weekend, so salads for me."

Alex rolls his eyes. "Babe, a burger won't kill you."

"No," says Kyle, "but it will make me fat again."

I want to slither out of this booth until I'm nothing but a puddle of human irritation on the floor.

"Um, Kyle," Clem says gently, "maybe you don't have to say fat like it's a bad thing."

Kyle gives her a puzzled look, but continues charging into a conversation about some teacher who dared to give him an A minus.

I wink at Clem, who reaches under the table to squeeze my kneecap.

For the rest of lunch, Clem, Alex, and Kyle chatter back and forth about choir and passing on the Prism torch to the underclass people, and Kyle and Alex's big plans to be the queer power couple of the century at Rice University this fall.

My mind wanders as I watch them and every other Clover City senior in this restaurant laugh and whisper and hug. All I can think about is Clem leaving me and Lucas choosing someone over me and how these are supposed to be the best years of my life, but how can that even be true? How is that even possible? If you would have told me just a week ago that these were the best years of my life, I would

63

have shrugged and said, "Sure, I guess. It's not bad, so it must be good." But this can't be it? Can it?

"So I told him he has to send the video in," Kyle says and nudges me in the side. "You're sending it in, right?"

I throw my arms up. "Yes! Okay? I'm going to send it in. I'm going to show the whole world that a random kid from a little Texas nowhere town can be the Fiercest of Them All. Are you happy?"

Kyle smiles a full twenty-watt smile. He doesn't get it. He's too damn noble to even read my sarcasm. "Yes," he says, like I've finally seen the light. "You go, queen!"

I could puke. I could vomit right this moment.

"I gotta go," I say, and look around for my nearest exit, but I'm quickly reminded that, oh yeah, I'm a huge tall, fat dude stuck in a tiny booth and there's no chance my butt is going over or under, so I turn back to Kyle. "Excuse me."

He doesn't move.

"Excuse me," I say again as I begin to scoot toward him, until he finally gets it and he and Alex move out of my way.

From across the restaurant, I can hear Tucker laughing loudly, and I know it's not directed at me, but I can't stop myself from feeling like I'm the butt of whatever joke has him so entertained.

I go out to the truck and wait for Clem and Hannah to finish their food. Part of me wants to ditch them and let them catch a ride with Kyle and Alex.

After a few minutes, Clem comes outside and whispers

something to Hannah, who hangs behind, plopping down on the curb.

Clem leans in through the passenger window and I have so much to say to her that if I make eye contact with her, it will all come spilling out.

"Waylon?" she asks. "What's the deal? Are you okay?"

I nod. "I'm good."

"Is it Kyle? I know he can rub you the wrong way sometimes."

"Yeah," I tell her as I start the car, and wave an arm out the window to Hannah for her to get in. "He just annoys me sometimes. I don't get why you like him."

She opens the door. "I don't get why you don't like him."

"You know why I don't like him."

She gets into the truck and in her gentlest voice, she says, "I don't think it's really fair to dislike someone because they lost some weight a few years ago."

Clem's always been the thin one between us. Growing up, we heard every joke. *Are you sure he didn't eat the third one in the womb?* And for a long time, it drove a wedge between us, especially when we were younger and we'd be in the pediatrician's office. Clem was always this shining example of perfect health, meanwhile I was routinely questioned about my eating habits and our mom was handed countless pamphlets about childhood obesity. I remember hating Clem for being skinny, but time and age helped me see that the only people confused by our differences were people who didn't matter. But there are still some things, like why Kyle makes me uncomfortable, that are hard for her to fathom.

I purse my lips together and call out the window to Hannah. "Come on! Let's go!"

"I don't want to talk about this right now," I tell my sister. I don't feel like having my emotions about something that felt very big to me dismissed. Because my problems with Kyle are so much more than that. For as much as I love my sister and as much as we have in common, maybe we don't know each other as well as I thought.

SEVEN

When all else fails, call Grammy. This has been my mantra since the first time I faked sick at school in first grade and both Mom and Dad called BS on me when I phoned them. When the secretary wasn't paying attention, I made one last-ditch effort to get out of school and called Grammy. I don't know what it was about that particular day. Maybe a bad day in gym class or maybe my teacher had caught me daydreaming, but I would have done anything to get out of school.

I gave Grammy my best performance, and afterward, she said, "I don't buy this sick act, but if you're calling me, it must be for a reason. Tell the secretary I'm on my way. I'll deal with your mother."

And that was only one of many instances where Grammy swooped in and saved the day, so not even Clem is surprised when I drop her off at school the next morning and announce that I will be taking a self-care day.

"Going to Grammy's?" she asks, fully aware that I've not been myself, especially since yesterday's lunch.

"I'll pick you up after school," I promise her.

"Mr. Brewer," calls Mr. Higgins from the carport where he's on morning parking lot duty.

"Shit," I mutter.

"How chivalrous of you to drop your twin sister off up front. I suspect you're going to find a parking spot and that I'll see you in first period?"

I nod mutely.

"Stupendous!"

Clem shrugs. "Sorry," she says quietly.

"Nothing to be sorry for," I tell her.

"Stupendous," she says in her worst Mr. Higgins voice. "I'll wait for you inside."

I circle back around and take a spot at the back of the lot. After hopping out and walking halfway across the parking lot, I double back because I forgot my backpack, and I can already feel my annoyance at merely existing today start to ramp up. Maybe if I can make it through first period, I can skip for the rest of the day.

As I'm walking into the building, Clementine comes barreling down the hallway. "We have to go to Grammy's!" she says breathlessly.

"What?" Panic spikes in my chest. "Is she okay? What's wrong?"

"There she is," Patrick Thomas sings as he steps in front of her, cackling in my face. "Miss America!"

"Are you high?" I ask him.

"Excuse me, Miss Patch?" says one of his younger goons in a voice so high it makes him sound like air escaping a balloon.

My chest begins to tighten. No. This can't be real. This can't be happening. Suddenly, my throat feels like sandpaper. There's only one way someone would know to call me by that name.

Clem grips my wrist. "Come on. Let's go. Ignore these guys."

Another guy who I vaguely recognize pretends to vogue, but does an awful job of it as he sings a nonsensical, barely recognizable version of "Lady Marmalade."

Around me, the entire hallway full of students is laughing. *At me.* They're laughing at me.

I turn to Clem, unable to hide the betrayal I feel deep in my bones.

I tear my arm away from her and look up just in time to see Tucker Watson grimace at this whole disastrous situation and turn away. *So glad I could disgust you*, I nearly spit at him.

I could hide out in Ms. Laverne's office, but that would require diving even deeper into the school. If Patrick Thomas has seen my audition video, everyone else has too, and if this is what I am greeted with after stepping five feet into the building, no thank you. Sorry, Mr. Higgins. I'm out of here.

I walk with purpose, my head held high and my shoulders squared, the whole way to my car as Clem chases after me.

I don't know how the video got out, but I do know that I shared it with one person and one person only. Besides, it's not like Clem was being so judicious in the first place about who she shared it with.

I get in the truck and Clem circles around to get into the passenger side, but I hit the lock button before she can open the door.

"Waylon Russell Brewer!" she says, shocked.

I shake my head and turn the radio on.

Clem comes over to my side and knocks on the window. "It's not so bad," she pleads. "Please let me in. We can handle this! We can do anything together! We're the Brewer twins, damn it!"

And that's it. That's the final straw. I roll my window down and turn to her. "Together? Really? Just like how you were going to go to Georgia without me? Or were we supposed to do that together too?"

Her jaw drops, and it's then that I know this is really happening. My twin sister, my best friend, is leaving me to go halfway across the country and she didn't even have the courage to tell me. She's not thinking about it or weighing her options. Clem's mind is made up.

It takes her too long to form a thought, to grasp her words.

I've already rolled my window up and am blasting Gaga's "Bad Romance." I reverse out of the parking lot, leaving my sister there, her jaw still slack.

EIGHT

It only takes a few minutes of internet sleuthing to piece together how this happened, and it all starts with Kyle Meeks.

Of course, it does. I slam my phone down in the passenger seat and grip my steering wheel as I try to inhale the good vibes and exhale the toxic anger that makes me want to crush Kyle Meeks and everything he loves until all that's left is ashes for me to sprinkle across a pit of rattlesnakes.

After a few moments, I pick my phone up again and begin to reread his text message.

> **Kyle: Waylon, I am so incredibly sorry! I shared the video to the Prism Club Facebook group. Or so I thought. I accidentally publicly posted it to my personal page. It was only up for 20 minutes. 30 tops.**

I pull up Facebook and find his post in the Prism Club, where he'd originally intended to post it.

Kyle Meeks (Moderator) → **Prism** (Group, 36 Members) ⋯
I'm so thrilled to share this FIERCEST OF THEM ALL
audition tape from our very own, Waylon Brewer. You go,
Waylon! We're rooting for you!

🕯11

Below is the video in its full unedited glory.

He even tagged me. This is what I get for saying Facebook is beneath me. (Honestly though, any platform where my own mother is sharing memes is not a safe space.)

The comments are mostly gentle and encouraging, which honestly softens me a little, but it doesn't matter because it's everywhere. Facebook. Twitter. Instagram. There are even a few reaction videos on Snapchat, Twitter, and YouTube. And all it took was thirty minutes before Kyle realized what he'd done and deleted his public post.

I haven't gone globally viral or anything like that, but there's no doubt that nearly every soul in this town has seen the video.

Mostly people are just laughing. But some of it is vitriol. Pure hate.

If my son dressed like this, I'd disown his ass.

I'm sorry, y'all, but this just goes against nature. God created this boy to be a boy.

What a perv.

Y'all can laugh all you want, but this boy must be possessed by demons.

In my day, boys didn't have time to wear skirts. They were busy providing.

Downfall of society, ladies and gents.

Some are even worse than that.

My phone rings.

My dad. Of course this would have made its way to him and my mom.

I think about sending him to voice mail, but that will only make things worse.

"Hello?"

"Son?" Dad's normally booming voice is soft around the edges. He clears his throat. "I, uh, your sister called your mother and me. Said some kind of video of you is making the rounds. You, uh, dressed in a . . . dress."

"I was in drag, Dad."

"Drag. Right. Like on your show, right? Anyone giving you a hard time?"

My chest tightens at the concern in his voice. "Just the usual suspects."

"You know, your mother and I would be happy to go up to the school and have a—"

"I think I'd rather take the day off."

I can hear my mom whisper something in the background and after a second, Dad says, "Of course. That's fine. Your mom wants to know if she can do anything."

"Gimme that phone," I hear her say.

"Baby?"

"Hi, Mom."

"You know we love you just the way you are, right?"

I can practically hear my dad nodding dutifully in the background. "Yup."

"And I haven't seen this video yet, but if you—" Her

voice catches. "If there's something you're not telling us about your gender i–identity or, uh, expression." She stumbles over those last few words.

"Mom," I say before she can go any further. "Thank you for being, like, basically the wokest middle-aged woman in Clover City, but I just really like drag and was messing around a little. The video got into the wrong hands and now everyone's seen it. That's it. But if I ever have any big gender revelations, you'll be my first call."

She sniffs. "Okay, good. That's good to hear."

"That's great, son," Dad says in the background. It's adorably frustrating that they haven't realized they can simply put me on speakerphone. My sister might be total trash right now, but at least I have the best parents.

"Wait," I say. "Did y'all know about Clem going to Georgia?" They must have. "Was I the only one in the dark?"

Mom sighs. "We told her that she had to tell you, and y'all know we don't like getting in between the two of you. But she should have told you instead of letting you find out . . . however you found out."

There's not much I can say to that. Mom has always frustratingly played Switzerland anytime Clem and I have had a standoff, only getting involved when someone's life was in actual danger.

"Well, what am I supposed to do next year?"

"Stick with your plan, baby," she says simply. "Go to Austin. I'll visit on the weekends!"

"That wasn't my plan. It was *our* plan."

"Well, then we'll make a new plan." She clicks her tongue a few times, before really dropping a truth bomb. "Baby, you both knew there would come a time when you'd take separate paths. There's no shame in taking your time while you find yours. Your father and I are in no hurry to shoo you out of the house. We'll figure it out."

"I'm going to Grammy's," I announce, not ready to confront the idea of living at home next fall without my sister. I'm going to Austin. That was the plan.

"Okay," she says after a long moment.

"Help her install that video doorbell, would you?" Dad asks, having taken the phone back.

"Sure." Though we all know that's more up Clem's alley than mine.

"It'll all shake out," he says.

We say our goodbyes and I love yous.

I shoot off a text to Grammy.

Fire up your commiserating engines. I'm coming over. It's been a rough day and it's not even 9 a.m. yet.

Revving it up now, she responds. **Putting a pot of coffee on too.**

NINE

When I get to Grammy's, she's on the porch waiting with two cups of coffee—black for her and black with sugar for me. Grammy says that anyone who drinks their coffee black probably likes it just a little bit when life stings.

And I guess that's true in a way, because as I sit there on her porch, sipping coffee while Cleo is wrist deep in her flower beds, I can't help but wonder what everyone at school is saying about me right now. Maybe Clem is in a death match for my honor, or perhaps Kyle is having an existential crisis about accidentally sharing the video and causing my mass humiliation.

Huh. That sounds nice, actually.

"Well, I saw your video on the Facebook," says Grammy as she taps her nails on the arm of her hot-pink rocking chair. "Delores down the road shared it from her grandson."

"Keith Fuller," I mutter, an epic bully from when I was in ninth grade who dropped out.

I lie on her bench swing, my limbs dragging off every edge and side as the chains creak beneath my weight.

When Dad first installed the thing I was convinced I'd break it if I even looked at it the wrong way, but he swore he'd reinforced it plenty and that if I broke it, it would be no big deal. He could just fix it. So for today, this swing is my fainting couch, and it's sort of comforting to know that my dad is still there to fix things when I break them.

"What'd you think?" I ask, feeling a little timid. Grammy has always encouraged me in everything, but we don't talk a lot about Clem and me being gay, which is nice, but sometimes I wonder if it's a topic Grammy is nervous to tackle. I'm wild with anxiety at the thought of everything I've so carefully kept to myself just being out there for everyone to see, but my ego still wants to hear her impression of it all.

"I think I ought to teach you how to do your makeup."

I laugh and relief swells in my chest. "Grammy, drag makeup isn't the same as regular makeup."

"Well, either way, we've got to fix that face. But honestly, Pumpkin, I found it charming. You've always been such a star. I wish you'd picked up theater or dance. I told your mama to get you started young, but she insisted that you'd find your passions on your own."

I sigh and reach down for a sip of coffee. Ah, it burns so good. "I have passions," I say.

I know. I should be super into theater or dance or something. But people who commit that hard to something kind of stress me out. In some inexplicable way, I feel embarrassed for them, but a tiny part of me has also always wanted to be them too. Like, I can't help but wonder how freeing it must be to love performing so much that you're okay with auditioning and not getting the part.

Choir, though, is the exact amount of commitment I'm comfortable with. There's something almost mathematical about how you either hit your note or you don't, and at least in our choir, there's little to no competition. And then there's the fact that if I'm going to be onstage, the only role I want to play is me.

"Well, you're still young," she says. "You've got plenty of time to explore every crevice of the world."

But it doesn't exactly feel like that. It feels like I'm supposed to know who I am right this moment.

"Clem's leaving me," I tell her. "She's going to Georgia."

She nods, eyeing me from over the rim of her coffee cup. "It won't be easy to see you two apart."

"So I guess I'm the only one who didn't know." I want to be angry at Grammy, but every effort to muster my disappointment fails.

"She didn't know how to break the news. I swear, the girl was losing sleep over it."

"We tell each other everything," I say, my voice catching on that last syllable.

Grammy is silent for a moment. "Maybe you don't. And maybe you shouldn't."

My mouth snaps open. She's wrong. We do tell each other every—well, maybe not everything. And, in reality, I don't want her to know *everything*. I think about her and

Hannah and her closed bedroom door. *Nope.* I definitely don't want to know everything.

"Fine," I say, even though it is very much not fine. Nothing about this is fine! "But this is an awfully big thing to leave out. I just . . . I thought we'd live together until we got married and then we'd be next-door neighbors and then our spouses would die before us and then we'd both die watching our favorite TV shows and then we'd all be buried in the Brewer family plot until we became one giant clump of dirt."

Grammy laughs. "Well, as lovely as that sounds . . . I don't think you're really taking into account what's best for Clem. Or for you!"

"Can we please talk about literally anything else?" I ask.

Cleo pops up from between the flower beds. "Oh my goodness, I watched the first few episodes of that television show you and Clem are always talking about? The one where winter is coming or what have you?"

"*Game of Thrones!*" I say. I'm on my third rewatch and am still reeling from the last season. "Well, you're, like, way late to the party, but welcome to the game of thrones! When you play the game of thrones, you win or you die," I quote back to her.

But her only response is her forehead wrinkling in confusion.

Bernadette steps out onto the porch, still in her lavender housecoat with a fresh cup of coffee in hand. "Are y'all talking about that throne game show?" She sits in the rocker next to Grammy. "You know, Peter tried getting me into that show when we were seeing each other and I couldn't get past the incest."

Grammy huffs. "There she goes again. You dated a thirty-eight-year-old man *once*. Once! And now you'll never stop talking about it! Peter this. Peter that. Someone mentions any little thing and somehow it's related to Peter."

I groan. "No, you've got to stick with it. You haven't even gotten to the mother of dragons. You haven't even seen Cersei in all of her awful glory!"

Bernadette rolls her eyes. "Peter and I were a brief flickering flame, but we left each other scorched. Forever changed, really."

"I really didn't need to know that," I tell her, but it feels good to come here and find these three women being their regular selves. My life might be upside down, but things are still normal somewhere.

"Well," says Cleo as she dives back into the bushes. "I found the show quite riveting, so I'll be watching and I don't want any spoilings."

"Spoilers," I tell her.

We spend the rest of the morning outside, talking shit about their neighbors and hearing about their next great big adventure, a trip to Palm Springs this summer. I try not to think too much about how nearly all my favorite people are three to four times my age.

★ ★ ★

"I'm so close to figuring it out," I say. On the floor, surrounding me in a semicircle, are the pieces of Grammy's old doorbell and her new doorbell. "I don't get how it didn't work."

"Does it have something to do with the password I set up on my iPad?" asks Grammy. "Or maybe if I restart my phone?"

I shake my head, not bothering to explain that the problem is the video doorbell and not her many devices it should link to.

The front door creaks open and Clem tiptoes through the doorway.

"Grammy called me," she immediately says in defense.

I look over to Grammy as she walks past me with a basket of laundry. "Traitor."

"I need a doorbell," she calls over her shoulder. "And you two need to come to a truce."

I turn to Clem as she sits down beside me. "I've installed and uninstalled it twice. Your problem now."

"Here. Let me see." She slides her glasses up her nose and takes a look at the instructions.

"Give me those," I say, motioning to her glasses.

She does and I clean them off with the hem of my shirt. "I don't know how you can see out of these things. They're so gross."

"Does this mean you're not mad at me?" she asks.

"Oh, I'm still plenty mad. Your glasses were just making it worse."

"I know you probably don't want to talk about it," she says quietly, "but not everyone at school had the same reaction as Patrick Thomas. In fact, a lot of people even thought it was pretty cool."

"I can't believe you shared that video to begin with. It was private!"

"I'm sorrrrrrry," she says. "I was really proud of you, and it's really nice to see you do something for yourself."

For myself? So that I'll have something to occupy my time with once she's gone and maybe she won't feel as guilty? "And how did Kyle even get it?" My words are venomous.

"Well." She clears her throat. "That is sort of my fault. He kept asking me to send it so he could show Alex, and so I did. I really didn't think he would share it so wide—"

"What were you thinking? How stupid can you be, Clem?"

Her cheeks flare red, an angry trait we share. "I was proud of you!" she says, her voice boiling over as she stands with the pieces for the new doorbell and the instructions.

I follow her to the doorway with my arms crossed.

"It's not like you're the shy type," she says, a screw between her teeth while she holds the doorbell plate in place. "And Kyle loved it! He was so excited for you."

"Kyle isn't the person you think he is."

"He only meant to post it to the Prism group, and he didn't do it maliciously. You've got to stop acting like he's always out to get you. Kyle is a good guy and I think y'all

82

could be really good friends again if you could get over yourself."

"Oh, that's nice. Pour some salt in my open wound."

She shakes her head and looks directly at me. "I need to talk to you about Georgia. I have to make a decision soon."

"Not right now. My brain is too full and I'm . . . I'm angry with you. Can it please wait?" It takes all my self-control to not completely turn on her and say all the vicious things running through my head.

She bites down on her lip. Clem hates indecision, and even though I'm sure she's already made up her mind about next year, it's still technically an uncertainty. "Sure. Of course."

I plop down on the couch with Grammy when she returns with a fresh basket of laundry to fold. We watch *Hollywood Squares* while Clem connects the doorbell to Grammy's, Cleo's, and Bernadette's phones.

I know I need to hear Clem out, but right now I've got too much on my mind. And maybe if I never hear her out, nothing has to change.

TEN

That night, I sit down at home with Mom and Dad and show them Monica Lewinsky's TED Talk about her scandal and explain to them that I need to disappear for two days.

"I need to wait out the news cycle," I say.

Mom side-eyes me over her shoulder as she stirs her spaghetti sauce.

"Hear me out. Prom court will be announced first thing Friday morning. If I can stay home for two more days, this whole thing will blow over and when I go back to school, everyone will be talking about prom court."

Clem looks up from her phone. "He's not wrong."

Dad looks to Mom, who eventually shrugs.

"Two days," he says. "No more."

"And no more fake sick days," Mom says. "The only way you're missing any more school after this before graduation is if you're on your deathbed."

"Morbid," I say. "But deal."

I spend the next two days trying and failing to make homemade facemasks out of eggs and avocados after reading a BuzzFeed article titled "30 Ways to Make Self-Care Happen on the Cheap." I do, however, try and succeed in finishing what episodes I had left of *The Great British Baking Show*. Mom and Dad also put me to work cleaning out the pantry and organizing Mom's extensive collection of Tupperware. It's not the glamorous two days chock-full of indulgence and mindlessness that I'd imagined, but it's better than the alternative. And I manage to elude Clem and her Very Important Discussion about Our Future. I'm so angry with her. I want her with me always and I want to push her a million miles away all at once.

When I finally go back to school, I walk in with my head held high, flanked by both Hannah and Clementine. I may not know Hannah very well, but I'm thankful to see her waiting for us in the parking lot.

Deep breaths, I tell myself, prepared to face Patrick Thomas at any moment, but Hannah and Clem walk me all the way to Mr. Higgins's class without a single incident. There is some pointing and staring, of course, but by far the worst of it is making eye contact with Tucker Watson when I walk into class and remembering the sting of his disgust the other day. Like it's not enough for someone to not like you—they have to be disgusted by you too. Is it because I'm fat? Gay? What is it, Tucker? Whatever. He's just another person I'll leave behind one day when I get out of this town.

I sit down, this time as far as I can get from Tucker, and moments later, Alex settles in next to me.

"Oh my gosh," he says. "Are you okay? Kyle said you

didn't respond to his texts."

"Is he surprised?" I ask, not bothering to hide how annoyed I am.

Alex nods and it's the closest I've ever gotten to an admission from him that he also thinks Kyle is a little bit awful. "Kyle can be . . . eager," he says. "You have to know, though, that he didn't post that video for it to get the kind of attention it did. Accidents like that happen all the time on the internet. Remember that time Jenna Martinez accidentally posted a picture of a wart on her you-know-what on Instagram? People eventually got over it." He sighs. "Kyle was just . . . he was so excited when you said you were auditioning and . . . you know, he would kill me for saying this, but he always talks about what great friends you two were through elementary and middle school."

"It doesn't matter what his intention was, Alex." My voice cuts, and I hate talking to Alex like this, but I also want it to sting enough so that somehow Kyle will feel it too.

For me and Kyle, history will always be divided into two distinctive chunks of time. BWL = before weight loss and AWL = after weight loss. And Alex isn't wrong. If you can even imagine it, Kyle and I were actual, genuine friends. But after he lost the weight, I couldn't handle the way he talked about his former fat self with hate and disgust. It felt like he wasn't only talking about himself. He was talking about me. Then, before I knew it, his whole world was Alex and the end of our friendship came all too naturally.

Being fat is hard enough without adding gay guy to the equation. The only gay guys anyone fawns over online are ripped with like twelve-pack abs or whatever. I know it's plenty difficult for other people too, but when you're straight and big, everyone is fine with you as long as you can be the person who lifts heavy stuff or fixes things or protects people. But when you're gay, if you want to be the object of anyone's desire, you better have washboard abs and a phone full of thirst traps. So in a very small way, I feel for Kyle, but mostly being near him hurts.

"Good morning, future adults. Welcome back, Mr. Brewer," says Mr. Higgins as he settles into his office chair and props his feet up on his desk before turning on the TV. "It's that time," he says.

Everyone likes to pretend they don't give a shit about things like prom court, but I can sense the electric energy in the air as that familiar intro plays on the TV.

Millie sits at her desk with Miranda Garcia, student body president, and Kyle Meeks, her vice president.

"Hello, CCHS student body. I'm here live in-studio with two very special guests," Millie says with a giggle.

Kyle and Miranda awkwardly wave, the both of them not sure exactly where to look.

"We're here today live to announce your prom court. Miranda, I believe you have our list of students in the running for prom king."

Miranda nods and offers a stiff smile. I swear, you turn a camera on and people (even stupid, charming Kyle) turn into robots. At least the two of them showcase how charming and relaxed Millie is on camera.

"We have four nominees for queen and four for king," says Miranda. "Your nominees for homecoming king are Mitch Lewis, Bryce Dooley, Tucker Watson—"

The whole classroom erupts in cheers and a few guys lean over to bro-grip Tucker's shoulder and offer their congrats.

Well, Tucker is on my shit list. Bryce is a piece of work, and even if he weren't, he would be by association thanks to his dad. Mitch is cool at least.

"And Hannah Perez?" Miranda finishes.

The room rumbles with whispers as Miranda leans over to Kyle and says, "Isn't that a girl?"

What is going on? Is this some kind of joke?

Kyle looks perplexed. "There's no rule saying that only male-identifying students can be nominated for king, so . . ." He turns to Millie. "We will, um, we will be speaking with our faculty adviser and double-checking the ballots on this one. I'm sure it was a misprint."

On-screen, Millie grins, though she's obviously a little perplexed, and blows into a plastic noisemaker. "Congratulations to the nominees! Can't wait to see who takes the crown." She turns to Kyle. "Take it away, Kyle."

He holds up a sealed envelope and tears into it. "These results were tabulated by our treasurer along with several faculty volunteers, and on behalf of the student body, Miranda and I would like to thank them for their service. Now for the results." He reads them quickly and his brow furrows for a moment. "Your nominees for homecoming queen are Bekah Cotter."

No surprise. She came out of the womb with a crown on her head and a baton in her meaty baby fist.

"Melissa Gutierrez."

Captain of the Shamrocks, the school dance team. Tucker's ex-girlfriend. She could give Bekah a real run for her money.

"Callie Reyes."

Former mean girl and former Shamrock, which should make for some good drama.

"And . . ."

Say Millie. Say Millie. Say Millie. We could use a wild card. That would change the news cycle, for sure. And give me someone to root for.

"Waylon Brewer."

That was not the wild card I was expecting.

ELEVEN

I am immediately called into the office, where Hannah is already sitting, slouched in a chair with her beanie pulled over her eyes.

"Um, what the hell is going on?" I ask her.

She pulls the beanie up over one eye and gets a look at me. "Oh, you haven't heard? We're next in line to the throne."

"Stop messing around."

She sits up with a sigh. "Just a bunch of idiots," she says. "Patrick Thomas probably got enough people to vote for us or someone rigged the vote. Either way, someone is making a joke of us. Nothing new."

"Maybe for you," I say. "But I've never been made fun of . . . on this scale." Unlike Hannah, I didn't join the town beauty pageant in tenth grade, which was basically an invitation to put a target on her back in some circles.

"How nice for you."

"You're not at all freaked out?"

She shrugs. "I've got a few weeks left here and currently my biggest concern is going back to class so I can tuck my phone under my desk and watch videos of hamsters sitting on miniature furniture inside customized doll houses."

"Now that's an internet deep dive I could get on board with."

Mom stomps into the office and says to Mrs. Bradley, "Where is he? I need to speak with Principal Armstrong. Immediately." She sees me sitting there with Hannah. "Oh my goodness. My darlings. We'll get to the bottom of this. Waylon, where's your sister?"

I turn to Hannah.

"She's still in class," she says. "But she's all fired up," she adds in a dreamy way.

Principal Armstrong sticks his head out of his office. "I believe we're still waiting on Hannah's grandmother."

Hannah stands. "She's at physical therapy, so she's going to be late. Besides, I'm eighteen."

I look to Mom and she doesn't object. "I'm definitely here for Hannah's benefit as well, and I'd be happy to relay any information to her grandmother."

The three of us sit shoulder to shoulder inside Principal Armstrong's office.

Mom sits between us with her purse in her lap. "Please explain to me exactly what happened here, Russ."

He eyes Mom at the use of his first name in front of students, but Mom doesn't flinch.

"I've spoken with the student government and the faculty volunteers who tallied the nominations. It appears that both Hannah and Waylon did indeed garner enough votes for their respective nominations. Their names were a surprise while the votes were being counted, but the consensus was that their nomination should be included in case they had legitimately tried to garner votes."

"So basically," I say, "a bunch of teachers thought I actually wanted to run for prom queen and that Hannah wanted to be king, so they let the student body president and vice president name us as nominees during the live announcements?"

Principal Armstrong loosens his tie. "Yes." He shakes his head. "We . . . they didn't want to discount the possibility, and perhaps there was a better way to handle this." He looks to Hannah, twirling a piece of gum around her finger, and then to me. "I guess I am to understand that these nominations were not the intended outcome?"

"Uh, ya think?" I ask, one step away from actually tapping his head to see if there's anything left in there.

He throws his hands up. "Every time I think I understand teens— You wanna know what, I'm going to take care of it."

"I expect apologies from the responsible parties," Mom says.

Principal Armstrong sputters. "We have no way of knowing who exactly is to blame here, but I will be vigilant about making sure that both Hannah and Waylon are not the victim of any further abuse, and their names will be removed from all prom-court-related things."

Hannah stands and pulls her backpack over her shoulder. "No need. They want a king? They'll get a king. Count me in. I'm running for prom king, Mr. Principal Man."

She's out the door before any of us can even react.

I look to Mom and then Principal Armstrong, who are both as shocked as I am.

"Uh . . . uh . . . give me a sec."

I run after her and find her in the hallway. "What the hell, Hannah? You can't be serious. What's your grandma going to say?"

She turns around with an innocent grin. "If I've learned anything in the last few years, it's that you've got to be the one who writes your own story. You don't think I see people making fun of me? I'm the Afro-Dominican girl with buck teeth. That's all anyone knows me as. I've been dating your sister since last summer and I bet that's pretty much all you even know about me."

I clear my throat, trying to suppress a little bit of guilt and what that guilt might mean. I haven't really taken the time to get to know Hannah, because I always felt like Hannah wasn't interested. "We are so close to graduation," I finally say. "So close to getting out of this stupid school, and you want to make a thing of this instead of just letting it die?"

She shrugs. "This can go one of two ways. We're nominated and step out of the race and people always remember that one time the two homos were nominated for prom court. Wasn't that funny? Or I could actually do this thing and then maybe someday everyone will remember how the gay girl with the crazy teeth took life by the balls and ran for prom king. Wasn't that wild? Wasn't she fearless?"

I stand there for a minute, waiting for her to say she's

kidding and that she's going to let all this blow over. But she doesn't. Instead, her posture only becomes more defiant. She's got nothing to lose. And for the first time, I think I'm actually seeing Hannah. It's as though this whole time the Hannah I knew was never Hannah at all. Only a shadow of her.

"Patrick Thomas and all the assholes who followed his lead might get to choose how this story begins, but I get to choose how it ends." She takes a step closer to me, and something shifts behind her light-brown eyes that makes me think that she's a little nervous to do this without me. "And for what it's worth, I think you'd make an incredible queen."

I watch her walk off down the hallway and her words vibrate through me like a tuning fork.

Back in the office, I find Mom and Hannah's grandmother talking to Principal Armstrong.

Hannah's grandmother looks just like Hannah if Hannah were sixty-four years old and wore chino pants and Clarks and got regular perms. She eyes me up and down as I stand in the doorframe. "The nose," she finally says to Mom. "Both babies have the nose."

Mom smiles and faintly touches her own nose with the tip of her finger, momentarily distracted by the thought of the three of us sharing a nose. Everyone has always said how much Clem and I look like Dad, and when I was a kid, I always felt bad, like it might hurt her feelings.

Hannah's grandma winks at Mom. I've been invited to Hannah's house many times, but if I'm going to be the third wheel, I might as well do it in the safety of my own home. I've only seen Hannah's grandmother a few times from a distance. Up close, I can see the soft lines around her lips and the silver hairs running through her curls.

I throw my hands up. "She's going through with it."

I expect Hannah's grandmother to be as outraged as I am, but instead she faces forward with her hands gathered on her purse in her lap. "It's decided then."

Well, there goes any possibility of grandmother interference. I sit down right outside the open office door as all three adults talk about the best way to proceed and how teens can be cruel and how social media has ruined us all—though Hannah's grandmother seems to have some interesting takes on Facebook. But the rest of the time, I listen to the three of them pretty much say all the things you hear adults talking about *this generation* say when they think we're not listening. Status update: we're listening.

But I can't get Hannah's words out of my head. I've spent the last few years of my life just getting by. Trying not to stand out. Most of my friends are adults who are at least double my age, and the one person I bare my soul to is connected to me by blood and therefore required to keep all the ridiculous and painful truth about me to herself. (She's not done a great job of that lately though, to be honest.)

I can't help but wonder . . . what if I just did this? What if I went all in? What's the worst that could happen? The end of my senior year is miserable? Someone tries to beat me up for wearing a dress? If someone is going to try to torment me for this, they've already made up their mind.

And then I envision something epic. Me as queen. Not just any queen. *Prom* queen. What if I not only did this whole prom thing, but what if I won? I don't even know if I actually want to do drag, but what a great way to leave high school in the dust and step into the future. The thing that really gets my blood pulsing, though, is the idea that things could be different. Maybe prom queen doesn't always have to be the same thin, pretty, and popular girl. Maybe the queen doesn't have to be a girl at all.

Prom is one giant charade anyway—a night where we play make-believe and pretend to be the adults we hope we might one day become. Elegant, refined, and a little bit sexy. That's not reality, though. Our real adult lives will be about bills and tough decisions and parents getting old and deciding to have families. Not evening gowns and tuxes and crowns. So if prom is one giant fantasy, why can't I be a part of the illusion?

TWELVE

I sit down beside Hannah in the home ec room on Monday after school. "When you manipulated me into actually doing this thing, you didn't say there would be meetings," I whisper to her.

"Surprise," she says. "There are meetings, I guess? I don't know. I'm not, like, some prom court expert."

"Well, you were in that pageant."

"As an act of protest," she reminds me.

"So what is this?"

She shrugs. "Something to keep me entertained until graduation."

After my conversation in the hallway with Hannah on Friday morning, I walked back into Principal Armstrong's office and told Mom to call off her dogs and that if Hannah was in, I was in.

Mom stared at me, and I could almost hear all the things running through her head that I knew she wanted to say, but instead, she turned to Principal Armstrong and said, "Well, you heard him. Let's make this official."

So here I am at prom court orientation, which I was not

aware is even a thing. I figured I would throw my hat in, make some posters, and leave the rest to be decided by the high school ecosystem fates, but it turns out that in Clover City, prom court is a *thing*, because of course it is.

"So if the pageant was a protest, did you get what you wanted?"

She side-eyes me. "I think that's a battle I'll be fighting for a long time, but I made a dent."

"Fair. Rome wasn't built in a day and blah blah." We're quiet for a moment, and it is becoming quickly apparent how much we're both missing our buffer, Clem. "What'd your grandma say about all of this?"

"¿Entonces ne te vas a poner un vestido?"

"Um, would it surprise you to know I got a D in Spanish?"

Hannah laughs and rubs her eyes. "Ds make degrees. She asked if this meant I wouldn't be wearing a dress. I told her she's lucky I'm even going to prom to begin with."

"I'm pretty sure that if you ever wore a dress, it would only be because you accidentally put both your legs through one pant leg."

She shrugs. "Fair."

"So . . . your grandmother . . . I've never actually met her. Is she cool?"

"Like, as in hip, or with the gay?" she asks with a laugh. "She has high hopes that I'll marry a girly girl so she at least has one granddaughter to dress up like a doll. Like Ellen and Portia, she says. So, yeah, she's cool with it, but it's been . . . a ride."

Tucker Watson comes in with his hands balled into fists in his pockets. As he walks past me, he gives me a nod. "Hey."

Was . . . did he just talk to . . . me? My stomach churns as I prepare myself for whatever awful thing he might say or do.

"Is this seat taken?" he asks, pointing to the chair next to me where my bag sits.

"Uh, um . . . yeah. Yes," I finally manage to say. He can barely look at me and now he wants to sit next to me. He's probably one of the jerks who voted for me to be nominated in the first place.

"You can sit here," Melissa Gutierrez says from behind me.

He looks at me for a long moment, like he's daring me to say something. "Cool," he says and then goes to sit with Melissa.

"Wow," Hannah says. "That was some real gay energy."

I shake my head. "Yeah, no. Guys like him are the reason I was even nominated to begin with. Besides, all my energy is gay energy."

Mrs. Leonard, a petite Black woman with her hair perfectly curled to frame her face, stands at the front of the room and throws her best spirit fingers to get our attention. "One, two, three, eyes on me."

"What are we in, preschool?" I mutter.

Hannah smiles. "I had her last year. She's a hard-ass, but she's perky about it. Hated her class. She was cool though. She wrote me a letter of recommendation for my college applications."

"Okay, folks, listen up. Congratulations on your nominations. We've got a great group this year and I'm excited to see how this turns out. Now, we are a town built on tradition, and prom court is no different. However, when I took over as faculty adviser, I decided that prom court should be more than a popularity contest, so that's why not only do the students vote, but the faculty do as well. I know what you're thinking—there are way more students than faculty—but faculty votes count as two votes while students count as one."

Behind me Melissa Gutierrez huffs. "That's not very democratic or whatever."

Mrs. Leonard smiles sweetly. "Did I say this was a democracy?"

"No, ma'am," Melissa mumbles.

Honestly, I may not have all the staff eating out of the palm of my hand, but I'm a big enough teacher's pet that this faculty vote thing might give me a fighting chance.

"Now, just because you were nominated does not mean you are eligible. Prom court students are held to the highest standard, so you must be passing all of your classes and on track to graduate. You are also expected to complete various tasks including community service hours, a staff appreciation project, and a school legacy project." She hands a stack of packets to Callie Reyes, who stands up and passes them out.

When Callie passes to Hannah, she playfully kicks her boot.

"You know her?" I ask. Callie has a mean-girl

reputation, and last I checked, she was on the dance team or flag-twirling crew or whatever. Definitely not the kind of girl I'd expect Hannah to be friendly with.

Hannah crosses her arms over her chest. "I guess you could say we're friends."

"Full of surprises," I tell her.

"Flip to the second page of your packets," says Mrs. Leonard. "There you will find the full list of expectations."

PROM COURT TO-DO LIST
- *8 service hours to the approved nonprofit of your choosing*
- *Faculty appreciation project*
- *Legacy project*
- *Feature and interview with school TV team*
- *Graduation eligible*

Bekah Cotter raises her hand. "Um, hi." She turns around from her seat on the front row. "Hi, y'all. This is so neat." She faces Mrs. Leonard again. "I was wondering if you could explain the two projects."

"Ah, yes," says Mrs. Leonard. "Each boy will be randomly paired with a girl and—"

Hannah's arm shoots up. "I think you mean person? Or, like, king nominee and queen nominee?"

Mrs. Leonard's brow furrows for a moment as she thinks about that. "Well, it is typically one king and one queen nominee . . . and, well, this year, we . . . well . . ." She motions to me and Hannah. "We have nontraditional nominees, so I suppose . . . okay . . . so."

I can see her brain doing somersaults, and honestly I can't blame her. I know that gender is fluid and that there's more than just male and female, but the actual reality of how Hannah and I fit into all this is . . . a little hard to define, especially for a small town.

"Let me start again," says Mrs. Leonard. "Each king nominee will be paired with a queen nominee to complete a project, which you will both work on together."

Callie groans. "A group project? Really? We can't even choose our partners?"

"Yes, a group project," confirms Mrs. Leonard. "And partners will be randomly chosen. Now, obviously this does not mean you'll each be running for king and queen as a duo, but you will work together. Staff appreciation is a project you'll complete as a thank-you to the staff on behalf of the graduating class. We've had breakfasts in the past. Car washes were another popular idea. Be creative. Your legacy project is a campus improvement you do on behalf of your class as a gift to underclassmen and future students."

"Like a construction project?" asks Bryce Dooley with disgust in his voice.

"What's wrong with construction work?" I ask. My dad might be the boss of his own company now, but not too long ago, he was working on other people's construction crews under the hot beating sun, and he still spends lots of time out there with his crew.

Bryce turns around. "I'm not really a fan of getting my hands dirty."

I roll my eyes. "And people call *me* a queen."

"All right, all right," says Mrs. Leonard. "Quiet down. The legacy project can be a physical gift, like planting a garden. But it doesn't have to be. It can also be something that changes the culture on campus."

"Like what?" Mitch asks.

"Starting a new club or tradition. One year, a cheerleader wrote a new cheer."

"How groundbreaking," says Melissa, and Callie laughs.

Mrs. Leonard takes two mixing bowls around the room and has the queen nominees pick from a bowl.

Callie reaches her hand into the bowl and holds her breath. Admittedly the stakes are high for Callie. Not only is Bryce, her ex-boyfriend, nominated, but so is her current boyfriend. She cringes as she reaches into the bowl and mutters a few prayers under her breath. Carefully, she unfolds her paper and sighs with relief as she sinks against Mitch's shoulder.

"You sure this isn't rigged?" asks Bryce.

Next up is Bekah. She unfolds her paper and reads, "Hannah."

She turns around and smiles, and Hannah gives her a thumbs-up.

Next is my turn. Either way you slice it, this sucks. Bryce or Tucker. Both are my own personal nightmare fuel, but at least Bryce doesn't pretend to be anything he's not.

I stick my hand in the bowl and close my eyes, as if that could possibly help anything, and let my fingers dance between the two remaining slips of paper.

"Waylon, you're going to have to choose eventually," Hannah says.

She's right. I pluck a piece of paper from the bowl with all the drama and flair deserving of a moment that is as extremely life or death as this one is.

I hand it to Hannah. "Read it."

She releases a long sigh. "Tucker."

Shit. I can't even make myself turn around to look at him.

"Howdy, partner," he mumbles from behind me.

I briefly sneer at him over my shoulder.

"Well," says Mrs. Leonard. "That leaves Melissa and Bryce. Prom is three weeks away, people. We will have weekly check-in meetings and I'll be speaking with each of your academic advisers to confirm your grade eligibility, but that's it for now. Put on those thinking caps and feel free to come by with questions any time you like. I'll see y'all next Monday!"

After she's done speaking, I wait for the room to clear before approaching her desk. "Mrs. Leonard?"

She looks up and smiles.

"You have excellent cheekbones."

She touches her fingers to her face. "Well, thank you. Is there something I can help you with?"

"Yes, I need to switch partners."

Her smiles fades. "I'm sorry, but unless your partner is ineligible, there is no switching."

I try another tactic. "Don't you think I should be paired

with a girl? Maybe I could switch with Hannah?" Way to throw a friend under the bus, but desperate times.

"Mr. Brewer, is it?" she asks. "Some things about prom court may be different this year, but one thing that is not changing is how I structure prom court."

"But—"

She gathers her papers and slides them into her red patent leather purse. "If you're going to run for queen, then do it all the way. What's that saying? Go big or go home? Go big, Mr. Brewer. Go big."

THIRTEEN

We live on the older side of Clover City in the kind of house that looks like it could be a dollhouse, with little shutters and a small porch. It's tiny, but it's enough room for the four of us, and even though Mom and Dad have come a long way since they first bought this place fifteen years ago, they both think it's wasteful to get anything bigger. So, even though Dad owns his own business and has as many employees as Bryce Dooley's dad at his car dealership empire. Dad doesn't think that just because you can afford to have bigger and better things, you should.

I, however, find comfort in material possessions and refuse to feel ashamed of it. Dad swears I get it from Grammy.

Regardless, if I'd known I would be trudging through sharp gravel and mud to get to Dad's construction site, I probably would not have worn my favorite teal crushed-velvet Doc Martens. Did I mention that it's only the third week of April and already sweltering? This weather is really not speaking to my footwear choices, but I spend so much energy making sure I don't stand out that I like to take advantage of wearing a few of my favorite pieces when I'm going places where I won't see anyone from school.

When I got home that afternoon, Mom was already busy making dinner, and she was in a great mood. I don't know why and it honestly doesn't matter, but when Mom is in a good mood, you're either with her or against her. Which is why she did not take kindly to me attempting to pick a fight with Clem the moment we sat down for dinner.

"How's my old friend Paulina out in Georgia doing?" I asked.

Clem crossed her arms over her chest. "Well, if you're ready to talk about this, let's get it out of the way."

"I don't think there's much to talk about, Clem. We made plans and you changed them."

She handed me the plates while she put out the forks and knives. "It's not that simple."

"Seems like it was pretty simple when you told Mom and Dad and Grammy."

"And Hannah, too," she added quietly.

"Oh, so Hannah knows too?" I wasn't surprised, but I was hurt.

"She's my girlfriend, Waylon."

"Yeah, and I'm your *twin brother*."

"Did you ever think that maybe there was a reas—" She threw her arms up and shook her head. "You know what? You're petty."

"Petty? I'm petty for caring that my sister went behind my back—"

"Enough," snapped Mom. "I'm not dealing with this

tonight. You two have to sort this out."

"Whatever," I mumbled.

"You." Mom pointed to me. "I'm putting this in a container and you're taking it to your father."

"Sure." I shrugged. "After dinner."

"Nope." She ducked down to rummage around in her cabinet of mismatched plastic containers. "You eat with your father. Clem and I will eat here."

My stomach grumbled then at the absolutely perfect moment, but if she could hear, she showed no pity on me.

At Dad's work site, a few of his employees wave at me as I soldier on to where Dad's truck is parked with all of his equipment. There are two kinds of trucks: there's my truck, a truck you can put stuff in and sometimes off-road in, and there's Dad's truck, the kind of truck that's made to survive the apocalypse and roads like this one. Which is why I had to leave my truck with all the other employees' cars and hoof it up the hill like a peasant. Of course, Mom piled me high with various containers so that the food wouldn't intermingle until mealtime, so I look like a wayward delivery driver with excellent taste in shoes.

A little farther up the hill, I see Dad hop behind the wheel of some heavy machinery. I balance the food in one arm and wave frantically before he gets busy doing whatever he's about to do and I get stuck waiting in the on-site office for hours. Not to mention that walking across a work site with him is like trying to get a bride across a reception hall without saying hi to anyone. (I was my cousin Claire's best boy/too-old ring bearer in eighth grade, and the sheer amount of people who wanted to talk to her made me so tired I could have slept under a banquet table. Also, my aunt Louisa made me wear dress shorts and knee-high socks like a sad British boy-child.)

"Dad!" I call as I step on a rock the size of a fist and lose my balance and all of Mom's carefully packed food. My feet are sliding and before I know it, my ass hits the ground, which is soft and sharp, and my head is pounding. I'm in the precarious position of my head being downhill and my feet pointing uphill, all the blood rushing to my brain. At least I've got a good view of my shoes, which— ugh—are covered in mud.

"Great. Just great."

Rocks tumble down the hill as someone races over to me. "Are you okay?" the voice calls, and before I know it, Tucker Watson's head is blocking out the sun above me.

What kind of fresh hell is this?

"Do I look okay?"

He squats down, removing a yellow hard hat and placing it on the ground, before scooping his hand under the back of my head. He hisses a little. "That was a rough fall."

"What?" I ask. "No Humpty-Dumpty fat joke?"

"I don't see any blood," he says. "Can you sit up?" With his other arm he braces my forearm and pulls me up, and I absolutely hate my body for even reacting with the tiniest thrill when his skin touches mine. I tell myself that the feeling in my stomach is revulsion.

"What are you even doing here?" I ask.

"It's called a job."

"Oh." I didn't realize Dad had high school students working for him, but then, why would he tell me who works for him?

Dad jogs down the hill and pats me on the back. "You okay, bud? This terrain is awful. You should have called. I would have come down the hill to pick you up."

"I'm fine," I tell him, deepening my voice, like that will somehow help me fit in here. "Dinner is not."

The three of us consider the trail of spilled containers leading down the hill, and after we pick them up, Dad tosses me the keys to his truck. "You and Tucker go get some Chicken Express for the crew. Dinner's on me tonight."

I pocket the keys. "I can get it by myself."

"Actually," says Tucker, "we have a school project to discuss, so that would be great. Thank you, sir."

"No problem, Tuck."

Tuck? *Tuck? Not only did my dad give him a nickname, but it also has a double meaning in very specific circles. So many things wrong with this situation.*

I march up to Dad's huge, honking beast of a truck and take off down the hill before Tucker even shuts his door.

"Buckle up, *Tuck.*"

We rumble down the hill, and not until we pull back into town do I say, "You never told me you work for my dad."

"I didn't know I needed to."

"Isn't it kind of weird that I see you every day in class and you never thought to mention it?"

"I guess neither of us say very much of anything to each

other." His voice is low and gravelly.

And whose fault is that? I make a wide turn into the parking lot of Chicken Express. This truck is the size of a boat, and not in a cute welcome-aboard-my-yacht way. "Well, I guess we should talk about prom court."

In the drive-through, I order enough fried chicken and sides to feed a football team and then some. After paying with Dad's card, we wait in what feels like a fragile silence for our food to be ready, the staff behind the window obviously annoyed by the size of our order.

"I know that neither of us are really thrilled by this partnership," I say. "Who knows? Maybe you wanted to end up with Melissa. Rekindle the flame or whatever."

The window opens and the woman on the other side begins to hand me bags of food, which I pile up in between Tucker and myself. If we're going to be in the same breathing space, at least I can separate us with a barrier of fried chicken.

Once we've pulled back out onto the road, Tucker says, "How do you know what I want?"

"You've made yourself pretty clear." I shake my head. "I can't believe I'm stuck doing another project with you. I'm so close to being done with this place and then the gods of high school throw down one last gauntlet." I roll my shoulders back in a sad attempt to relieve the tension in my body and in this truck. "You know what? Never mind. What are we going to do for these projects?"

Tucker shrugs, totally chill and completely unmoved. "We could do a breakfast like Mrs. Leonard said."

I shake my head. "That's not inventive. Me winning this thing is a long shot, but I'll die before I'm boring. What would you want if you were a teacher?"

He laughs. "A day off."

That gets a slight smile from me. "Fair, but I don't think we have that kind of authority. What about, like, a spa day?"

"That sounds really awkward. I use three-in-one shampoo, conditioner, and body wash, so I don't think that's really my speed."

And admittedly, outside of the occasional sheet mask, I'm no pro either. "Well, do you have any ideas for the legacy project at least?"

He shrugs. "I could build something. Like a bench. Or a planter box."

"Are you trying to flex on me? I can build something with a piece of wood and four legs too."

Tucker watches the road disappear behind us through his rearview mirror and smiles. "I didn't say you weren't good with your hands."

"Not explicitly."

"And I didn't want to end up with Melissa, for the record."

"Good for you. I don't really keep up with all the straight romance gossip. Sue me." I can't tell if he's trying to say he doesn't mind that we're partnered up, but honestly, I don't care. My time left in high school is limited and I'm sure not wasting it trying to be friends with some guy who can't even follow through on a class project.

"Can I ask you a question?" he asks.

"Can't promise I'll answer."

"Was the video real? Did you really want to audition for that show?"

"Does it matter?" I ask as the truck chugs up the hill.

"To me it does."

I swallow audibly. I'm not going to give this guy an inch. "I think I love fried chicken more than my family."

He leans back and takes a whiff of our fried surroundings. "I would die for two things: a real-life Ewok and fried okra."

"Wow, does the student body know you're a nerd?" I park in front of the trailer office and hit the e-brake.

"*Star Wars* is pop culture. In fact, I would say that being a nerd is mainstream." He shakes his head. "It's not like all those old movies make it out to be. You're not just a jock or a nerd or a rebel or hot. There's a whole group of guys on the football team who straight-up throw down every weekend over tabletop games. Melissa, my ex? Yeah, she's captain of the dance team, but she's also president of the regional National Honor Society and she kicks my ass at *Red Dead Redemption 2* and *Call of Duty*."

"That's different. Those people are popular people drifting into nerd territory. They're already cool, so whatever they do is cool—but show me the kid on the debate team who tries to join the football team without catching any flak, or the fat gay boy running for prom queen who's not a joke. Show me those people making it and I'll believe your little theory about cliques and social food chains being a thing of the past." I hand him a bag of food. "Let's go."

We take the food inside and Tucker goes to let all the other guys know that dinner has arrived.

I sit inside Dad's office and we eat chicken wings over paper towels.

"So, this prom thing . . . Mom says you and Hannah are sticking with it. You know, buddy, I'm a small-town guy, but that doesn't mean I'm small-minded."

"I know, Dad."

He bites into his second wing and takes a swig of unsweetened iced tea. "But that doesn't mean other people in this town aren't. And I don't want what those people might say or do to stop you from being who you're meant to be."

I put my chicken down. It's so hard to look people in the eye when they're so sincere like this. It makes my chest tighten and my eyes water. "Thanks, Dad."

"But I also don't want you to do anything that could hurt you. Or . . . not everyone is good, son." He looks out the window at the setting sun on his work site.

He's scared for me. And I don't want him to be. Except that I'm scared for me too sometimes. "Dad, I . . . me and Clem both . . . we still have to live our lives, and right now that means saying a big F-you to everyone who tried to humiliate me and running for prom queen. If me being prom queen is such a joke, what better way to get back at them than to take myself seriously."

He wraps his hand around my arm. "How'd I get such a badass kid?"

"I don't know," I say. "A wait list. Is that how these things work?"

He chuckles. "You better head home. And tell your mother her dinner was delicious."

I stand. "Could you give me a ride back down that cursed hill? You already owe me a new pair of shoes."

"Only if you do one thing for me."

"What's that?"

"Talk to Clem. It's got your mom real upset, and when your mother is unhappy—"

"We're all unhappy."

FOURTEEN

Mr. Higgins wrestles with the remote, trying to power down the TV after morning announcements. "Damn thing," he mutters.

There's a knock at the door as it opens a crack and Kyle pokes his head inside. "Mr. Higgins, I'm so sorry to interrupt. This will only take a moment."

"Sure." Mr. Higgins tosses the remote on his desk. "Did the office need something?"

Kyle nods, and pulls an office memo from his pocket. "I've got a message." He unfolds the paper and begins to read. "Alex Wu, you received a phone call. It was from my heart." He reaches into his back pocket and pulls out a long velvet rectangular box.

Beside me, Alex gasps, and a few rows over, Tucker fidgets in his seat while others chuckle and some let out a choir of *aww*s.

Kyle steps forward and pops the box open. Inside are two matching teal bow ties. "Will you go to prom with me?"

Alex nods furiously and jumps up to hug Kyle, but before

their embrace can turn into a kiss, Mr. Higgins says, "All right, all right. Very cute. Everyone, save the promposals for passing periods and after school."

Kyle backpedals toward the door. "Sorry, sorry!" He waves to Alex and blows him a kiss.

Well, that was sickeningly cute. Despite how annoying I find Kyle, even I have to admit that matching bow ties was a pretty damn precious idea.

At lunch, me, Clem, and Hannah head to Harpy's and I claim our semicircle booth in the corner. By the time I got home last night, Clem had locked herself in her room and, from what I could tell, was on the phone with Hannah, so we haven't talked like I told Dad we would. Of course, we're talking, but we have this ability to table our fights until the right time. Maybe it's from living in such close quarters our whole lives.

Kyle and Alex walk into Harpy's, their fingers intertwined, and sit down with us.

"Okay," says Clem, popping a fry in her mouth. "Give me every adorable detail."

The two of them lean toward her and begin to paint a scene, shamelessly embellishing.

I turn to Hannah. "So what have you and Bekah cooked up for your projects?"

But she's not looking at me. Instead she's waving over a group of white girls I vaguely know in the same way I know everyone in this town, and Millie Michalchuk is among them. The group slides into the booth behind us and Hannah points at each of them, but I can barely keep up. "Amanda, Millie, Ellen, and Willowdean. Where's Callie?" she asks.

The chubby blond one who I recognize as an employee here swivels around. "She and Mitch are working on some prom court thing." She waves to me. "You can call me Will."

I nod. "I'm Waylon."

"Oh," says the thin girl with silky dark hair, "we know who you are. And I'm Ellen."

Millie giggles. "You're kind of a legend."

I smile at that. "Millie, right?"

She nods.

"I'm sort of like your biggest fan," I gush.

"Whoa," says the girl next to her in a cute tracksuit. "That's gonna go right to her head."

"It's nice to be appreciated," says Millie matter-of-factly. She nudges the girl beside her. "And this is Amanda."

"But seriously," Willowdean says. "We will do anything we can to help y'all win this thing. And honestly, I need all the distractions I can get."

Hannah grunts. "We stand no chance of winning. We're here to make a statement."

Willowdean rolls her eyes. "This is how she was with the pageant."

Hannah smirks and holds up a finger. "Let's stop pretending you entered that pageant to win."

"She's right," I say. "We are most definitely not winning."

"Hey now," Millie interjects. "That's not the kind of

attitude that will take the crown."

Hannah rolls her eyes. "Y'all know Bekah will win, and maybe Bryce or that Tucker guy. He seems boring and inoffensive enough to please the masses."

"I wouldn't say that," I blurt.

The five of them all perk up at that.

"I wouldn't know . . . for sure . . . about him being boring," I add. "But I haven't exactly had good experiences with him in the past."

Will leans her head against the windowpane and takes a long sip of her root beer float.

"Is she okay?" I ask the other girls.

"I'm fine," Will says.

"Anyone who says they're fine isn't fine," I tell her.

Ellen touches a hand to Will's leg.

Behind the counter a tall cute white guy with shaggy honey-colored hair reaches for the intercom. "Uh." He clears his throat and all the girls except Hannah squeal. "This is . . . my name is Bo and this is for my girlfriend, Willowdean."

Now he's got the attention of the entire restaurant.

Ellen gasps and pokes at a frowning Will. "Oh, Will, look!"

"Who cares about prom?" Will mutters.

"He's trying," Ellen says, and pushes Will out of the booth until she's standing. "Give him a chance."

Will huffs a sigh and crosses her arms.

Bo flips through something on his phone and then puts it down on top of the intercom buttons so that it acts as a makeshift speaker as the opening notes to a song I remember Grammy humming along to when I was a kid begins to play.

Ellen clutches her hand to her chest. "It's Dolly! Awww! He's speaking her love language." She leans across the table and whispers, "He's been sort of MIA lately."

"Oh," Hannah says with a hint of suspicion in her voice.

In a key I didn't even know existed, Bo begins to sing, "Baby, when I met you there was peace unknown, I set out to get you with a fine-tooth comb. . . ."

Bo steps toward her and takes her limp hand. He pulls her to him and wraps his arms around her, placing his chin on top of her head, and she looks a little bit like a rag doll, but you can see her whole body soften as she slowly warms to him. After two more verses, the chorus hits, and half the restaurant is singing, "Islands in the stream, that is what we are, no one in between . . ."

Bo and Willowdean dance, and we're all captivated, honestly. Forget matching bow ties. This is the kind of promposal dreams are made of. Cheeseburgers and Dolly Parton and the kind of love that feels lived in and complicated.

The song ends and every single one of us erupts into applause. "Prom! Prom! Prom!" a few people even chant before getting hushed.

"Willowdean," says Bo, swooping down on one knee.

Wow. He's really going all in, isn't he?

"Will you go to prom with me?" he asks.

"Ho-ly shit," Hannah says far too loudly. "Now that's a promposal."

Willowdean's faces shuffles through various reactions before she asks him something in a voice too low for any of us to detect.

Bo stands and shakes his head.

Ellen hisses painfully. "Oh, this is not good. Abort, abort, abort, abort."

Willowdean's brow furrows and her lips sink into a frown again as she pulls her wrist free and walks out the door.

"And that's my cue," says Ellen as she scoots out of the booth.

"And that's our ride," says Amanda.

"It was nice to meet you," Millie whispers to me as she scoots out of the booth, a milkshake in one hand and a boat of fries in the other. "I'd be happy to give you a tour of the news studio." She winks. "Anything for a fan."

As they file out the door, Bo pushes through the line of people waiting to place their orders to get past the counter and into the back room.

"Ooooh, that stings," I say.

Alex slumps back against the booth. "Is it weird that I think it's sort of very romantic in a doomed way? Like, he put himself out there."

Kyle smiles. "I love you." He claps his hands together. "So I have news."

"Are you pregnant?" I ask.

Clem snorts, but stops the moment she realizes we're still in a weird place.

Kyle gives a thin, impatient smile. "No, we are not expecting, but my parents are leaving town next weekend to visit my great-aunt Connie in Del Rio, and I, Kyle Meeks, have decided to host my one and only high school party."

Our table falls silent. "I'm sorry," Hannah says. "But did you have a stroke? Did an alien species invade your body?"

Beside Kyle, Alex bounces with excitement. "This is the real deal, y'all. A real party with real booze."

Kyle takes Alex's hand. "We've already made a plan for what parts of the house will be off-limits and who's on our invite list. Think of it as well-designed chaos."

"Ahhhh." Hannah nods. "You know how our peers love an organized house party."

"I'm sure it will be great," Clem says.

Hannah reaches into her pocket and slams down a crumpled-up red flyer. "Not as great as this."

Clem picks up the paper and reads, "All-ages night at the Hideaway! Bring a friend! Bring ten! Amateur Divas of Drag Contest! Cash prize!"

Her eyes light up as she turns to Hannah. "Is this that bar you were telling me about? With the Dolly drag queens?"

"Oh my God," says Alex. "I've never been to a drag show. I can't go to college without having been to a drag show. That's like showing up to college a virgin."

"Virginity is a construct," I pipe in, hoping that no one notices the flush in my cheeks when I think about how maybe I never went far enough with Lucas. Or maybe we went too far. Who knows?

"Well, we're going to this thing on Saturday," Hannah proclaims and then points at me. "And you're coming with."

I don't want to go. All I want to do is spend every weekend until graduation holed up in my room with reruns of *Fiercest of Them All*. "I guess it sounds fun," I finally say.

"It's a date then," says Kyle.

FIFTEEN

On Friday morning, when I walk into first period, Tucker hands over his phone. "Your number. I need it."

I look down at his lock screen to find a picture of a dog wearing a Princess Leia costume. "Who's your girlfriend?"

"That's Duke, and he's a very good boy," he tells me.

"In drag."

He grins, and I realize that he's got one of those goofy, lopsided smiles when he's not trying to be cool. "Leia's my favorite. Duke's more of a Han, but I dressed as Han. I needed a Leia."

"Well, I'm sure one day you'll find the girl to be your Leia. Or maybe you'll have to play dress-up with your dog forever."

"I could think of worse things."

I try not to smile, but I do. "Fair." I type in my number and save it under first name: Waylon; middle name: Your; last name: Queen.

He checks my work. "Well, my queen, intel says we're way behind the curve on these projects. In fact, I've heard

Bekah and Hannah are nearly done with their projects and Callie and Mitch are halfway done. Not to mention our volunteer hours."

I gasp. "Hannah has been radio silent."

"Well, if she's working with Bekah, she's in it to win it."

"What about you?" I ask, my brow arched. "Are you in it to win it?"

"I'm in it to not bomb this thing and look like a total dick."

"Well, that might take some work." The last bell rings and we take the only two seats left, side by side on the last row.

"What about tonight?" I ask. "We could get together and come up with a plan."

"I have to work."

If he didn't work for my dad, I'd say he was full of shit and trying to flake on me all over again. "Tomorrow?"

He shakes his head. "Got plans."

While Higgins is taking attendance, he leans over. "Did you just call me a dick, by the way?"

"Indirectly."

His gaze narrows into a simmer as the morning announcements begin, and I have to remind myself to breathe.

I spend Friday night as the Lord intended: watching *Fiercest of Them All* bonus content and drag makeup tutorials that make contouring look like an art form. Hannah and Clem go out, and even though they dutifully invite me, I'm not really up for being their date-night third wheel, as romantic as that sounds.

On Saturday morning, I wake to a text from Tucker that is time-stamped 4:23 a.m.

Tucker: So no breakfast for the teachers. No spa day. What about oil changes?

You were thinking of me at 4 in the morning? I type, before hitting the backspace button until the message box is blank again. If I think too much about him and four a.m., I start to wonder what his room looks like and his bed and what he wears to bed and—I type a message back. When in doubt, give them snark.

Waylon Your Queen: I never took that course at Masculinity Prep.

The moment my message goes through, the three little dots indicating that he's typing a response appear.

Tucker: I could teach you. You could be my assistant.

Waylon Your Queen: I'm not really the assistant type.

Tucker: I'm running low on ideas here. And I guarantee no one's ever done this before.

Waylon Your Queen: Don't you need some kind of certification to work on people's cars?

Tucker: It's not like we're charging. Think of it like changing your mom's tire.

Tucker: My dad was a mechanic, so I've got everything we could need.

Waylon Your Queen: Have I mentioned how much I dislike manual labor?

Tucker: You can be the beauty. I'll be the brawn.

Waylon Your Queen: Fine. But we have to wear matching coveralls.

Tucker: Yes, your highness.

Clem steps through my open door, catching me mid-giggle. "What's so funny?"

My smile falls. "Nothing."

"We need to talk, Waylon."

I let out a long groan and bury my head in a pillow.

"I'm tired of this weird, polite silent-but-not-silent treatment you're giving me. You won't even yell at me!" She sits down on the corner of my bed. "I'm not leaving until we talk."

I'm not ready for this conversation. I don't think I'll ever be. "So if I say nothing, you won't abandon me for Georgia?"

She shoves my shoulder. "That's not fair."

I close my eyes and inhale deeply, trying not to say something I'll regret. "What's not fair, Clem, is that we had a plan."

"You keep saying, but *you* had a plan, Waylon. It's always been *your* plan. We were supposed to go to Austin Community College to figure out who we wanted to be and what we wanted to do. But I know those things already. I want to go to engineering school, and I got in. Dad has spent his whole life building and fixing things and now I want to learn how all those things work. I want to know the science and reasoning behind it all. Isn't that great? I know what I want to do and someone is going to let me do it. Can't you be happy for me?"

My shoulders sink. "Honestly? I'm having a really hard time with that. I'm not sad that you know what you want to do." Except . . . maybe I am. Maybe Clem knowing what she wants not only makes me feel like a failure, but also deeply lonely. "You could have told me this months ago and I would still have had time to make other plans or at least process this. We've been connected at the hip for eighteen years, Clem. If you're going to pull the rug out from under me, you could at least give me a little more warning. Were you just going to leave one day and call me from the road?"

She scoots down the bed toward me, and begins to undo her braids, which is code for *you can play with my hair*. "I love being your twin. It's one of the most important things I am, but we can't always be Waylon and Clem. Sometimes you have to be just Waylon and I have to be just Clem. Didn't you ever wonder what your plan would be if it weren't something that had to work for both of us?"

My eyes well with tears. "No, actually, I hadn't. I just. I thought it would always be the two of us."

Her expression softens at the sight of me letting my guard down. "I'm sorry I didn't tell you sooner. I was scared. It was wrong. Everyone told me so, even Hannah." She grimaces. "I was so scared you would hate me."

"I don't hate you," I mutter. "I wish I could. That would be way easier. Instead my stupid, stone-cold heart only cares about a few people and you happen to be one of them. I build up walls, Clem, I know that. But it makes it so much harder when someone inside the wall hurts me, because I'm not in the business of letting people in."

"Oh, I know all about your walls," she says with a sympathetic frown.

I sigh so hard my lips sputter. "And now I don't know where I'm going or who I want to be and I made that stupid video and what if that's all anyone ever knows me for? What if I'm always that fat gay kid with the embarrassing video who ran for prom queen?"

She loops her arm through mine and leans her head on my shoulder. "You're Waylon. Before the video. After the video. With me. Without me."

I was so ready to live our lives out in Austin, but the thought of being there without my Clementine makes me feel like I'm trying to find my footing in a pit of quicksand. "And God, why Georgia?"

She smiles sheepishly, and I immediately know she's about to drop another bomb. "Well, I was wait-listed at UT, but I also got into the University of North Texas, and then a few others. One in Florida and another in Arizona, but, um, Hannah actually has a full ride at the Savannah College of Art and Design. We'd still be four hours away, but—"

"Oh." I want to snap back with something pithy, but this hurts a little too much for me to come up with a venomous response. She's just twisted the knife. It's not that she's going somewhere else on her own. She's going somewhere with someone else. A someone else she chose over me. "What happens if . . . what if y'all . . ."

"What if we break up?" she asks smartly, and it's one of those moments when I can perfectly see the features that make us twins. The pointed nose. The sharp line of our brows. The freckles that won't quit. "I talked to Mom about that. I didn't want to go all the way out there and feel like I'd made some huge mistake. But I'm not going out there for Hannah. I'm going out there because it's the best school I was accepted to and Hannah being nearby is simply a perk."

I nod silently, studying my hand clutching my sheets.

She touches my wrist. "And maybe I'm making a mistake. But you have to let me make my own mistakes too, Waylon. And speaking of mistakes, I am really, truly sorry about the video. It wouldn't have gotten out there if I'd been a little more careful. I know Mom always says I'm the glass half full and you're the glass half empty, but sometimes I wish I could anticipate the worst like you can. It might have saved you from this whole ordeal."

I look up at her then, and find her eyes watering and her neck and ears red. All sure signs that she feels awful. "It's okay. We can't all wield the power of pessimism. It's a gift and a burden. Besides, what's done is done, and who knows? This whole experience might not be the worst thing to ever happen to me. Stay tuned."

"Are we okay?" she asks, her voice cracking. She timidly draws back a little, preparing herself for whatever my answer might be.

"I don't know. I'm sorry. I just . . . I feel like this can't just be magically fixed." It's the truth. "It's going to take me a while to get over all of this. But I need you. I can't believe I'm doing this prom queen thing. And with Tucker Watson of all people."

"*Tucker?* Don't we hate him for some reason? Remind me again."

I can't help but laugh. When it comes to transgressions against me and the ones I love, I'm like a librarian with a perfectly organized catalog of memories. "Ditched me for a group project, forced a teacher to redesign the seating chart so he didn't have to sit next to me, and most recently, he shushed me."

"Ugh, what a jerk." She says it with extra outrage just for me.

"Thank you. Your loyalty is noted and appreciated." I pull her close to me for a hug, and even though it doesn't feel the same as it always has in the past, it feels good.

I really don't know how to get over this and where to go from here, but Clem and I aren't just friends or regular brother and sister. Being a twin means being there for each other even when your relationship isn't fully functioning. I think other people would take some time away from each other and really figure out their feelings, but Clem and I live across the hall from each other and we share a car, so we have no choice but to figure this out as we go.

We spend all day vegging out and watching highlight reels of our favorite YouTube videos until it's almost time for us to get ready. "What are you wearing to this thing tonight anyway?" I ask, reaching for her wavy hair, which still smells like coconut. I might give her a hard time about her braids, but I do love the way they hold the smell of our shampoo like she's straight out of the shower.

Clem points down at her frayed cutoff jean shorts and Dad's old undershirt that she cut into a tank top. "This?"

"Um, no," I tell her. "Negatory on that, captain."

I stand up and yank her to her feet. "If we're going to have our Brewer Twins Go to a Gay Bar premiere, we're going to look fabulous. We have to make a statement."

"And the statement can't just be 'Look at me. I own clothing'?" she asks hesitantly.

"Don't ruin this for me," I warn.

Next door, in Clem's room, I tear through her closet searching for anything we can work with, but it's mostly jean shorts, black leggings, holey T-shirts, and a few short nineties-throwback dresses that aren't awful but aren't great either.

"Does this still fit you?" I ask, holding up a baby-blue spaghetti-strap dress with little daisies all over it.

"Um, that's the dress Mom made me wear for Easter in seventh grade."

I throw it at her. "Try it on."

With my back turned, she does so. "I can't believe you're making me try on a dress from middle school. The last time I put this dress on, I didn't even have boobs. If I even wore a bra with this dress, it was probably for theoretical purposes—ooh. Ow!" She grunts. "Okay, ta-da."

I turn around.

"I don't think Mom ever envisioned my Easter dress

quite like this. Should I wear the cardigan that she bought for this?"

I snort. "Definitely not." Clem's once-ladylike seventh-grade Easter dress is now a mini with slip-dress vibes. "I can't believe that thing even fit over your head. And not that I'm invested in your boobs in any way at all, but everything looks to be in tip-top shape."

"Thank you?" she says with slow confusion.

She reaches up to part her hair to rebraid it, but I swat her hands away. "The head of creative did not approve your Wednesday Addams braids."

She pouts. "But I can feel my hairrrrrr."

"Yeah," I say. "That's part of the whole having-hair thing."

She wiggles like her follicles are growing worms. "Okay, fine."

I nod. "You look, like, really cool. Like, I don't want to sound super Podunk or anything, but you could easily be going out to some kind of indie-band show in New York City or something. Austin at the very least."

She looks down at her dress. "I feel ridiculous, but I guess I like it."

We sit down on the ground in front of each other with her pile of unused makeup. "You should know I've only done makeup the one time."

"Well, you should know that I never wear makeup, so I won't be able to tell the difference."

I dig through our spread and come up with a silver eyeliner and use it to draw little stars in the corners of her eyes before handing her the mirror and letting her apply her own mascara. I top it off with a black lipstick from a few Halloweens ago, and then I lean back to appreciate my work.

"You look stupid good. Okay, I gotta get ready. Wear those combat boots." I point out the black ones with the neon-blue shoelaces sitting in the corner.

"Those are Hannah's," she says.

"Nothing says high school lesbians in love like wearing each other's combat boots."

"Well, that's accurate," she admits.

I throw up my best spirit fingers in an attempt to curb my nerves at the thought of attending MY. FIRST. GAY. BAR. "And now I must transform."

SIXTEEN

It feels really fucking good to dig into the side of my closet I've preserved for future Waylon adventures. I might not be living my post–high school dreams just yet, but it feels like for one night only, the future is here. Or at least a preview of it.

With my fingers, I swipe a translucent shimmery eyeshadow over my cheekbones and use a clear gloss on my lips. I salvaged my new boots that fell prey to mud earlier this week and pair them with black leggings I stole from my mom and never gave back and a black T-shirt with a velvet robe Grammy was donating that "fell out" of the bag before I dropped the rest of the items off at Our Lady of Peace Women's Shelter.

Outside, as we're getting in the truck, Hannah says, "Whoa, y'all look like—"

"We're old pros who have been to a million gay bars and aren't even a little bit nervous," finishes Clem.

"I was going to say like people who googled 'what to wear to da club,' but sure, that too."

I hold my robe out like a cape and take a twirl. "We're

not nervous for the club. The club is nervous for us."

"You look amazing too," Clem says to Hannah as they share a quick kiss.

And Hannah does look great in skintight black jeans and a white tank top. She's smudged a touch of matte gray eyeshadow across her lids, and it's the perfect addition to make her light-brown eyes sparkle. Tonight, her hair is pulled back from her face with one side swept back in a French braid. Hannah always looks like the kind of girl who could kick your ass, but tonight she looks like the kind of girl you'd be begging to kick your ass.

"Not to be a total creep, but is that side boob you're rocking?" I ask.

Hannah blushes instantly, but instead of telling me to shut up, she curtsies and says, "Indeed it is."

It's not that we're all different versions of ourselves tonight, but it's like we turned up the volume a little, and it makes me excited for what could be.

As we buckle up, Hannah says, "Y'all know this is basically like a honky-tonk, but gay, right? Not at all classy." She's got that nervous energy that spawns anytime you're about to share something you love with someone and are suddenly thinking of all of its flaws you're usually indifferent to. "Y'all are, like . . . really dressed up. Way more than usual."

"Be the class you wish to see in the world," I tell her as I hit the gas and haul it out of Clover City.

I've heard all kinds of things about the Hideaway, which is right outside of town somewhere in between nowhere and the middle of nowhere. Depending on who you talk to, it's a breeding ground for carnal sin or it's a place where the most unlikely of dreams come true.

The reality, however, is just as Hannah promised it would be. A gay honky-tonk.

"I was promised drag queens," I remind her as we pull into the gravel parking lot.

"This place looks . . . rough," Clem says as she takes in the clusters of people in the parking lot and dotted around the edges of the building, some smoking, others vaping, and some sitting on the hoods of their cars. The clientele ranges from teens to elderly. A few look like what you would expect to see at a country-looking place like this, but some look like people you would see at the grocery store or the mall, and then there are a few who overdressed for a night out. Honestly, I think I might share an immediate and mutual understanding with anyone who would overdress for a night out at a middle-of-nowhere gay bar.

We join the line at the door, and a big, burly guy checks our IDs before slashing big X marks across the tops of our hands with black permanent marker.

As we're funneled in through a short but narrow hallway, Clem says, "Alex and Kyle should already be here."

"Oh, joy," I say.

And if Clem had any sort of response to me, it's lost to boisterous laughter and a constant buzzing of conversation over Katy Perry remixed with One Direction. Is this heaven? Am I dead?

Actually, based on the smell—cigarettes, sweat, a sickly

sweet something, and the faint scent of mildew—this most definitely is not heaven, but it's a dark little corner of the universe full of oddballs and misfits, and even though I've never been a fan of crowds or loud noise, I feel at home. For the first time ever, I have the freedom to blend in or stand out. It's something I never thought to wish for.

"Follow me," says Hannah as she takes Clem by the hand, who then takes my hand.

We form a chain link as we slither in and out of people and around tables until we've made our way to a small circle table where Alex and Kyle are waiting. The table is made to hold three, but we squeeze in and make it work. Alex is wearing his usual skinny jeans and rumpled T-shirt, and Kyle looks like a missionary in his Sunday khakis and lavender polo shirt. There's letting your mom dress you, and then there's looking like you let your mom dress you. Kyle is definitely the latter.

Immediately, Alex and Kyle dive into a conversation with Clem and Hannah while I scope the place out.

There are so many little clusters of people who look just like us—a little bit uncomfortable and a little bit astonished. What's so special about being the small-town gay kid in a room full of small-town gay kids? But my whole heart feels full and I'm scared to join the conversation at my table for fear that I might start crying for no reason. So this is what it feels like for so many of the people I've known my whole life. This is the comfort of effortlessly blending in.

I feel at ease in a way I never have before, and I didn't

realize how distancing it was to watch queer people through a television screen or a computer monitor without ever feeling this kind of close proximity. This kind of safety in numbers.

From across the room, I see Corey and Simone, a Black girl with a nearly shaved head who I recognize from the wrestling team, and wave. They're sitting with a small group of kids—some who I recognize and some who I don't. I think I missed the boat on Prism, but I'm starting to wonder if maybe I haven't always been so alone and if, in reality, there's been this little queer network all around me.

The muscled man from the front door takes the stage and he's greeted by a few wolf whistles and squeals. "Now, come on, y'all. I damn well know y'all aren't here to see little ol' me. Put your paws together for the one! The only! Leeeeeeeee Way!"

A shorter queen who I think might be East Asian struts out onstage. She's dressed in a gold fringed sequin shift dress and her blond wig looks like it could potentially be half her body weight. "Welcome, welcome, welcome to amateur night!" she sings into the microphone.

"I just got chills," says Alex.

Hannah whoops loudly, catching us all off guard.

"You *know* her?" I ask.

She smiles slightly, and it's too dark to see if she's blushing, but the way she covers her cheeks with her hands makes me think that she is. "Lee's an old friend."

I shove her shoulder. I can't believe I never knew. This

may be my first drag show, but I've definitely heard of Lee. She's a West Texas legend. "You buried the lede here, Hannah!"

She shrugs. "I didn't want to get y'all excited in case she wasn't here. I don't know." She shakes her head. "Besides, it's been a little while. She might not even remember me."

"You're not very easy to forget," I whisper to her.

She takes a big sip of water from her plastic cup, searching for anything to do besides respond to me, and even though Hannah likes to pretend she's an old gay pro, I can tell this night means something for her too.

"But first," Lee says. "Y'all know I've got to christen the stage with a song. Dale, give me something to work with. And last call to sign up for tonight's main event! Sandra has the clipboard up at the bar."

"Oh my God," Kyle says. "You should totally sign up, Waylon. Give Pumpkin Patch time to shine."

"Pumpkin Patch is currently on hiatus." And then, because it strikes me as a possibility, I say to the entire table, "But I swear on Carmelo, RuPaul, Lady Bunny, Divine, and every other drag icon imaginable, I will kill any of you if you even dream of signing me up without my express permission."

Clem nods solemnly and Kyle's lower lip protrudes in a pout.

Lee turns her back to the crowd and begins to shake her hips on beat with the opening notes of Shania Twain's "Man! I Feel Like a Woman!"

"Let's go, girls!" The whole bar, myself included, sings

along. I don't even need to close my eyes to easily imagine myself up on that stage.

After Lee's song, the bartender runs the clipboard up to the stage. "Ahhh," says Lee. "A few new names and a few old. Let's kick this off right, y'all, with a dear friend of the Hideaway and everyone's favorite pizza restaurateur by day, Peppa Roni! Show 'em what you got, Peppa!"

A short, round queen steps onstage and I can quickly imagine what Peppa might look like out of drag, a graying gentleman with a receding hairline and a potbelly. But here, Peppa Roni is basically a living tribute to Miss Piggy herself.

Peppa performs Madonna's "Like a Virgin," followed by a surprisingly touching rendition of "Somewhere Over the Rainbow" that has me dabbing my eyes before any tears ruin my makeup.

The night is full of ups and downs. Some performers are absolutely tragic and have me drowning in secondhand embarrassment, while others are so good they make me wish I had the courage to get right up there on that stage with them. There's lip-synching, dancing, and even a little bit of comedy.

Dollar bills fly when each of the queens makes the rounds in the audience. During an especially memorable performance of Taylor Swift's "Bad Blood" from a muscled and tattooed queen named Snicker Doodle, Snicker focuses in on our table and reaches for me, cupping my chin as she lip-synchs. I feel my whole body being drawn in by her and for a brief moment, it's like this whole night was orchestrated for me and me alone.

After the show and once a queen (Peppa Roni) has been crowned, I search for the bathrooms.

"Line starts here," says an older man in a purple silk shirt with the kind of jeans my dad would call "dress jeans."

"Thanks," I say, and line up behind him.

"First time?" he asks.

I smile nervously. "Is it that obvious?"

"Nah. Just the kind of place where a new face stands out."

"Well, I plan on coming back," I inform him, even though it's something I've only just now decided for myself.

The bathroom lines aren't defined by gender, but they are equally long, so I just choose one and wait.

Finally, I make it to the front of the line and do my business as quickly as possible. When I walk back out, I collide head-on with someone a little bit taller than me. "Sorry," I mumble.

And then someone tugs on my hand. It's Hannah. "There you are," she says. "Come on. I want to introduce you to Lee."

I look over my shoulder to see who it was I ran into, and heading for the exit with a sudden sea of people between us is Tucker Watson, a slight grin on his lips. He is immediately swallowed up by the darkness of the parking lot, but for half a second, our eyes lock.

I just—did I really just see Tucker Watson? Here? "I'll be there in a minute," I tell Hannah.

She grasps my hand firmly. "Oh, no you don't. This

place is a mess of people and I'm not about to make Lee wait."

"But—" Anything I might have said is lost to the buzz of the crowd. My brain won't stop replaying that single moment on a loop. Tucker Watson. In a gay bar.

Hannah leads me and Clem down a narrow hallway behind the stage, where a tall white man in leather pants, a tank top, and a leather jacket stands guard.

"Hey, Dale," says Hannah.

The beefcake man known as Dale takes Hannah in a hug, momentarily sweeping her off her feet. "I thought that was you," he says. "Where's your whole crew?" he asks.

Hannah blushes and reaches for Clem's hand. "I wanted to bring my girlfriend—"

Dale holds a hand out for Clem. "Did our little Hannah just say she has a girlfriend? Pleased to make your acquaintance. I'm Dale, the man behind the queen."

Hannah beams at the phrase *our little Hannah*. This is all very sweet, but it's taking every bit of self-control I have not to run back out there and track Tucker down.

Clem curtsies. "Clementine, and this is my twin brother, Waylon."

Dale turns his attention to me. "Oh, Lee's going to love you both. Y'all come on in." Dale pushes the door open and calls out, "Lee, honey, are you decent?"

"Am I ever?" Lee pipes back.

"You've got some . . . younger visitors, my dear. Keep it PG-13."

Lee gives a gruff chuckle. "Y'all enter at your own risk."

The three of us file in with Hannah leading the way.

Lee gives a shriek at the site of Hannah and pulls her in for a hug. Hannah lets out a goofy laugh and squeezes her eyes shut tight as Lee holds her closely. It's a good hug. You can tell. I'm jealous. Her presence is enough to make me forget about Tucker for just a moment.

After their reunion, Clem and I both introduce ourselves.

"Oh, y'all have a seat," Lee says, and the three of us squeeze into a dusty old plaid love seat while Dale perches on Lee's makeup counter.

"This place is incredible," I say, looking around at this haven of a dressing room with an entire wall dedicated to wigs from floor to ceiling and another wall reserved for all things costuming, from dresses to sewing machines to bolts of fabric.

"Well," says Lee, "every girl needs her beauty closet."

Dale scoffs. "Closet? More like gallery."

Lee smiles at him dotingly. "Well, it started out as a closet, and then you transformed it." Lee looks to Hannah. "Now, catch me up on all the happenings. How are my girls doing? Willowdean came around here a while back with that boyfriend of hers."

Hannah grimaces. "Yeah, they, uh, hit a rough patch."

"He proposed," I blurt. "I mean promposed. In front of a whole restaurant of people. It was . . . adorable until it was awful. She sort of walked out without giving an answer. It was a car wreck, but I couldn't look away."

Lee's eyes widen. "Oh my."

Hannah shakes her head. "I think they're . . . school's ending soon. We're all going our separate ways—"

"That kind of stuff will make you silly," Dale says.

Lee nods. "Ground shifts around you and you figure out the fastest way to fall is to stand still. But sometimes when we know we need to take a leap, we're jumping off the wrong cliffs."

Dale takes Lee's hand. "They're good kids, though. Either it works out or it doesn't. No matter what, none of it is time wasted."

Lee sizes up me and then Clem. "Twins, huh?"

"Yes, ma'am," I say, but then take in the lack of wig and the sweatpants and T-shirt. "Or sir."

"Either'll do," she says. "Y'all look like a couple torna-does about to take on the world. Where are y'all off to after graduation?"

Clem takes Hannah's hand. "I'm heading to the University of Georgia and Hannah is headed to Savannah and Waylon—"

"Has no clue what he's going to do. I've dabbled in drag," I admit, my voice lowering and my cheeks burning with immediate embarrassment. I can't believe I just said that out loud to a real-life drag queen. "But . . . my plans for the future recently shifted." I decide not to throw Clem under the bus. "And now I'm trying to reconfigure, I guess. Not a lot of options currently."

Lee swats a hand at the air. "At your age, the world is nothing but a buffet of options, baby."

Dale affirms her with a nod. "Well, we better let y'all get home before you go turning into pumpkins on us."

We stand and say goodbyes, and both Lee and Dale embrace me in a hug. "The House of Way is always taking applications," Lee whispers.

"Hannah, you text us when y'all get home safely."

Hannah nods and doubles back for one last hug from Dale.

As we walk back out through the bar, I search for Tucker, but he's nowhere to be found. The House of Way is fresh on my mind as I start the truck, but the thing I really can't get out of my head is the memory of Tucker Watson and our gazes linking in the middle of the only gay bar in a hundred-mile radius.

We drive home and behind us the Hideaway stands like a lighthouse, and even as it grows smaller in the distance, we still feel the warmth of its beacon light.

SEVENTEEN

That night, I lie in bed with my phone dangling from my fingers, an open text message to Tucker on the screen. The flashing of the cursor is the only thing keeping me awake. I type out failed texts one after the other.

Maybe I was hallucinating, but were you—backspace, backspace, backspace.

Did my eyes deceive me—backspace, backspace, backspace.

Stalking me now, are you? Backspace, backspace, backspace.

I'm guessing you didn't make the hike all the way out to the Hideaway just to see me. Backspace, backspace, backspace.

I try once more.

What other secrets are you keeping?

I hit send and stare at my phone for . . . as . . . long . . . as . . . I . . . possibly . . . can . . .

The next morning—no, I check my phone, afternoon—I stumble out of bed in search of the source of the scent of freshly cooked bacon.

As I'm walking down the hallway to the kitchen in the silk robe I wore last night, I say to whoever will listen, "Do you think Miss Piggy knows how good bacon tastes?"

"No, but I bet Kermit does," says a voice—a voice belonging to—

"Tucker!" I screech. "What the hell are you doing in my house?" I pull my robe tight around me, but he still definitely saw me in my boxers. Tucker Watson stands in the middle of my kitchen in jeans and an undershirt, chugging a glass of water. "Is this a hallucination? Do I have a tumor? Is this a stroke? Is that smell burning toast?"

"No, no, no, and yes," says Mom as she walks past me, teasing her fingers through my hair. "Your sister definitely burned toast at one point this morning."

Tucker puts his glass down on the counter and wipes his mouth with his forearm. He nods toward Mom. "Thank you, ma'am, for the water. I better get back to it." He looks to me. "Morning, Waylon."

"To what?" I ask, still completely shocked at this boy's ability to show up in the most unlikely places like a damn leprechaun.

"You will do no such thing," Mom says to him. "You sit down and have some bacon and eggs. I was about to make some fresh toast for Waylon."

I blink at the pair of them until my head suddenly realizes that oh-holy-shit-I'm-in-my-underwear-in-the-middle-of-my-kitchen-with-Tucker-Watson. "I'll be right back," I say before racing down the hallway to the bathroom.

"Great," I mutter as I notice the mascara and glitter

smeared down my left cheek. Nothing says *I have my shit together* like waking up at noon with last night's evidence all over your face. After a quick sink scrub-down and some deodorant on my pits, I piece together actual clothes and take a second shot at my grand entrance.

Tucker is sitting at the kitchen table, twiddling his thumbs, like this is the most normal thing in the world and he's been at my kitchen table a million morning/afternoons before.

I take my seat just in time for Mom to serve up fresh toast and orange juice. "Thank you, Mommy Dearest."

She swats me on the head with a dish towel before taking her cup of coffee back into the living room, leaving Tucker and me with a bowl of eggs and a plate of bacon covered with a damp paper towel.

"So, you're at my house for breakfast," I venture.

He scoops eggs onto his plate and piles it up with bacon. "Well, not actually for breakfast. More like brunch. But I never turn down breakfast. Even this late in the day. Long night?"

"Uh-uh," I say, wagging a finger at him. "I ask the questions. What are you doing at my house on a Sunday? Scratch that. What are you doing at my house at all?"

"Your dad asked me to look at your mom's alternator."

"Well," I say with a disappointed huff, "that's a perfectly reasonable explanation."

"But I don't think that's what you really wanted to ask me," he says with a smirk as he hunches over his plate like someone might take it.

"So then why don't you tell me what I really want to ask you?"

He eats a slice of bacon in one bite and washes it down with a swig of orange juice. "You're wondering if I think Peppa Roni was really the most deserving queen last night or if her win was nepotism."

"Cut the shit. Why were you at the Hideaway?" I ask.

He leans toward me and rests his chin in the palm of his hand and clears his throat. "It was an all-ages night." He shrugs. "Sounded like something fun to do on a Saturday night."

"So are you saying that you're . . ." After almost two years of fooling around with Lucas behind closed doors and constantly wishing for something more, but knowing deep down that it wasn't for me to pressure him, I'm not about to put myself in a similar situation with Tucker.

"I'm saying I went to a show at a bar on all-ages night." He doesn't say it quietly or loudly. He just says it.

"And you were only there for the fun of it? At a gay bar?"

He shrugs and smiles playfully. "I like the atmosphere."

"Wait. You've been there before. What about Melissa?" I ask, trying to read between the lines.

"What about Melissa? She's my ex-girlfriend. It'd be kind of weird if I took her out on a date. Don't you think? If you're wondering, though, she was a big Peppa fan, too." He stands up. "I better get back out there."

"So you're not going to swear to beat the shit out of me if I tell anyone I saw you at the Hideaway?"

"I'm not trying to keep secrets." He walks out the door to the garage.

I wait for the door to shut behind him before I let out an exhausted sigh. Did I wake up in the Twilight Zone today? I know that technically he doesn't owe me any kind of answers, but I can't get the image of him out of my head. His coy smile, neon lights blurring behind him.

I finish up my breakfast and shuffle out to the living room, unable to help how mopey I am. Mom sits in her recliner and is playing mah-jongg on her iPad while catching up on her DVR.

Dramatically, I spread out on the couch next to her recliner, daring her to ask me what's wrong so I can tell her all about the way everything in my body right down to my guts is twisted into a knot and that I feel restless and aimless and just . . . less.

She doesn't take the bait.

"Sweet of that boy to come over and look at the car. I told your father I'd take it in this week, but he insisted. He's taken a real shine to that boy."

"Maybe he can adopt him," I say. "Swap me out for a more useful model."

She chuckles at something on her iPad or at me and my endless misery. Probably both.

"Where's Clem?" I ask.

"Hannah's."

Ah, yes, living her life without me. It's like when we were in middle school and we both agreed to stay up late the night before a history test and blow off studying for reruns of *Keeping Up with the Kardashians*. Except when I passed out, Clem studied without me. Only one of us failed the test the next day.

"Are we going to Grammy's for dinner?" I can feel my questions needling at her.

"That's the plan." She sighs, closes the cover on her iPad, and stands. "I need a pedicure. And you're clearly emotionally afflicted in some kind of way."

I moan. "Is it that obvious?"

"All right, up and at 'em! We're getting these little piggies painted and you're driving."

I run to grab my keys. "I'll meet you outside! But I get to pick your colors this time."

She flips her hair. "Pea-green toes can be very elegant, thank you very much."

As I'm running back through the kitchen after putting on my shoes, Tucker's there washing his hands in the sink. He shakes his hands out, unable to find a towel. Sunlight cascades down his face, like a damn Instagram thirst trap come to life.

I reach into a drawer and hand him a fresh dish towel, breaking the moment and snapping myself back to reality. "Here."

"Thanks." He dries his hands and hangs the towel over the edge of the sink.

"I'm sorry," I say, "you don't owe me any kind of explanation about why you were at the drag show last night."

He smiles, the lines around his eyes wrinkling. "I kept wanting to go up and talk to you."

"Me?" I ask. "We don't even know each other. Or even like each other for that matter."

Tucker shakes his head. "Waylon, I've known you my whole life. And I've never said I don't like you."

"I mean, I guess we know each other in the small-town kind of way. But you haven't exactly been friendly to me in the past."

He's so close. It's so quiet. Dad is gone. Mom is outside. Clem is at Hannah's. It's just me and Tucker, this boy I've known for my whole life apparently, but who is still such a mystery to me.

"Oh, and you've never been a jerk before?"

I suck in a breath. "That's not the impression you left me with."

Tucker bites down on his lip. I think our rib cages might be made of magnets, because no matter how hard I try to pull back and knock some sense into my head, I can't seem to stop myself from—

"Waylon! These toes are done waiting," my mother calls from the garage.

I take a step back, gasping. "Be right there!"

Tucker doesn't seem at all fazed.

"I better go," I tell him. "You have to go."

"After you," he says smoothly.

I snatch the keys off the counter and march outside in my most awful cargo shorts and polo shirt. "Let's go, Mom."

"Oh, Tucker," Mom says. "Thank you so much."

"Yes, ma'am. Anytime," he tells her, on his best

behavior. "I texted Mr. Brewer the info on what parts we need to order. I'd be happy to install them for you when everything comes in."

She cups his cheek. "You are such a wonderful help. I insist you join us for dinner tonight."

"Oh, ma'am, I've, uh . . . I can't this evening, but thank you."

She points a finger at him as she gets into the passenger door of the truck. "You'll not elude my dinner invitations again, young man."

"Yes, ma'am, I'll take a rain check," he says as he closes the garage door behind him.

The moment my mother is fully seated in the car, I reverse out the driveway. "Well, now hang on a minute," she says. "Let me put my seat belt on. And we didn't even see to it that Tucker got on his way okay."

"Mom, I guarantee you on a Sunday afternoon, there's a wait at the nail salon, and if anything is wrong with that boy's truck, you and I are the last people on earth who could offer him any help."

In the rearview mirror, I watch as Tucker steps out into the street, his hands in his pockets, as we drive away.

EIGHTEEN

I barely sleep on Sunday night thinking about the prospect of seeing Tucker on Monday morning in first period. But when Monday morning finally comes, Tucker is nowhere to be found.

I think about texting him, since we have a prom court meeting after school, but what am I supposed to say? *I think you might be gay and please don't bail on this dumb meeting we're supposed to attend?*

As I walk to choir, Alex bounces at my side. "Wasn't Saturday night absolutely epic? And next Saturday is Kyle's big party. You're coming, right? Would karaoke be fun? Do our peers appreciate karaoke?"

I pat his shoulder gently. "I think you might want to rethink the karaoke."

Alex's shoulders slump and he nods.

Across the hallway, I see Simone, who was also there this weekend. I wave and she smiles cheerfully. I feel a twinge of regret for not getting to know many people during my four years here. I turn back to Alex. "But I guess it's always good to have activities planned as a backup? Karaoke could be fun, I guess."

"Yes!" His puppy-dog energy surges. "Now, that's a party planning tactic I hadn't thought of. Backup activities."

In the choir room, Clem and Kyle are already sitting on the risers.

"Ask him," Clem says to Kyle.

I settle in next to her with a slight feeling of dread. "Ask me what?"

"You should know," says Kyle with absolute earnestness, "that I've never even unintentionally broken the law, so I'm not entirely comfortable with this potential situation, but—"

"They need booze," says Clem. "For the party."

Kyle sucks air in through his teeth and winces. "And now I'm making you all accomplices. I'm sorry, but I remember you being . . . friendly with Lucas Campbell."

"Ohhhh," I say, immediately aware of where this is headed. Kyle doesn't know the full extent of my fling with Lucas, but he did happen to walk into the gas station once while I was walking out of the back room. "I don't . . . Lucas and I . . ." Lucas is not only the recent high school graduate gas station attendant. He's also one of the only people in town who will sell beer to minors, but he won't sell to just anyone. And sure, I know for a fact that Lucas would sell me whatever I wanted, but it would require actually seeing Lucas, which is a thing I had hoped to avoid forever, basically.

"Come on," Clem chimes in. "We've never been to a

real high school party, Waylon. This is our chance to make one last memory of our time here."

The three of them—Clem, Alex, and Kyle—look at me with hope in their eyes. And it's true. None of us were ever invited to the wild high school parties where people get wasted and dance on tables or make out with six people in one night. We could invite Millie and Amanda and Ellen and Willowdean and all the other kids who were never cool enough to be on someone's list and for one night, we could run the show.

"Fine," I finally say. "I'll see what I can do."

Alex kisses me on the cheek and Kyle lunges at me in a hug. "Thank you, thank you, thank you," they both sing in unison.

Surprisingly, their close proximity isn't awful.

After school, in the home ec room, everyone partners up in their assigned pairs automatically, so it's just me left sitting at the back of the room at a tall tabletop desk, like the kinds we have in science classes, getting ditched all over again. Déjà vu.

"Good afternoon, prom court," Mrs. Leonard says in a teacher voice.

"Good afternoon," a few people mumble back.

In front of me, Melissa and Bryce have a whispered argument that results in Melissa scooting her chair a full two feet from him.

"Is everything all right, Miss Gutierrez?" asks Mrs. Leonard.

"Um, no, actually," Melissa says.

"Come on." Bryce groans. "Really?"

Melissa throws up a hand to silence him. "My partner seems to think our legacy project should be a yearly official publication of the Hot or Not list."

"Is that really still a thing?" I ask.

Callie, Hannah, and Bekah turn to me, varying shades of irritation on their faces. "Yes."

Mrs. Leonard shakes her head. "Bryce, that is highly inappropriate. Melissa, I'm sure Bryce meant that as a joke."

"Does it even matter if he did?" Melissa asks incredulously.

Just then, the door swings open and Tucker dashes inside, straight to where I'm seated. "Hey," he says to me, still panting. "Sorry I'm late, Mrs. L." He turns to me. "Sorry."

"Where were you today?" I ask in a hushed voice.

"Anyone else like to share an update on where they are with their projects?" asks Mrs. Leonard. "The only group I've seen complete one of their tasks was Hannah and Bekah, when they served an omelet bar in the faculty lounge on Friday morning."

"Actually," Bekah says, "Hannah found a small support group in town for families whose kids have recently . . . come out."

Hannah nods encouragingly at Bekah. "It's called Parenting with Pride."

Bryce says something under his breath and Callie hisses at him.

"They're about to lose their meeting space at the library," Bekah continues, "and they've been given access to use another space, but they need help cleaning it out, so if anyone needs more volunteer hours . . ."

"We're in," I tell her.

She turns and smiles at me. "That would be great."

Tucker's hand shoots up.

"Yes, Tucker," says Mrs. Leonard.

"Yes, ma'am, Waylon and I were actually hoping you could help us get excused from classes on Wednesday, because we would like to offer teachers free oil changes and we would need the whole day available."

Mrs. Leonard gasps with delight. "Now, that is an incredible idea. So out of the box! I'll see what I can do, gentleme—gentlepeople."

"So I guess this means I should learn how to do an oil change," I whisper.

Tucker reaches under the table and touches my thigh. "I got you," he says, his gaze still concentrated on the front of the room.

His hand lingers there for a few seconds, before he pulls back and my brain turns to static for the rest of the meeting.

After our prom court meeting, I decide it's best to get this over with and drive to the Gas n' Go. I park on the side of the building, and there's only one trucker filling up while the rest of the parking lot is completely empty except for Lucas's truck.

Yanking down my visor, I give myself a good look in the mirror. I swear, every day I have more freckles. One morning I'm going to wake up and find out I've turned into one giant freckle.

I practice a few faces in the mirror, from fierce indifference to seductive gaze to calculated chuckle.

"You can do this." I smile. "I'm so happy for you both," I say. "You took him to meet your parents? How precious. Oh, wow. He's so slim and trim. What a bod. You work out together for fun? How darling. You bench-pressed him for giggles? So adorable."

After making sure everything is zipped and buttoned and smoothed, I saunter into the gas station, the bell above me ringing as I pretend I'm still wearing the robe I wore to the Hideaway this weekend.

Lucas is organizing cigarette cartons behind the counter and doesn't notice me.

I clear my throat.

"Just a second," he mutters.

"Lucas."

"Waylon?" He turns slowly at first, but then once he realizes it really is me, he hops right over the counter.

Ugh, why is he such a charming little puppy?

A display of mini flashlights clatters off the counter and we both reach down to pick it up, our heads colliding.

"Ohhh, ow," I say touching my hand to my head.

"Here, let me." He gathers up the flashlights and they immediately spill out of his arms and back onto the floor.

"No, you know what?" He smirks, leaning back against

the counter. "Never mind. I'll get them later."

"Hi," I say.

He reaches for my hand at the precise angle I know is just out of reach of the security camera. "I've missed you."

I don't even try to hide my shock. "You have?"

"Well, yeah, of course. You were one of my closest friends and then you just . . . stopped coming around."

I pull my hand back and cross my arms over my chest. "I wouldn't exactly call us friends, Lucas. And if I recall, you were ready to ask someone to be your boyfriend. Someone who wasn't me. What, did you expect me to come up here and check in on you? Oh, yeah, let me just go hang out at this gas station, so I can see how my old fling's new fling is going."

His expression hardens into hurt. "I thought you were supportive of me. I even told my parents."

And at that my heart does twinge. "How'd they take it?" I ask gently.

"I think it's safe to say they're still taking it. Some days everything is normal—eerily normal—and on other days they act like I'm sending them both to an early grave. But they didn't kick me out, so that's a plus."

I hate that not getting kicked out is the sunny side to this difficult situation, but I've heard of this exact thing going a lot worse for plenty of people.

"Well, that's good. I'm—I'm proud of you." I shake my head. "But that's not what I'm here for. I need . . . beer. And liquor. And a lot of it."

He shakes his head. "I don't really do that so much

anymore, and I definitely don't supply for big parties if that's what you're getting at. Too risky."

"Come on," I tell him. "It's one shindig for a bunch of queer kids at school."

"Listen, if this was only you and Clem wanting a six-pack or a bottle of Everclear, I could make that happen, but a whole party? I'm not looking to get in trouble."

I take his hand again and channel the same argument Clem used on me. "I never got invited to any of the parties in high school like you did, Lucas. I've never had that classic high school rager experience. This is my one chance. Help me. Please."

He sighs. "Is it true you're running for prom queen?"

I nod.

"God, you're way too fucking cool for this place."

That gets a laugh out of me. "Tell me that again after I've been stuck in this place for forty-plus years."

"Nah. You'll leave us all in your dust. Besides, you and Clem are off to Austin the minute you walk across that stage." He smiles. "All right, you got a list?"

I hold up a folded piece of paper between two fingers. "As a matter of fact."

I was in this stockroom only two weeks ago and already it feels so much smaller than I remember. Perched on the desk in my usual spot, I wait while Lucas puts together a pile for me, which is growing to be much larger than I expected.

"Kyle Meeks is throwing this party?" he asks.

"The one and only."

He rolls a keg over to the back door. "The student government nerd?"

"Along with his boyfriend, Alex."

Lucas shakes his head. "Those two always stressed me out."

"What's so stressful about two well-adjusted gay boys who have their lives perfectly planned out right down to what flowers will be at their wedding?"

He laughs, leaning against the keg with his feet crossed at the ankle. "So I'm not the only one?"

"Oh, I've spent plenty of time thinking about how they make me feel like I must have missed part of orientation day at gay camp." My voice is bittersweet.

"You know," he says, uncertainty in his voice. "You always kind of made me feel that way too."

My brow furrows in shocked confusion. "What are you talking about?"

"You know what I mean," Lucas says. "You're so sure of yourself. You always have been. You've never been sorry for who you are."

"Well," I say, "It's pretty hard to hide it, Lucas. No matter how hard I try—and I've tried plenty—it's everywhere. The way I walk. The way I talk. I didn't wake up and pray to be a walking gay billboard." Sometimes falling more on the femme side of the spectrum sends me into a massive thinky, feelsy spiral. I don't hate those pieces of myself, even if they sometimes scare me. Those attributes are part of me, but it's just a small sliver of who I am. And yet for so many people, it's all they see. It's the whole package. Fat. Femme. Judgments made. Case closed.

"I didn't mean it like that. I know that . . ." He closes his eyes for a minute and flexes his fists, like he's physically gathering the right words. "I know that people assume I'm straight. And I don't usually correct them, because it's easier that way."

I sigh. I think this is the most we've spoken ever. Our mouths were busy doing . . . other things. "I know you know that. I'm just hurt, okay? You hurt me when you told me you were ready to come out. I thought you were ready to come out for me. But that's silly, because coming out isn't for anyone but you. I thought it meant that . . . that you'd want to be together."

He clutches his hand to his heart and cuts across the stockroom to me. "Oh, Waylon, I'm—" He shakes his head, and I can see him connecting the dots about how exactly I might have come to that conclusion. "I'm so sorry. If it helps, Rashid totally freaked out when I told him. I think he might like me, but maybe he's just not—"

"I don't need all the details," I tell him in the kindest way I can.

"Right. Of course," he says, riddled with embarrassment. "I meant what I said, though. I do miss you."

He leans into me then and parts my legs with his thigh. My body begins to react almost immediately, and the semi I managed to hide when Tucker touched my thigh is still fresh enough in my memory that I pitch a tent almost instantly. (Yes, Tucker simply touching my thigh got that much of a reaction out of me. Thank Goddess for table-tops.)

Lucas brushes his lips against mine, softly at first, nudging me, and then with more force. It's the kind of kiss that makes me want to yank him even closer until our bodies meld into one heap of limbs and sweat, but—"Stop," I say, my voice too soft at first. "Stop." This time my voice is more firm. It takes every ounce of self-control I have to pull back from him.

"I'm sorry," he says instinctively.

"For what?" I ask him. "Dumping me the first time or toying with me just now and making me your second choice?"

He opens his mouth, but nothing comes out.

"My life is a lot of things right now, and not much of it is good, Lucas, but one thing I know for sure is that I can't be anyone's second string. Honestly, I'd rather be alone. At least then I know I'll have chosen myself."

"I'm—I'm sorry," he finally stutters. Tears well in his eyes, and he lets out a grunting sigh.

I stand up and start heading to the back door. "I know you've got a lot of shit to sort through right now too, but maybe you should think about just being with yourself and putting yourself first before you can do that for anyone else." I almost hate myself for even saying it, because it's the kind of bullshit advice people give that they can never actually act on for themselves, but there's still truth to it. There's still something to be gleaned.

I do something that surprises even myself. I reach out to

Lucas and I pull him to me in a fierce and tight hug.

He grips onto me and hiccups, holding back tears. It's enough to make my eyes water, and before I know it, I'm blinking back tears too.

I didn't know how much I needed this. To just be held. To be held without expectations or exceptions. And so we stand there for a moment in the back of a grimy little gas station, two lost boys.

"Come on," I finally say. "This booze isn't going to load itself."

"Friends?" he asks.

I nod. "Messy former-friends-with-benefits friends."

NINETEEN

"Come out already!" I say, banging on the bathroom stall.

"Do I have to wear the bow tie?" Tucker asks.

"It's a look," I explain. "Besides, I paid money for it, and I wouldn't call my current financial situation thriving."

"To be clear, when you said matching outfits, I thought you meant like T-shirts from Walmart."

"I'm going to pretend that you didn't just insult me," I say. I'm not insulted by the implication that I would shop at Walmart. I'll shop at whatever store has clothing that will fit my body. What I am insulted by, however, is the notion that I would ever believe a T-shirt constitutes an outfit.

"I can't promise the bow tie will last." Tucker kicks the door open.

I gasp. "My vision! Yes!"

I turn around to see both of our reflections in the mirror. The first thing my brain wants to notice is how I'm fat and he is not, which is extremely apparent in our matching outfits, but I force myself to look past that. We both wear white coveralls and red bow ties with red-and-white-striped page boy hats. My idea was candy striper/milkman turned mechanic chic. Mrs. Leonard got us out of classes for Wednesday, so we both separately spent Tuesday scrambling around for important supplies. Matching uniforms, I decided, were very important supplies. We also had to get an announcement out to the teachers, but I pulled some strings with Kyle, who used his office aide hour to print and copy flyers for the faculty mailboxes. To be fair, I had just discreetly delivered a whole ton of booze to his house the night before. He owed me.

Tucker runs his hands over his name embroidered on his chest. "This is pretty cool," he admits.

"My grammy embroidered them with her machine." A fashion sense like hers is not direct from the rack.

He nods. "Grammy gets five out of five stars. But you know this white is totally impractical, right?"

I flip my invisible hair. "I never said my vision was practical."

The two of us head back out to the parking lot, where our trucks are parked side by side. I brought a few boxes of doughnuts and Mom put together a few thermoses of coffee, while Tucker brought every supply for changing oil we could possibly need.

"Does she have a name?" I ask.

"The truck?" He smiles. "Xena."

"Xena? As in the warrior princess?"

"The one and only. What about you?"

"Beulah," I say.

He nods with admiration. "Beulah and Xena. They make a good couple."

Why does the idea of our trucks being in a long-term committed relationship make me want to puke but also twirl around the parking lot like Julie Andrews? "I don't think I've ever seen campus this early in the morning," I say, changing the subject.

"Oh, I have during football season. Kind of peaceful, right?"

I begin to set up a little coffee bar on the bed of my truck using a tablecloth Mom lent me.

Tucker pulls a pen and clipboard from his backpack.

"Smart."

He sets up all the tools and oils he might need in the bed of his truck.

"So why'd you miss school Monday?"

"Work," he says simply.

"What?" My dad is not an easy boss, but would never, and I mean never, let a high school student work through the day. He rarely even hires high school kids, because he doesn't want to interfere with school.

"Not for your dad," he clarifies. "At my, uh, dad's shop."

I nod. "Were you just helping out?" I wonder why he doesn't only work for his dad. That seems like plenty to keep him busy.

"You could say that."

"So you have two jobs?"

He laughs. "Only one that pays."

"Do you mean your dad doesn't pay you?"

I pour a cup of coffee for myself and hold one up to offer him.

"Dad's shop is hanging on by a string and he doesn't always get it together to open up the shop in the morning, so I've got to fill in sometimes. If we're not open, we're not making money, and if we're not making money, we don't have a roof over our heads. My job with your dad is how I pay for gas and food and basic stuff we need."

"Wow." I don't even have one job. Sometimes I'll do odd jobs over the summer, but Mom and Dad have always told me and Clem they didn't want us working during the school year. "You said your dad doesn't always get it together . . ."

He takes a sip of coffee and watches me from over the brim of his cup. "Must be nice to have a dad who has it together."

He doesn't say it in a judgmental way, but I still feel very judged.

"Well, good morning, good morning," says Mr. Higgins, way too much pep in his step for this early. "Did someone say complimentary oil changes?"

"Uh, heck yes, we did," I say, taking the clipboard. "Let me get you signed up."

He dangles a set of keys in front of my nose. "Be careful with this beaut." He points over his shoulder to a fading champagne-colored Toyota Camry. "My Delilah . . . she's the only woman in my life."

"I find that so surprising," I say dryly.

Tucker claps Mr. Higgins on the back. "We'll take good care of Delilah."

Mr. Higgins hands over an envelope. "Group project in class today, so you two are paired together and need to get this in to me by tomorrow night."

"You mean we have to change your oil *and* do homework for you?" I ask.

Mr. Higgins laughs maniacally and walks off into the building.

"You're like some kind of Disney villain!" I call after him. "But not in a fabulous way."

Tucker laughs. "Well, this sucks. I have to work tonight. For your dad," he clarifies.

I yank the folder out of his hand. "I'll bring you dinner and we can work on it during your break. I've got some sway with the boss man."

"Did you just ask me out on a date?"

My cheeks warm and suddenly I want to yank this bow tie off my neck. Or maybe I want to yank the bow tie off *his* neck. "Oh," I manage to say. "If I ask you on a date, you'll know."

Ms. Laverne pulls up next, cutting right through the tension vibrating between us. After I help her out of the car, she hands me her purse to hold while she unties the silk scarf wrapped around her head. "Couldn't risk messing up my new do." She holds a hand out to display a warm-blond curly wig.

"Stunning," I tell her. "Absolutely stunning."

She clears her throat. "Thank you, thank you. I thought I might get you to weigh in on a couple of styles I was considering, but I haven't seen you in my office too much lately."

"I'm so sorry," I tell her. I really am. Gossiping with Ms. Laverne is always one of the best parts of my week. "I've been really busy with prom court."

"No, no, no," she says. "It's a good sign. You've got your wings! Finally!"

"What do you mean?"

She takes her purse back and digs out her keys for me to take. "Baby, any time someone is in my office it's because they're sick or they're hiding, and it's usually the latter. I'm glad to see you're not hiding."

I take the keys from her and give her a slight smile. I feel pretty uneasy having this conversation with Tucker so close by. "Thanks," I say quietly.

"Do me a favor and roll up the windows if you see any stormy-lookin' clouds."

"Yes, ma'am!" I call after her as she heads into the building.

The next hour is a flurry of teachers and organizing the faculty parking lot and writing down makes and models and making notes like whose driver's side door needs jiggling and whose brake sticks and whose radio won't turn off once it turns on.

But finally the last bell of first period rings and the whole parking lot looks like the rapture just happened and the only two people left on Earth are me and Tucker.

"Man," he says, looking over the coffee station. "Those teachers demolished the doughnuts."

"It's scientifically impossible to say no to free dough-nuts."

Tucker surveys the lot. "We're going to have to divide and conquer. I'll show you how to do the first few and after that we'll split up. I'll give you similar cars so you're not hunting for oil filters."

We start with Mr. Higgins's car. I help Tucker jack the car (something I've done before) so that we can both crawl under.

With the light of his cell phone, Tucker points to a nut. "You see this thing?"

I nod, wiping back a bead of sweat and immediately regretting my decision to agree to this.

He positions a pan between us. "First thing we do is empty out the old oil." With a gloved hand, he unscrews the nut and oil spills out over his hand and into the pan, splattering on both of us.

"Seriously?" I ask, motioning down to my coveralls.

"I told you white wasn't the best choice."

"Hmph. Well, at least we'll wear the evidence of our labors."

"So we let this drain and then screw this guy back in, then we go back up top to put in some new oil."

"That's it?" I ask.

"Pretty much."

The oil drains and we both shimmy out from under the car. As Tucker pours in the oil, he explains that every car will take a certain kind of oil, and using the labels on the engine and on the bottles of oil, he shows me how to figure out which car gets which oil.

"You bought all this oil?" I ask, wondering how much he must have spent.

He shrugs. "I wanted our project to be special," he says. "I know changing oil sounds like a stupid idea, but there's nothing people hate more than going in and having their car worked on. Especially teachers who only have weekends off. I thought we might stand out. Besides, I think you've got an actual shot at this thing."

I laugh. "Is that some kind of joke?"

"Waylon," he says. "I'm serious. You could win. I'm not saying, like, right now at this very moment, but if we win over some teachers and make waves with our legacy project, you could get some people behind you in a major way."

I roll my eyes, but oh my God the Julie Andrews spinning feelings are kicking into overdrive. "This town is not ready for me to be their prom queen."

"What do you mean when you say *this town*?"

"You know what I mean. These people. This place. Sure, there are handfuls of great people, but most of these people are small-minded losers."

He leans on the hood of Mr. Higgins's car—something I'm sure Mr. Higgins would not appreciate. "Maybe you should give people a chance to surprise you. Have you ever thought that maybe you're using *this town* as an excuse to not put yourself out there?"

"What are you talking about?" Defensiveness builds in my voice. Goodbye, Julie Andrews.

"Maybe you should turn your volume up to ten and see

if these people can handle you. Maybe you're not giving them a fair shot at accepting you. Go full Waylon on this town. That's how you win this thing. I saw you on Saturday night."

"I'm full Waylon, thank you very much." I dig my toe into the cracked pavement until a small bit of gravel loosens. "But what would that even look like? To go full Waylon."

He shrugs. "Do the prom court panel in drag. Dress for school like you dressed at the Hideaway. You looked like a totally different person that night."

My cheeks flush and my heart thuds against the wall of my chest.

I follow him to the next vehicle, which is a truck and doesn't require a jack, so we both shimmy under, and this time I unscrew the nut and drain the oil.

I groan as the oil spills over my hand.

"That's it," he says. "Waylon Brewer getting messy."

"Literally the opposite of everything I aspire to."

As we're standing up, I point to Mr. Higgins's car. "Why do we men always name our cars and boats and inanimate objects after women? Beulah, Xena, Delilah."

"Well, I can tell you what my mama would have said about that. She always said men made their objects women because the only thing we teach boys about girls is that they're objects."

I nod thoughtfully. "I think your mom was onto something. Lucky for Beulah, I would never objectify a woman."

We take on the next car, an old minivan with wood paneling.

"I'll take this one," Tucker says. "These older cars can be tricky."

"I won't argue you on that," I say.

While he's cranking the jack, he says, "So you're a twin? What's that like?"

I shake my head. "Only the best and worst thing in the world."

He laughs. "How so?"

"Well, we want to be together all the time, but then it's like always being with someone who knows you a little too well and feeling like you can't even be spontaneous sometimes. And then every decision I make takes Clem into account." I slide the tray under the car for him while he crawls under. "But then sometimes she doesn't do the same for me . . . I don't know, it's complicated. We're so codependent, but I also wouldn't change us for anything."

"What do you mean, she doesn't do the same for you?"

I launch into the entire story about Clem and college and keeping it all a secret from me, and when I'm done Tucker emerges from beneath the van with a few more stains than he had going in.

He sits there on the pavement for a moment with his arms propped up on his knees. "That's tough."

"What can I say? My Clementine knows what she wants."

"But what do you want?" asks Tucker. "To go to Austin?"

I laugh bitterly. "Me? I knew what I wanted. She's the one that changed course without even telling me."

He shrugs. "You could go to Georgia with her."

". . . I could." I reach a hand out to help him up and he takes it, but once he's standing he doesn't let go.

We stand, eye to eye, close enough for me to smell the coffee on his breath. "But you won't," he says.

"I don't really like the idea of following her out there, if you get what I mean."

He smirks. "Yeah, you don't strike me as a follower."

I pout and cross my arms, yanking my hand free of his. "It's just really shitty of her."

"God, Waylon, maybe this isn't even about your sister." He rolls his eyes.

"I'm sorry, but are you frustrated with my feelings about my own life?"

He shakes his head and walks off.

"Say it!" I yell to him. "You can't roll your eyes at me and then say it's nothing."

He whirls around and throws his arms up. "You have cool-ass parents. They're not on you about your future, and you can basically do anything you want with your life. Your sister changed plans without telling you and that sucks. I get it. But you're not stuck here."

"Like you?" I ask. "Sorry," I say immediately. "That sounded shittier than I meant it to."

He nods. "It's fine," he says with a gruff voice. "It's true."

"I'm sorry." And I really am. I don't know Tucker's whole story, but based on what I do know, my grass is definitely greener. "My mom calls it a complaining spiral.

I start and I can't stop and even if there is a bright side, it's hard for me to see."

He shakes his head. "You should be able to be upset. That really does suck about Clementine lying to you. I think you're really cool and . . . I think one day I'll get to tell people that I knew you before you were an even bigger deal than you are now."

"You think I'm a big deal?" I ask, my gaze searching for his until he looks up with that slight smirk and our eyes meet.

He chuckles. "I don't know how it's scientifically even possible, but I can see your head expanding as we speak."

I nod knowingly. "My ego is very responsive." If only he knew how much I doubt myself and how poorly equipped I am to handle the future. But then, he's one of the few people in my life who doesn't see me as part of a two-person twin unit. So maybe he can see something I can't.

He hands me a fresh set of gloves. "Are you ready to fly solo, little bird?"

I take the gloves. "Here's hoping I don't absolutely destroy some teacher vehicles."

We spend all morning circulating the faculty lot and shuffling cars around. It takes me about four or five cars before I do one whole entire oil change by myself, and even after that I still have questions on almost every car, but I'm pretty impressed with myself.

I'm halfway under a Honda Accord when I hear the sound of a car lock chirping. Beside me my dad squats down and says, "Thought I'd bring you boys lunch."

"Music to my ears!" I pull myself out from under the car and give him a big oily hug.

"Come on now," he says. "This shirt was clean."

I give him a look. "Sort of," he clarifies. "Tuck!" Dad calls. "Lunchtime!"

And even though I'm slowly coming to tolerate Tucker, the familiar nickname grates on me.

Tucker's eyes light up at the sound of my dad's voice and he jogs over.

"Tacos," Dad says, nodding over to his truck. "We can eat in the cab if y'all want. Blast some of that AC."

The moment he mentions air-conditioning, I realize how sweaty I've become. I'd been in such a zone that I honestly hadn't even noticed. All those years Dad worked under the Texas sun, I wondered how he did it. He always said it was about getting into a rhythm, and I'd never quite understood what he meant about that until now.

We pile into the truck and devour a bag of tacos. Tucker and Dad talk about guys from work and an upcoming project Dad is trying to land. It's like watching my dad talk to a peer, and for some reason, watching the two of them interact makes me a little bit jealous, but I stuff that feeling down when I remember what Tucker said about me being lucky.

After lunch, Dad sticks around and watches me change the oil on a Subaru. He hovers and tells me things I already know—well, admittedly, things I've only known for a few hours. Thankfully, right as I'm about to absolutely explode and tell my dad to drink a gallon of motor oil, Bekah Cotter calls out to us from the courtyard. "Hey, y'all! Could I talk to you two?" She waves to Dad. "Hi, Mr. Brewer!"

"How do you know Bekah Cotter?" I ask in a whisper.

"What? Scared your dad's popular?"

I laugh. "Not even a little bit."

"I play softball with her dad."

"Got it. Dad, I better—"

He throws his hands up. "I hear ya loud and clear. I'll get out of your hair."

"I love you! Especially when you bring me tacos!" I call after him as he gets into the truck.

"Hey, Bekah!" Tucker says as she draws closer.

She smiles at him, bouncing on her toes. Ah, yes, she definitely thinks he's cute. There's a twinge in my stomach and I can't tell if it's jealousy or the tacos.

"I needed to talk to y'all about some prom court biz," she says.

"This sounds juicy," I say.

Her eyebrows jump up and down excitedly. "Volunteer hours."

I grimace.

Bekah doesn't miss a beat. "Hannah has us all signed up for after school on Friday."

"I usually help my dad out on Fridays, but I'll see if I can get out of it," Tucker says.

Bekah grins. Eyeballing our uniforms, she says, "Oh, now this was a good idea."

"You think?" I ask.

"Oil changes?" She nods feverishly. "That's like a real thing people need. Melissa decorated teachers' doors and I heard a bunch of them were actually annoyed because she got glitter everywhere."

"Glitter is dangerous," I say. "You don't wield glitter. Glitter wields you."

She leans in to add, "And Bryce didn't even help her."

Tucker rolls his eyes. "Flake. Probably thinks he can phone it in."

Bekah nods knowingly. "But I think y'all actually stand a chance here."

Something about hearing that from Bekah, the kind of girl who the social hierarchy was built for, actually makes me believe it might be true. Cue Julie Andrews.

TWENTY

"I can't believe you spent an entire day in matching out-fits with Tucker Watson and the only word you have to describe it is fine," Clem tells me. "That guy's been on your shit list for years."

"Well, while I'm very honored to know that you keep track of my shit list, which is very long and thorough, it really was fine. It wasn't awful. It wasn't great. It was fine." Except it wasn't fine. It was confusing. And dare I say fun? "Honestly," I tell her as we pull up to our driveway after school, "I'm way more concerned with pulling off all this prom court crap. And we haven't even broached the topic of my prom attire. We have less than a week and a half, people."

"Do what I'm doing and rent a tux," says Hannah.

"One does not simply rent a tuxedo," I say.

Hannah and Clem are silent, the two of them blinking at me.

"I mean, you *can* rent a tuxedo," I say. "I don't techni-cally own one, so I guess I would have to rent one too, but . . . I don't know. I didn't actually imagine myself going to this thing, so I never thought about what I might wear, and now we're actually going to prom and"—I can feel myself getting flustered—"so now I can't even begin to think about what the perfect outfit might consist of. Do I play it classy with a plain black tux? Do I lean into my queen nomination fully and go in drag? I've never walked more than a few steps in heels and—"

Clem pats my shoulder. "In through your nose and out through your mouth."

I roll my shoulder away from her hand. It might just be clothing, but it's also so much more than that. If I win—a very big and unlikely *if*—then this look is going in the yearbook. Hell! Even in the newspaper. And if little ol' Clover City is about to crown my ass prom queen, they're going to be stunned when they do. And then there's the fat factor. Finding the perfect thing to wear to prom is difficult, but being fat and bringing my vision to life could turn out to be impossible.

"I think you should dress in whatever makes you feel powerful," says Hannah. "When I'm in a suit, I feel like I'm the chief executive president commander empress of the world."

"Yeah," says Clem. "You have to figure out what your power suit is."

"Great. No pressure."

"Do you need a pep talk? You're smart. You're beautiful. You have impeccable taste. You're ahead of your time.

Our generation is lucky to have you."

I pucker my lips into a frown to stop from smiling. "Thanks."

She takes my hand and presses a kiss to my knuckles. "This pep talk has been brought to you by your twin sister."

At home, Mom finds me hanging upside down on the couch. "Baby, you look like a damn tomato with all that blood rushing to your head."

"I'm trying to trigger my creative juices," I tell her.

She sits down beside me. "By hanging upside down on my sofa? With your shoes on, I might add."

I slither off the couch onto the floor as gracefully as I can, which turns out to be not at all. "I'm trying to figure out what to wear to prom. And you know I have a hard enough time finding clothes as it is."

As the primary buyer of my wardrobe, she nods knowingly. "I'll have a look-see around town and let you know what I come up with."

"Thanks," I say, even though the thought of my mom picking out my prom outfit is even more stressful than trying to fulfill my own vision.

When I tell Mom I'm heading up to Dad's work site to do homework with Tucker, she insists on sending food. This time, though, I don't make the mistake of hiking up the muddy hill myself, and instead call Dad to chauffeur me.

"Did somebody call an Uber?" he asks as I get in.

"Primo dad joke," I tell him. "Like, you're two steps away from wearing socks with sandals and only watching movies based off true stories."

"Watch out," he says. "One day you'll be old too."

"I may be old, but I'll always be fabulous," I tell him.

"Your grandmother's genes are strong as hell, aren't they?"

"They are," I say. "But don't let her find out. Hey, I meant to ask: How long has Tucker worked for you?"

He thinks for a moment as he parks in front of his on-site office. "Well, I don't hire anyone under eighteen and he just came of age this year, so I guess a few months."

I nod. "Did you know he spends a lot of time running his dad's shop?"

He turns off his ignition. "I did. You know, Charlie, his dad, hasn't had it so easy. He's got a real problem with the bottle and lots of guilt to contend with. We went to school together, his dad and I did." He pauses. "Sounds like you've taken a real shine to him."

"Well, we got stuck doing this prom stuff together," I explain.

"Doesn't seem like a bad guy to get stuck with." He winks and nudges my arm.

I wrinkle my nose and shake my head. "Did Mom put you up to this? We are definitely not having this conversation."

"I'm just trying to bond with my son," he says as I slam the passenger door behind me.

"Then take me shopping!" I tromp up the stairs and

Tucker is already waiting for me. He's changed since this afternoon. Now he wears light-wash jeans that are forever stained with dirt, oil, and paint, with heavy work boots like the kind my dad has always worn and a faded Texas A&M T-shirt.

"I come bearing gifts of leftover casserole and home-work," I announce. "Indeed. I don't know what it is, but I know there's cheese."

"Don't mind if I do," he says as he takes the food from me and pops it in the microwave, which is pretty gross on the inside and has definitely seen its fair share of exploded lunches. He punches a few buttons and then turns back to me. "So, we have one project down and one to go. The faculty were super into it. And, of course, homework."

"None of them were really into doing my customer ser-vice survey," I tell him, tucking my chin into my shoulder, like I'm emotionally wounded.

"Oh, come on now." He moves to the other side of the room where I am, leans up against the counter next to me so that our shoulders are brushing, and crosses one leg over the other. "It was less a survey and more you cornering staff members and asking them how likely they were to vote for either one of us on a scale of one to ten."

"There was a very nice mint in it for them if they answered. Those white puffy soft ones."

He patronizes me with a sliver of a smile and a nod. "Those mints do get me every time. But teachers want the day to be over more than students do," he says. "We still have to plan our legacy project. This one's gotta be huge, though," he says. "Like, think viral."

I groan. "I hate that it's called a legacy project. It makes it sound like we're dying." I fall silent for a moment, trying to think of something. "I don't know. I mean, we could build a bench. Or, like, get the broken vending machines fixed. Or paint some dumb mural with a bunch of kids holding hands around the world."

He shakes his head. "What's something that would have changed your whole experience at school? The kind of thing that would've helped you leave this place with close to zero regrets?"

The microwave dings before I can answer, which is good, because I don't have an answer. I want to stand out. I want to fit in. But I've never done much of either. The only place I've ever felt like I'm right where I'm supposed to be is Clementine's side. I'm not really leaving school with regrets, but I'm not leaving with many memories either. I've only got a few weeks left, and if I'm going to stand out or fit in, now is the time.

I let my mind wander to my own personal Fancy-but-Not-Too-Fancy Utopia. A place where beautiful gowns and sweatpants are equally revered. Perfect climate control so that I never walk into a room feeling like a sweaty mess. A place where no one looks at you like you need to eat a salad when you choose to eat a burger and a place where anyone can hold hands or kiss or not do any of those things without anyone else caring. That's a laundry list of things, but if I could start anywhere, where would my utopia begin?

"Really luxurious bathrooms," I finally say as he's shoveling the casserole onto two different dishes. "Like with fainting couches and mints and free tampons and shit for people who need them and really fancy soap."

He laughs, really laughs, his head shaking as he chokes on a bit of casserole. My stomach jumps a little at the sound of it and all I want to do is make him laugh again. "Okay, yes, a fancy bathroom to poop in would be fantastic, but I'm talking about something that would change everything for you."

"You underestimate the power of luxury," I tell him, as the irony of this dingy little trailer really sinks in.

He has another bite of the casserole and lets out a delicious sigh that gives me chills. Then he points his fork at me. "Try again."

It takes a minute for my brain to work, because his sigh is on a constant loop. I clear my throat and force myself to think. "Honestly, if I could just be me. That's it. That would change everything. If I could just be the version of myself that exists in my head, but in real life all the time, that would have made high school better. Maybe then I would have run for prom queen because I wanted to and not because some knuckle-dragging Neanderthal nominated me."

"Full Waylon," he says knowingly, like he can perfectly imagine exactly what form that might take. "But if you think about it, everyone feels like that. Don't you see it everywhere you look?"

"Oh, come on," I say, a little outraged by his inability to

see what I see. "People like Melissa and Bryce and Bekah and even Mitch and Callie—those people always get to be themselves without getting eaten alive."

"I'm not saying the stakes aren't high for you—they are, but take Bekah, for instance. She's more than a baton-twirling blonde."

I shrug and drag my fork through my food. "Bekah and I are not the same. Bekah is hot. I'm a fat gay guy who has a female alter ego."

He takes a huge bite of food and keeps talking—which is somehow gross and adorable. Who have I become? "First—maybe there's more to Pumpkin than you think. Maybe spending more time as Pumpkin might help you feel more like . . . you."

It's the first time I've really heard someone talk about Pumpkin like she was a legitimate thing and more than a silly nickname from Grammy. Like I could actually build a life around being Pumpkin by night and Waylon by day. And like maybe in order to fully be Waylon, I need to let myself be Pumpkin.

"And B of all . . ." He looks down at his near-empty plate. "You're pretty hot yourself," he says softly.

That should make me blush. I should feel a fluttering in my chest. I should be asking him a zillion questions right now. But the truth is his words make my stomach turn, and I lose my appetite faster than I can push my food away.

I've tried not to spend too much time thinking about the differences between me and Tucker, but this morning when I saw us both in the mirror in our matching outfits, it was more apparent than ever. We're both tall, except he's broad and trim where my shoulders seem to slope down like I'm some kind of penguin, and my gut pooches out to complete the whole look like I'm not just a penguin. I'm a penguin with a beer belly. I try not to think too much about my body, and the fact that I can't confront that part of myself embarrasses me. It makes me feel weak, but honestly, I don't even like to look too long at what's underneath my clothes. So hearing Tucker call me hot doesn't make me feel good. It makes me feel uncomfortable and patronized. At least with Lucas, there was less talking and more fumbling in the dark.

"We need to start on this homework," I say quickly, and pull Mr. Higgins's folder from my backpack.

He clears his throat, his cheeks flushed. "Right."

For the next hour, we fill out worksheets, I share my leftovers with Tucker, and he makes us awful break room coffee. And slowly my brain forgets about the extreme discomfort I felt at the sound of someone calling me hot. Everything that's been a source of pain or worry for me over the last few weeks falls away until it doesn't matter, because Tucker Watson and I are sitting across from each other with only a narrow table between us. If this table wasn't here, all I would see is his thigh laced between mine and the inside of his foot resting against mine. It's a silent, unacknowledged touch that makes everything inside of me roar to life.

TWENTY-ONE

Ms. Jennings holds her hands up, fingers stretched out, triumph written all over her face as we hold the final note of our graduation medley. She snaps her hands shut, and we stop in unison. With a teary-eyed grin, she nods. "Perfect. Just perfect."

"Ms. Jennings," Kyle says, "can you please go to college with us?"

"You pretty much look young enough to be a senior in college, anyway," Alex chimes in.

"Suck-ups," I mutter.

"But it's true," Clem whispers as she peels a piece of purple nail polish from her thumbnail. "She looks young enough to be in our class."

The bell rings and the thrum of noise in the hallway is immediate. "Okay," says Ms. Jennings over the commotion, "I'll see you all next week. And Waylon, if you could stay behind for a moment, that'd be great."

"Ooooh!" Clem pokes at my side. "Someone's in trouble."

I roll my eyes and toss the keys her way as she joins

Hannah in the hallway. "This teacher's pet would never. I'll meet y'all at the truck."

I hover at Ms. Jennings's desk as the last student scoots off to lunch. Being asked to stay behind after class by a teacher will forever make me anxious.

She closes the door behind her and turns to me. "It's been a big couple weeks for you, huh?"

She's talking about prom, but the video too, which I'm sure she saw. "That's an understatement."

She nods, her lips twitching into a sad smile. "That thing people say about high school being the best years of your life? It's a lie."

"I'd hoped that was the case."

She crosses her arms and leans against her desk. "I hear Clem is off to Georgia with Hannah. Have you given any thought to what's next for you?"

I shrug. "Community college maybe. I don't know. We were supposed to go to Austin, but that's not . . . well, she's going to Georgia."

"Community college is a good option," she says. I can tell she's not lying, but she's not telling the whole truth. It's like she's waiting for me to say some kind of magic phrase as a sign that it's safe to let her guard down.

"Too bad there's no college courses on drag," I say with a laugh. In Clover City, you either go off to school or you're stuck here forever.

Her face lights up. "Teachers aren't supposed to say this, and this might be crossing a line, but . . . I wanted to say . . . college isn't for everyone, Waylon. Or it doesn't have to be. And . . . if you're really serious about drag, I know some of the best queens in Texas. It's not really ideal career counseling to encourage a student to pursue a career in drag, but it's a real art form and I think you could really thrive. You know, right down the road, we have our very own—"

"Lee Way," I finish for her. "She's amazing."

She pushes her glasses up into her hair and laughs. "Well, I'm glad to know we have similar taste. Lee is a dear friend. At least I haven't had an awkward run-in with you at the Hideaway. Though, if I had, you wouldn't be the first student or former student."

"Oh, I've already had an awkward run-in of my own there," I say, sounding much more experienced than I am.

"Listen, Waylon, I want you to know that I'm here for you. After graduation, too. Of course, if you need any letters of recommendation for school . . . or an introduction, just let me know."

"Thank you," I tell her with as much genuine gratitude as I can muster. It really does mean so much to me. She sees something in me, and if she sees something in me, maybe I can see something in me too. "And Ms. Jennings . . . you're the shit."

She chuckles. "Back atcha."

Out in the parking lot, I head to my truck with an extra bounce in my step.

"There he is!" calls a voice.

I double back, glancing down the aisle of cars to see a

whole ton of seniors hanging out in the beds of their pickup trucks. It's not just any seniors, though. It's decidedly popular senior guys, most of whom are football players.

"Pumpkin!" calls Bryce.

Patrick Thomas and another guy named Aaron echo him. "Pumpkin!"

Beside them, Tucker stands, leaning up against his brake light. He gives me a single nod.

Bryce lets out a gut-busting laugh. "You two freaks have the same shirt on," he says, pointing at Patrick.

I look down and then to Patrick, and sure enough, we both have on the same bland polo shirt. Teal with a yellow stripe across the chest.

Patrick laughs. "Yeah, it's like the supersized version of me."

"Wow. So clever," I say dryly. "A fat joke. So groundbreaking."

"You want to get in on our senior prank plans?" Bryce asks as he regains his composure.

None of these guys outside of Tucker are people I have any interest in making plans with, and speaking of, what is he even doing with these human skid marks?

"Yeah," says Patrick, "this is equal-opportunity prank planning. Fairies welcome. A friend of Tucker's is a friend of ours."

"How progressive of you. I think I'll pass." I spare a glance at Tucker. I almost find myself asking, *You're not really friends with these guys, are you?* His gaze narrows on the gravel, the vein in his neck twitching.

Oh, so last night he tells me I'm hot and today he can't make eye contact with me in public. My blood begins to boil. This is what I get for letting him in.

"Let us know if you change your mind," says Bryce. "If you're not in on the prank, you might find out that the prank is on you."

"I'll take my chances," I mutter as I walk off to find Hannah and Clem. I look down at my stupid polo shirt. If it didn't mean wearing my undershirt or taking my chances on what the lost-and-found has to offer, I'd rip this damn thing off right now. I've spent years trying to fit in with these two-dimensional lumps of shit and they still treat me like this. I hate myself for spending all these years trying to blend in.

I'm done hiding.

TWENTY-TWO

"Welp, we want to thank you lot for being here tonight to help us out." Pastor Rich, a tall, gawky white guy who definitely owns a collection of braided belts, turns to his wife, Sheila, and takes her hand. "We want this little church of ours to be a place for everyone, and we're so happy to officially have the space to host Parenting with Pride. Hannah, it was so good of you to bring your friends."

Hannah gives Pastor Rich two thumbs-up, which is honestly something I never thought I would see with my own two eyes.

"Sheila and I will be over in the chapel working on a few things, so come find us if you need anything." Apparently, Grace Chapel didn't always meet in a chapel. They used to meet in the shopping center in between Lonestar Tae Kwon Do Academy and Down for the Count, the boxing gym. But after years of saving, they were able to buy the dilapidated Clover City Church of Christ. The building behind the chapel houses a couple of classrooms, including the one where Parenting with Pride will be meeting.

Sheila, a short East Asian woman with round hips and rosy

cheeks, takes her husband's hand. "Everything you should need is right over there in that corner. We've got drinks in a cooler and we'd love to order y'all some pizza later."

I gulp loudly. This is starting to feel very much like youth group, which is very much not my scene.

The minute they're gone, I turn to Hannah. "This feels like a trap."

She laughs and starts to hand out brooms and trash bags. "Don't worry. They won't spritz you with holy water."

"Pastor Rich and Miss Sheila are way nicer than my pastor and his wife," Bekah says. "One time I wore spaghetti straps to church and Pastor Troy asked his wife to give me an extra choir robe so I wouldn't tempt any of the men during service."

"That's disgusting," Clementine says and pretends to retch.

Hannah playfully rolls her eyes at Clem, because I guess when you're lovesick, everything your significant other does is adorable. "Hey, where's Tucker?" she asks, suddenly aware that our numbers are down.

"He texted and said he was running late. He should be here soon." I take a look around to survey the work ahead of us. Scum-covered windows. Broken blinds. Grimy floors littered with trash and moldy books. It's a mess so bad that you have to wipe away dirt to more dirt and so on and so on until finally you reach the decaying surface.

I take a broom and Clem a trash bag while Hannah and Bekah start on the windows. We turn on some music, and after a little while, Willowdean and Amanda show up with extra gloves in hand.

"Thanks for helping us out," Hannah tells them.

"Any reason to escape my brothers for the night," Amanda says.

Willowdean nods. "I don't mind cleaning as long as it's not my room. Or anything adjacent to my room."

"That's a mood I can get into," I say.

We all fan out into different parts of the room. After a few minutes of working, Willowdean lets out a sigh.

Amanda puts an arm around her. "You could try talking to him again."

Willowdean pulls a latex glove over her hand. "It's kind of hard to talk to someone who's not talking back to you."

Hannah snaps her fingers in agreement.

"I don't get it," I say. "You're mad because he invited you to prom?"

Willowdean begins to pluck trash off the ground and put it into the trash bag Amanda is holding out for her. "He's so hot and cold. One minute, he's ghosting me, and the next, he's doing these huge grand gestures like asking me to prom in front of a restaurant full of people. We would be at work and he would just run off after our shift when we would normally hang out, or he would be busy texting other people when he'd invited me over, and when I asked if it was another girl, he was, like, offended that I'd even think that. What else was I supposed to think? And now prom is coming up and I don't have a date and I never thought I'd ever care about that, but I guess I do." Her nostrils flare as she lets out a loud huff.

"If it makes you feel less alone, I am very, very much dateless and I'd love to hang with you at prom," I tell her.

"Me too!" says Amanda. "It'll be great. We'll all be together. Why is it that we work so hard to get through twelve years of school and somehow the pinnacle of it all depends on whether or not you have a date for one random night?"

"She's not wrong," I say.

Amanda tips her invisible cap to me.

Willowdean musters a smile and nods. "Thanks, y'all."

"Cherry Bomb" comes on through the speaker, letting me know this is definitely Clem's playlist, and Hannah cranks the volume up. "Less talk. More work!"

After a few songs, Tucker jogs into the room, sweat beading down his jaw. "Sorry I'm late," he says, trying to catch his breath.

I hand him my dustpan. "Did you *run* here?"

"Uh, yeah, actually, I did," he says, slumping against a collapsing desk.

"In jeans?" It's hot enough today that you could break a sweat sitting perfectly still. Running in jeans? That's asking for swamp ass.

"I think the people of Clover City would prefer I keep my pants on."

"Speak for yourself," says Willowdean from across the room with a laugh.

The blush in Tucker's cheeks spreads up his ears, or maybe he's just flushed from his two-mile run. "I was having car trouble, so I left the truck at school and hoofed it."

"You could've called me," I tell him, even though I'm even more pissed now that he's late, and having to give him a ride after that incident in the parking lot would have made my day even worse.

"I didn't want to bother you," he says as he lifts the edge of his T-shirt up to wipe the sweat off his face, giving the whole room a look at his abdomen, which isn't jacked but is much more defined and tan than anything below the collar of my shirt has ever been.

"Or you didn't want to be seen with me?" I ask, very clearly remembering the way he refused to look at me in the parking lot and determined to not be swayed by the sight of his chest for the second time in the last month.

He grits his teeth but says nothing.

I hand over my broom. "I think I'm going to pass the broom torch to Tucker and start working on those windows outside," I say. "I could use some air."

Tucker takes the broom and stands there while I grab some supplies to take with me.

Clem eyes me thoughtfully. "You want some company?"

"Nah, you stay here."

I take my window cleaner and squeegee outside to pout in private.

From inside the sanctuary, Pastor Rich and Sheila are singing along to the Beach Boys while they paint once-faded walls a crisp but warm shade of white.

Church was always a social thing for my parents, but once Clem and I came out, we all sort of drifted away from Sunday service. And honestly, it was for the best. We wouldn't have been welcome anyway. But this little place doesn't seem so awful. Maybe a church that hosts a support group for parents of queer kids can't be all bad.

The door around the front of the building creaks and I hold my breath in anticipation of who it might be.

"Hiya," Clem says as she turns the corner. "Not who you were hoping?"

"I don't know. Maybe. Yes."

She takes the squeegee from my hand. "I wipe. You spray."

"Yes, ma'am," I say, and knock my hip into hers.

"Spill it," she says. "What's the deal with you and this guy?"

"I think we hate each other. Or I thought we did. And then I saw him that night at the Hideaway and—"

She gasps and in a whisper voice, says, "Oh my God! I knew that was him. I saw him from across the room and tried pointing him out to Hannah, but he was gone." She leans back, arms crossed. "Huh. Tucker Watson is into the menfolk? I had no idea! He's so . . ."

"Straight!" I finish for her. "Or not, I guess. I don't know."

"Well, did you talk to him about it?"

I shrug. "Sort of. But I didn't really know how to be like, so were you just spectating at the gay bar or were you participating?"

Clementine stares at me dumbfounded. "I guess he could have been there . . . to be there, but what eighteen-year-old straight boy goes to a gay bar to just . . . go?"

"I know. And he's been really hard to read . . . but sometimes, for just a moment, he says the exact right thing, and it makes me feel like . . . my whole body is glowing." I hate myself a little bit for even saying that out loud, but there it is.

"Waylon," she says, her voice soft and patient. "I want you to be happy. I want you to fall in love and find something and someone that brings you the kind of joy you only see in movies. But I can't watch you fall for another guy who's still in the closet."

I shake my head. "I can't. I won't. Everyone's on their own time, but I think I might finally be finding my place, and it's definitely nowhere near any closets. Unless it's an immaculately organized closet Marie Kondo style with my dream wardrobe."

"I love mess," Clem says solemnly, quoting the goddess Marie Kondo herself.

"But we don't love other people's half-in-the-closet messes."

"Amen," she says.

"Besides, I won't have you here to pick up the pieces."

Her lips puff into a frown.

"No, I'm sorry," I say. "I didn't mean that in a passive-aggressive asshole way. I meant it in a literal way. I don't want to say the idea has grown on me, but . . . I think you should go to Georgia." The words are out of my mouth before I have too much time to think about them. I've felt this moment slowly dawning on me for a little while now.

"Not that you needed my permission."

She drops the squeegee and throws her arms around me. "I'll visit. You'll visit. We'll FaceTime every day."

I wrap my arms around her and press my face into her shoulder. "Don't forget me," I say so quietly that I almost hope she doesn't hear.

"Impossible," she squeaks.

I step back and take her hand. I can't imagine who we would be without each other and I never want to know, but it's time for us to take a few steps apart. Just enough space for us each to grow a little broader. A little stronger. A little brighter.

"Besides," I say, "if anyone can survive being half a country apart, it's us."

She bites down on her lip, tears welling as she nods. "What will you do?" she asks.

"I don't know," I answer honestly. "But when I do, you'll be the first to know."

A knock on the window startles us, and I let out an embarrassingly dramatic scream.

From inside, Hannah waves and sticks her tongue out.

I spray the spot over her face with window cleaner and blow a raspberry.

I still feel uncertain, and part of me might always think that this is Clem choosing Hannah over me, but no matter why she's going or what I think, I have to let her go. I have to try.

TWENTY-THREE

"Can you please explain how exactly you got us all volunteering at a church?" Amanda asks Hannah as she slurps a hunk of cheese off the tip of her pizza. "Did Millie possess your body in your sleep?"

All seven of us sit on the steps of the chapel with two extra-large boxes of pizza and cups of lemonade like Sheila promised.

Hannah shrugs. "Me, Bekah, Tucker, and Waylon need the volunteer hours for prom court."

"Well, sure," I say, "but that doesn't explain how exactly this happened. Honestly, I didn't realize there were enough gay kids in Clover City for there to even be a need for some kind of parental support group."

"You'd be surprised," Hannah says, and bites down into her slice.

We all stare at her, waiting for her to finish that thought.

"Oh, fine," she says as though it's such a pain for her to say more than six words at a time. "Rich and Sheila took me in when 'Lita kicked me out."

"What?" I ask, completely shocked. I've only met

Hannah's grandma once or twice, but she always seems so proud of Hannah.

"The summer before ninth grade," she confirms.

"But your grandma is so cool," Amanda says. "Why would she do that?"

Hannah looks to Clem, and I get the feeling this isn't a story she freely shares often. "I never came out to my 'lita. She caught me kissing my cousin's friend the summer before ninth grade. She went weeks without even making eye contact with me. When I tried to talk about it, she'd start praying, like directly at me, like I was some kind of demonic force. It was terrifying, in a way. I felt like somehow I'd become the monster in the story without even realizing it. Her pastor told her I was an abomination and she told me I had to go to church camp or get out."

Clem grips Hannah's knee. "I wouldn't call that place church camp."

My jaw drops. "Your grandma tried to send you to a pray-away-the-gay camp? Oh my God, Hannah, I'm so sorry."

"It's fine. I didn't go." Hannah laughs bitterly. "Rich and Sheila were always a little nosy. Honestly, it kind of annoyed me sometimes. These dopey-ass neighbors next door always in our business. But when Sheila saw me crying on the front porch, she invited me over for some lemonade and then that turned into an offer to let me stay in their guest room."

"Wow," says Bekah with a drawl, her bright-blue eyes round and wide. "That breaks my heart."

"I only stayed with them for two weeks. I expected

them to try and, like, 'fix' me or something. But it wasn't me they were worried about fixing. Rich spent a lot of time going over to 'Lita's and talking scripture with her. Speaking her language. I moved back in three days before the first day of school. It hasn't been easy. She still doesn't get a lot of things, but she left her church and has been the secretary for Grace Chapel ever since." She looks around at us all, completely entranced by her story. "Ta-da?" she says. "The end? Can someone else talk please?"

"Willowdean!" someone yells from across the darkening parking lot.

Ellen, fresh off a dinner date with her boyfriend's parents, sprints toward the chapel. "I saw him!"

"What?" Willowdean stands and rushes down the steps toward Ellen.

"Bo!" Ellen yells. "He was out to eat with these two old guys."

"What?" She throws her arms up. "What are you even talking about?"

"Am I supposed to understand what's happening?" I ask Clem under my breath.

She shakes her head. "I . . . think her boyfriend's cheating on her with two older gentlemen?"

"I fully expect Wendy Williams to show up and tell us who the father is."

"Wendy Williams doesn't do paternity tests on her show," Hannah clarifies.

Clem grips her knee. "Do you mean to tell me you're a Wendy Williams fan?"

Hannah snarls but then pinches two fingers together. "A teensy fan."

Tucker stands, stretching his arms wide so that the edge of his T-shirt rises over the top of his jeans an inch or two. "I'm going to get back to work."

"I'll join you," says Bekah.

I watch the two of them walk through the patch of overgrown grass, bugs buzzing to life under the setting sun as Bekah's soft laugh echoes.

My chest is tight and my throat feels dry. I wonder if I've simply made up the last few weeks of my life. If it's all in my head.

Clem nudges me.

"They'd make a cute couple," I say.

"Bekah would make a cute couple with a coatrack," Hannah says.

I nod. She's got that right.

"Come on," says Clem. She stands and takes my hand, and the two of us, along with Hannah and Amanda, make our way back to the old building while Ellen and Willowdean stay in the parking lot, losing their shit over two old mystery men.

After a few more hours of cleaning, the room is ready to be painted and the floors sanded. Pastor Rich and Sheila cheerfully sign our community service forms and invite each of us to their first Sunday service in a few weeks.

The two of them sandwich Hannah in a hug, and when she starts to squirm, Sheila reaches for Clem. "Now, both of y'all need to come over one night with Miss Camile before you leave."

"Oh, 'Lita is already planning a peach-themed going-away party."

Bekah's phone buzzes. "Oh, shoot, my sister's here." She turns to Tucker. "We could give you a ride."

"I'm giving him a ride," I say before Tucker has a chance to answer. "Prom court biz," I add through gritted teeth.

Bekah smiles and her bright-blue eyes bounce from me to Tucker, who nods. "Well, I'll see y'all later," she says, excusing herself.

As we all head our separate ways, Tucker follows me to my truck. "You really don't have to give me a ride."

"You going to run home now too?" I ask.

"I was thinking more along the lines of a stroll."

"Get in," I tell him. "But I'm surprised one of your good buddies wasn't here to pick you up."

He doesn't take my bait and we drive in silence until I roll to a stop at a red light at a totally empty intersection. "So how is it that a mechanic's car breaks down?"

He throws his head back with a laugh, his stubble-covered Adam's apple bobbing. "A shitty truck is still a shitty truck."

"Do you need a ride in the morning to pick it up?" I hate myself for even asking, and I rarely stir before eleven on a Saturday morning, but I'm starting to feel like I'm not in control of my brain.

"Nah. I'll get the tow truck so I can fix it in the shop."

"Hey, Tucker, were you embarrassed of me today? In

the parking lot with Bryce and Patrick. Is that why you wouldn't look at me? Because if you're embarrassed to be seen with me, it's best if we go our separate ways now."

"No," he says firmly. "God, no." He runs his hands down his thighs, pushing so hard his nails turn white. "I was being stupid and I—"

"I'm sure being paired with me for prom court hasn't been . . . easy on you," I say, laying the guilt on thick just like Mom.

"I wasn't embarrassed by you. I was embarrassed to be seen with those asshats."

"Well, you didn't do a great job of showing it. Aren't those asshats your old football buddies?" It's hard not to feel his answer isn't some kind of cop-out.

"I'm not going to tell you I haven't spent years hanging out with those guys or pretend like I haven't known them my whole life. Your parents dump you in peewee football when you're a kid and in a place like this, that means you're basically stuck with the same guys forever. But I don't really think of them as friends. They wouldn't, like, help me out of a bind or anything."

"My dad tried to get me into football," I tell him. "Second grade. I didn't make it past the first practice." I try to imagine, for a moment, what things would be like today if I'd stuck with it. Maybe I'd be the best queer football player Clover City had ever seen. Or maybe I'd be just another meathead, suppressing who I really was.

He grunts. "You should have stuck with it. Turns out football is super gay."

"Is it really now?" I ask, my hands immediately sweating. This is what I was trying to explain to Clem. Endless mixed signals!

He bites down on his lower lip, eyebrow arched. "Trust me."

I wonder if he can hear my heart pounding. My mouth is dry and my palms are slick on the steering wheel. "Do you remember in sophomore year when you asked to switch seats so you didn't have to sit next to me?"

He grimaces. "You gonna make me answer for all my sins tonight?"

The click, click, click of my blinker is my only response. I want to let Tucker in. I want to be friends. But I can't do that without retreading the past. I have to know why he despised me. He has to say it out loud or else the wondering will never end.

"I felt bad. I felt bad about ditching you on our group project, and I—I had stuff going on and then when we were seated together that one time . . . I figured if I didn't have to see you, I wouldn't have to think about it. And I wouldn't have to think about you."

My heart stops and all I can hear is that he thought about me. Years ago, before I even knew who I wanted to be, he thought about me. I felt so entirely alone, and I wonder what would have happened differently if when we first met up for that group project, I asked Tucker to stay for dinner or walk to Sonic.

I want to ask him why he ditched me to begin with and what kind of stuff he was dealing with. But I can barely even register that we're here at his dad's shop where they live in the apartment above, and he's practically out of the car before I'm even in park.

"I gotta go," he says in a hurry, but before he can even shut his door, his dad is rambling through the dusty gravel toward my truck with a graying mutt who I recognize as Duke trotting behind him.

"Thanks for the ride," Tucker says. "I'll text you later."

I might be petty, but Mom didn't raise me rude, so I call past Tucker, "Hi, Mr. Watson."

Duke dodges past him and walks right up to the open door to investigate me. I reach my hand across the seat for him to sniff and he carefully nudges the top of my hand with his wet nose. Our family dog, Griff, died when I was thirteen and Dad was too heartbroken to let us get a new one. A dog is high on my list of priorities once I'm a fully functioning adult.

Mr. Watson doesn't even look up at the sound of my voice. I can see him in Tucker. The shoulders and the shape of their lips. The way their noses gather into a square point at the end. In many ways, Mr. Watson looks like a deflated version of Tucker, but with a smattering of sun spots.

"Dad, why aren't you in bed?" Tucker asks in a stern voice that sounds so foreign coming from him.

"I, uh, lost the s—key to the apartment," he slurs. Mr. Watson pats down the front of his jeans and his back pockets like the keys might somehow miraculously appear.

He looks so much like Tucker. It almost makes me uncomfortable. Tall and broad, but softer. He's overdue for a haircut, with curls gathering at the nape of his neck, and his skin is papery and translucent. I bet that before Tucker was as big as he is today, helping his dad into bed was much more of a task than he could easily handle.

I feel suddenly protective of younger Tucker, and I hate myself for being so venomous with him and quick to assume that the whole situation between us was about me entirely.

"You're that Brewer boy," he says. "The queer one."

"That's me," I cheerfully admit. I'm plenty used to being the queer one.

"Good for you," he says, giving me a hearty thumbs-up.

Tucker turns back to me and whispers, "Sorry."

"Your daddy worked so hard for that business of his." Mr. Watson shakes a finger in my direction. "Shame you won't be the one to be taking it over."

"Oh," I say, taken aback. That took a turn, but I'm quick to remind myself that Mr. Watson is an alcoholic and the last thing Tucker needs is me getting into a scuffle with his dad. "I'd run the whole thing into the ground." Even though I could totally take over the family business if I wanted to, but yeah, sorry, my heart's not in the construction biz. This hair is too good for a hard hat.

Sorry, Tucker mouths through a grimace, apologizing again. That's all it takes for everything to get through my thick skull to my brain. It wasn't me who Tucker was embarrassed of when we were younger. It wasn't me who he didn't want to be seen with during our group project.

I can't believe I didn't piece it together sooner, but I can sense his frazzled nerves over anyone seeing this side of him. Whoever Tucker brings into his life is committing to more than just him, and judging by the tension radiating from him, he knows it. And somehow, I take a little bit of pleasure in witnessing this. Not because I like to see Tucker suffer, but because seeing the most difficult corners of his life makes me feel closer to him. It makes me want to keep him close.

"Maybe one day, Tuck'll turn this place into something," he says. "My castle." He gestures around to the run-down garage, with its broken gas pumps and cracked windows. Tucker catches his elbow before he trips.

I lean across the seat, toward the open passenger window, and give Duke a well-deserved scratch on the head. "All due respect, Mr. Watson, but I think Tucker is meant for much, much bigger things."

Mr. Watson lets out a short, acerbic laugh.

I know that this guy is probably just fine when he's sober, but I don't think I've ever wanted to punch someone else's dad like I do right now.

Tucker smiles tightly, pulling his dad toward the door. "Come on, Duke. Inside." He looks up to me, and I can see the million thoughts passing just behind his eyes about what me meeting his dad might mean to him. Uncertainty. Discomfort. And even a little bit of relief. "Thanks for the ride," he tells me.

"Anytime."

TWENTY-FOUR

On Saturday night, me, Hannah, Clem, Alex, and Kyle are all gathered around Kyle's family's dining room table.

Kyle looks over a clipboard. "Alex, baby, you did one last sweep for breakables? Did you get my mom's framed photo of Nana on her wedding day? The one in the hallway bathroom."

"Yes, for the tenth time," Alex says. "Can I please start making those blue frozen drink thingies I found on Pinterest?"

Kyle sighs. "I don't want us to blow through our ice supply too quickly. Once it's out, it's out."

"We could run to the store," says Hannah, her voice flat and bored.

"Not if you've even had a drop of alcohol," says Kyle. "So if you plan on being the party mom, that's on you."

Clem reaches under the table to squeeze Hannah's hand in an attempt to diffuse obvious irritation.

I raise my hand, which I can immediately tell Kyle greatly appreciates by the way he nods at me.

"Yes, Waylon."

"Um, who exactly did you invite to this party?" I ask.

"Yeah," says Alex. "You've been very cagey with the invite list."

Kyle clears his throat. "Well, I invited the Prism Club. And the choir."

The only thing that cuts the silence is the whirring of the ceiling fan in the living room.

"Do you know how much booze I got?" I manage to say. "There's enough alcohol in your shed to get a small country hammered."

"I wanted it to be a special night," Kyle says. "A party for *us*. Not *them*."

For the first time since I've known him, I can see Alex's blood begin to boil. "But we don't want it to be us versus them. We want to be them! And throwing a badass party is a step in the right direction." He lets out a frustrated shriek and storms out.

This ship is sinking fast. I look to Hannah. She nods, instinctively.

"We could call the rest of the prom court," I offer.

The doorbell rings.

"I'll get it," says Alex. "Our one single guest has arrived!"

"Do whatever you want," says Kyle as he pushes back from the table. "It's probably the pizza guy," he calls to Alex. And then to us, or maybe to no one, he says, "I try to do one adventurous, wild thing and plan a memorable night for us to tell our kids about, but no, it's not enough. I didn't invite the right people. Well, fine, Waylon. Invite them. Invite the jocks and the cheerleaders and the popular kids and the stoners. Sue me for wanting to have a party with people who actually like and respect me."

Clem looks to Hannah and shakes her head while Hannah is very clearly biting her tongue.

Kyle marches off to the door to help Alex with the pizza.

"Should I break it to him that like and respect are both very strong words?" Hannah asks once the coast is clear.

"You two are awful," says Clem.

"This party is going to be less exciting than an overnight sleep study," I say.

"I said you were awful," Clem says. "I didn't say you shouldn't call your prom squad."

I step out to the backyard, where Kyle's pool glitters under a canopy of string lights, and hold my phone to my ear. I can't believe I'm doing this.

"Waylon?" asks Tucker, shouting into the receiver over the sound of a jackhammer in the background.

No turning back now.

"Hey," I say, unable to help myself from shouting back. Neither of us have even so much as texted since last night.

"Is everything okay? You've never called me before." He continues to yell, even after the noise behind him quiets.

"I can hear you," I tell him.

"Oh, sorry."

"And I'm fine." He's right, though. I've never heard his voice on the phone, and now that I have, it might be something I need to hear again. "What time do you get off work tonight?" I ask.

"I'm putting in overtime right now, so I guess whenever I want."

"How do you feel about a party?" I ask. "And how quickly can you help me get half the school here?"

"I feel like watching Netflix and eating cold pizza, but I could be persuaded. As for half the school, I've got a few group texts going that could fill a house in thirty minutes."

In the forty-five minutes it takes for anyone else to arrive, Kyle stress-eats a whole pizza and then begs Alex to forgive him through a locked bathroom door while Hannah and Clem run out for a few extra bags of ice.

I hang out in the living room, nibbling on pizza while the strobe lights from Kyle's karaoke machine dance around me.

When Hannah and Clem return, they've brought with them Willowdean, Ellen, her boyfriend Tim, Amanda, Callie, Mitch, Millie, and a boy holding Millie's hand who I've seen around school with her.

"This is the party?" Callie asks when she sees me eating pizza solo by strobe light.

"I've never been to an unsupervised party like this before," Millie says with a giggle.

The guy holding her hand, with thick black hair and a caramel-brown complexion, who also manages to make a sweater vest and loafers look cool, gives her a kiss on the cheek.

She wraps her arms around his waist. "Malik stole a box

of wine from his parents' stash," she whispers.

"A box of wine to myself sounds like the kind of party I need right now," says Willowdean.

Malik laughs. "I was thinking the box could be more of a communal situation. I don't know much about box wine, but solo box wine sounds sort of depressing."

Millie nods thoughtfully.

Ellen takes Willowdean's hand and pulls her closer, whispering something to her.

Clem and Hannah emerge from behind them with bags of ice.

"There's a freezer in the garage," I tell them.

"Come in, come in," says Kyle, sweeping down the stairs as he pulls Alex behind him, and Alex's eyes are a little bit puffy and red. Drama in paradise! "There are refreshments in the kitchen and libations as well. Please leave your keys in the cookie jar to help me monitor drunk driving."

"I've got no desire to drive drunk," says Amanda, "but I don't think you're going to get many people who are willing to give up their car keys."

Before Kyle can respond, the doorbell rings. "I'll get that!" Alex says, and moments later a flood of vaguely familiar people we've all sort of known since kindergarten trickle in.

"Make yourself at home," Kyle says, but his voice is drowned out by laughter and banter, and soon, our new guests have found the kitchen and the beer.

After that, it's a near-constant stream of people coming through the door. Some ring the doorbell. Others don't.

Someone helps themselves to Kyle's parents' sound system, and soon music is pumping through every room of the house.

Me, Hannah, and Clem laugh ourselves silly as we watch Kyle try to rope off the upstairs using an old winter scarf.

A few people from Prism seem a little startled by the crowd at first, but apparently underage drinking and the end of the school year are the ultimate unifying factors for teenagers everywhere.

"Am I at the right party?" a voice behind me asks.

I turn to find Tucker, freshly showered with still-damp hair and a six-pack of root beer dangling from his fingers.

Kyle rushes between us, one second away from asking someone to take their shoes off in the living room, when Tucker hands him the soda. "I wasn't really sure what to bring, but I thought I should contribute."

Kyle gasps, momentarily distracted from his mission. He clicks his tongue. "A host gift! How thoughtful! Let me put this on ice."

Tucker shrugs and Kyle's off again.

"Well, he's going to love you forever and ever as long as you both shall live," I say. "If you leave now, there might still be time to escape him."

"Nah," says Tucker. "I'll take my chances."

A swarm of guys led by Bryce walks past us and someone pats Tucker on the back.

"What's up, man?" he asks, and bumps fists with basically the whole football team.

Once they're gone, I hold my fist up. "'Sup, bro?"

Tucker goes to bump my fist, but instead his fingers snake around my wrist. He tugs me toward the back door. "Come on, let's see what's going on out here."

He drags me behind him and I think my whole heart is in my throat, because a boy—no, Tucker Watson—is holding my hand in front of practically our whole class. I guess technically he's leading me by the wrist, so maybe it doesn't really count as hand-holding, but it mother-freaking counts for something, because from across the room where Clem and Hannah sit curled into each other on the couch with red cups in their hands, my sister points at me, her jaw slack.

Holy shit, she mouths.

TWENTY-FIVE

Outside on the patio table, the umbrella has been removed, and there is a very intense game of beer pong happening. And if my eyes don't deceive me, at the center of it all, Alex is surrounded by half the baseball team as they cheer him on. "I'm going to kick so much beer-pong ass in college!" he shouts.

In the deep end of the pool, a few guys are competing to see who can land the biggest cannonball while two girls sit on the edge, giving scores on a scale of one to a million. And in the shallow end, the cannonball waves lap over Callie and Mitch while they make out partially clothed. Like me, Mitch has a flabby chest that is clearly visible through his T-shirt, but that's definitely not stopping him now.

"Get a room!" someone shouts.

Tucker and I settle onto a set of lounge chairs in a darker corner of the yard, where a small cluster of people are passing a joint. It's shocking to me that this whole side of high school has existed right under my nose. What else have I missed out on? I feel like I've only been with these people while we're under adult supervision, but something about being at this party levels the playing field, so it's almost not even a shock to see Alex reign over a whole bunch of jocks and Mitch getting it on with one of the hottest girls in school.

"You want a drink?" Tucker asks. "I'm going to grab a soda. You can drink around me, by the way. I just . . . don't. Save my seat?"

"Yeah, sure. I guess I'll take a beer."

The moment he's gone, Clem comes out of absolutely nowhere. "Um, hi," she says, her breath warm and boozy. "What aren't you telling me? Did something change on the way home last night?"

I cover my face with my hands. "Nothing." I shake my head. "Everything, but really nothing. But go, go, go before he comes back."

Hannah tugs at her hand. "Don't ruin your brother's game. Come on."

Clementine pouts. "Fine, but I want details later."

"Details later," I promise. "Go, go, go."

"Okay, but first." She holds my head and presses our foreheads together. "You're a badass. You're perfect. You're a work of art. You're fierce. You're probably Mom's favorite. I'm a little bit drunk. And there's oregano in your teeth." She boops me on the nose with the end of her braid and disappears into a crowd of people.

"Shit," I mutter and rub my thumb over my teeth, hoping that does the trick.

When Tucker returns, he hands me a red cup and stretches out beside me.

We lean back and I sip on my beer, which I've never really cared for, but tonight the crisp frothiness of it feels just right, and I think I might be getting a contact high from the cluster of stoners. Being here with all of these people makes me feel microscopic. Almost like I did at the Hideaway. Like I'm a tiny part of something much bigger.

"I have an idea," I say after a few minutes of staring at the canopy of lights until they become one massive starry blur. "I think we should dedicate one whole wall on campus to truth. A place where anyone—absolutely anyone—can write a secret or a truth or a wish or a hope."

Tucker swings forward so that he's straddling his lounge chair and raises his soda can. "Okay . . . that could work. We could even have a group of students sign up every semester to repaint the wall."

"A clean slate," I say. "And you can write anything. A misconception about yourself. How you wish people would treat you. Who you really are."

"Yes! We gotta get with Mrs. Leonard on Monday. I love this idea. It's so simple." He clinks his can against my cup and then takes a drink. "Cheers to us."

"To us," I say. The word *us* catches in my throat.

"About last night," he says, his voice fragile. "I'm sorry if my dad was rude. He's not himself when . . ."

"It's okay. You have nothing to apologize for."

"He hasn't been himself since . . . you remember that my mom died back in middle school, right?" he asks softly, and almost like he's a little embarrassed to be doing this at a party. "I always expect people to just know and sometimes they don't, so it's easier when I ask even if it's a little awkward."

"Oh," I say, suddenly remembering him being gone for a few weeks and a few different churches in town raising money for expenses and Mom signing up for meal trains. "I do remember now. . . . Wait," I say. "It was a car wreck, wasn't it?"

He stares down into his soda can, swishing it around, and his lips curl into a sad smile. "Eighteen-wheeler swerved. She died instantly. He lived." He sighs and his jaw twitches. "And because he feels so bad about the living part, he's slowly drinking himself to death."

I swallow. The air between us is heavy, and I want more than anything to reach across the distance we share and hug him. I've never wanted to touch someone so badly that it made my fingertips hurt. I wonder if Tucker even had time to grieve his mom before he was faced with the reality of an alcoholic father. "I'm so—"

"Please don't say you're sorry," he interjects.

My mouth snaps shut and I nod like a fool.

He looks up at the lights twinkling above us.

I want to tell him that I wish he didn't have to take care of his dad and that someone should be there to take care of him and that maybe we could take care of each other someday, but as I'm taking another sip of beer, a second-story window opens and Kyle Meeks climbs out.

"What the hell?" I say.

Kyle sits on the ledge of the window and screams, "ALEX WU! ALEX!"

Alex emerges from the crowd of baseball players and

onlookers who have gathered around the beer pong table. "Kyle?" He looks up. "Kyle! Christ! Kyle, get down! Get down right now! I'm coming up there."

"No, no, no," Kyle says, his voice slurring, and it's evident that something has definitely happened to Kyle since I last saw him and I think it involves his blood alcohol level. "I'm coming to you," Kyle says as he begins to stand, fighting to maintain his balance on the sloped roof.

Everyone outside gasps and a whole mess of people flood out of the house to see what the hell is going on.

"He's gonna jump! This kid is gonna jump!" someone shouts.

"Cannonball! Cannonball! Cannonball!" another person begins to chant, even though no one else joins in.

"Alex Wu," Kyle says. "I love you with my whole heart and my very big brain and every one of my two hundred and six bones."

"Boner," someone snorts.

Others let out a soft *awwww*.

"Um, should I go help him?" Tucker asks.

"Maybe?" I say.

Kyle slips a little before steadying himself again.

"Definitely," I confirm.

Tucker hands me his soda and sprints into the house.

Kyle wobbles and then braces himself on the window frame. "I'm sorry, Alex. I'm sorry for being a party pooper."

"You're not a party pooper," Alex calls to him.

"Not anymore!" Kyle says, pumping both fists into the air. "I'm a party maker!"

The whole crowd erupts in cheers and hoots.

Behind Kyle, the light shifts as it appears that Tucker enters the room.

"Behind you!" someone shouts.

Kyle spins around with an en-garde stance and nearly falls off the roof, which could either be awful or fine, depending on how much air he gets and if it's enough for him to land safely in the pool and not splat on the concrete.

Tucker catches him by the elbow and says something quietly. He is way too good at taking care of drunk people.

After a moment, Kyle nods and begins to climb back inside.

I unclench the fists I didn't realize I was making.

A few people boo, and at the sound of that, Kyle wiggles out of Tucker's grasp and takes a running leap off the roof. "I LOVE YOU, ALEX WU!" he shouts.

Alex screams and I close my eyes tight, because I may not exactly like Kyle, but I also don't want to see him belly flop onto his parents' patio.

I open my eyes in time to see the splash as he lands in the pool. The entire backyard full of people absolutely loses it, chanting his name. "Kyle! Kyle! Kyle! Kyle!"

Someone spots Tucker, who is now leaning out the window, watching the action unfold.

"Tucker! Tucker! Tucker!" the crowd says, changing their tune.

Tucker shakes his head and turns away. At least he's got some sense.

But then he whirls around and launches himself through the window, cannonballing fully clothed into the pool. I hope his phone is waterproof.

With that, everyone starts dropping into the pool. Some people kick off their shoes and others undress completely down to their underwear.

But I stay right where I am, fully clothed and dry.

When Tucker surfaces from his cannonball, he whips around, his eyes searching until he sees me. I watch as he dives to the bottom of the pool and swims under people, through legs and arms, until he makes it to the edge of the pool closest to me.

With one finger, he beckons me closer.

I shake my head, fear and hope building inside me in equal measure.

He nods.

I stand up, kicking off my shoes and removing my socks. I shuffle to the edge of the pool where his fingers grip.

Taking a second to roll up the legs of my pants, I sit on the edge of the pool. Behind Tucker, Clem and Hannah fling themselves into the pool, their hands linked. Nothing in my life has ever felt more real than watching everyone I know have the time of their lives while I sit on the edge, only letting my feet get wet.

"Nuh-uh," says Tucker, tugging at my ankles. "All the way."

I cling to the concrete like it's the only thing that can save me from drowning. "I'm good. I'm fine."

To my left Willowdean and Ellen rip off their jeans and

jump in side by side followed by the guy who came with them. Even Millie and Malik are in the shallow end, holding each other close. Beside Tucker, Corey and Simone sit on the diving board with their feet dangling in the water and their heads resting on each other's shoulders.

Millie, Willowdean, and Mitch especially catch my eye. The other fatties. Their wet shirts cling to them and you can see everything clothing is meant to hide. Rolls and dimples.

But when this shirt gets wet, the only thing the whole school will see is Waylon Brewer and his man boobs.

"Come on," Tucker pleads. "For me."

I hold my breath and scooch a little closer to the edge.

The last time I got in a pool with anyone who wasn't my family was when I took swimming lessons in fourth grade. I wore a shirt the whole time, but not even a shirt—which I swore to the whole class was only meant to protect me against sunburns—stopped the laughing and pointing.

But then I think about Kyle Meeks professing his love to Alex in front of everyone. And I think about Millie sitting behind her news desk every morning. And even Willowdean and her dashing boyfriend, who was humiliated for love in front of that whole restaurant. I think of Lee Way and Peppa Roni and even Mimi Mee. And Tucker, who moments ago told me about his mom dying.

I decide that probably no one at this party will die if they see a fat boy in a wet T-shirt bobbing around in the water with another boy.

I slither in and Tucker holds a hand out for me, but it doesn't stop me from submerging completely in the water.

Under the surface, I hear Tucker let out a wild laugh, so I open my eyes against the sting of the chlorine, but Tucker's gone.

I push off the floor of the pool, but he's—

"Marco." His lips are so close that they brush my ear.

Under the water, he takes one of my hands, and all the blood in my body rushes to—well, definitely not my brain.

"Polo," I say, my voice raspier than I mean for it to be.

"Marco," he says, kissing my neck.

I gasp. Chills run down my spine. We're in a literal sea of people. This isn't just him tugging on my wrist. This isn't some indecipherable touch. This is lips on my neck. His lips. I can barely breathe. I want to kiss him. I want to do very filthy things with him that I can't do in a pool full of people.

"Waylon!" Clem's voice carries across the pool.

I turn around and there she is, waving in the shallow end. "A bunch of us are going inside for karaoke!"

"I should go," I tell Tucker. I want to stay. But I'm terrified. I'm terrified of what people will see and what they'll say. This whole time with Lucas and now Tucker, I was so concerned about being their secret, but maybe they're not the only ones living in fear.

"What are you going to sing?" he asks.

"I didn't say I was singing."

"Waylon Brewer," he says, "don't you get it? This is the night you say yes."

"You already got me in the pool," I say with a laugh.

"One yes down," he says. "A million to go."

We wade into the shallow end, and since we're one of the first to get out of the pool, we're lucky enough to find towels.

Tucker wraps a towel around his waist and them shimmies out of his wet jeans underneath before kicking them into the grass. He catches me watching him. "What? You were on me for running in jeans last night and now you're judging me for stripping down," he says. "You gotta get those off."

"Um . . ." Well, yes, he is right. My legs feel like two drowning sausage links. "I need to find the bathroom."

"I'll wait for you in the living room," he says.

Inside, I search the whole downstairs for a closet or a room that might have something I can temporarily clothe myself with. The bathroom is locked. The guest bedroom is being used by two mystery people rolling under the blankets, so my last resort without going upstairs is Kyle's parents' bedroom.

I open the door to find a random girl crying into a phone. "Get out!" she screams, and continues to sob.

"Sorry, sorry, need the bathroom."

She throws a pillow at me and nearly pegs me in the head, but I duck into the bathroom just in time.

Inside the bathroom, I see the reality of my situation. Wet dog times ten. I wish I could be like the kids in the movie who go swimming at parties and walk around in oversized T-shirts or traipse around in their underwear. But I'm not there yet. I don't know if I ever will be.

But I do like the idea of saying yes, like Tucker said. Waylon two weeks ago wouldn't even be at this party, let alone stay after going for a fully clothed swim.

My pink T-shirt that reads ON WEDNESDAYS WE WEAR PINK is something I like to think of as a crossroads between New Waylon and Old Waylon. It definitely says something about me, but it's also inconspicuous enough to go unnoticed. Either way, it is soaked through, and as I feared, you can see everything. But for some reason, the sense of dread I was expecting is lacking.

There's so much I need to think about and mentally digest, but right now I need a costume change.

Swinging open Kyle's parents' closet in their master bathroom, I quietly say, "Sorry, Mr. and Mrs. Meeks."

It turns out that Kyle's dad's clothes are too small and Kyle's mom's clothes are . . . well, they fit, but they're not what I would call the kind of statement I'm looking to make.

I settle on a teal floral pair of sweatpants and a T-shirt that reads MY SON IS AN HONOR ROLL STUDENT AT CLOVER CITY ELEMENTARY. I give myself a quick look in the mirror, and say to no one but myself in the deepest southern accent I can manage, "Kyle, come hug your mother." That makes even me laugh. Or maybe I'm a little drunk. Can you get drunk off one beer?

As I'm closing the closet door, I notice a mauve silk robe hanging under a towel. I would normally never wear something like that in front of the whole school, but what the hell? I'm already nominated for prom queen. And it reminds me of Grammy. I could use some Grammy courage right about now.

I pull on the robe, which I quickly discover is more polyester than silk, and tie the sash tight at my waist.

"What the hell?" says the girl who was on the phone, but who is now tucked into bed, watching *Frozen* on TV.

"Don't I look fabulous?" I ask.

She shrugs and nods.

"I hope you feel better," I say as I close the door behind me.

"Thanks!" she calls.

In the living room, Willowdean and Ellen are standing on the coffee table in T-shirts and underwear; Willowdean's reads *Tuesday* on the butt. She's a little bit of a mess, but I feel seen, to be honest. "Two doors down, we're laughing and drinking and having a party," they sing.

Tucker waves me over to where he sits on the floor. Hannah and Clem sit beside him on the couch, squeezed onto one cushion. "I like your sister," he says.

"I like your . . . friend," Clem says.

I narrow my gaze, but she keeps bopping her head along to the music.

My fingers are splayed out on the carpet between me and Tucker, and I watch from the corner of my eye as he inches his hand closer.

The song finishes, and Alex takes the microphone from Willowdean and Ellen.

"Awww, come on!" they say. "One more."

"I fear those two have discovered karaoke for the first

time," says Hannah, "and now there's no going back."

"I love the legendary Dolly Parton as much as anyone, but that was your third song in a row. Time to pass the mic," Alex says.

Before the words are even out of his mouth, Kyle yanks the microphone away from him. "Me, me, me, me!"

My spine goes ramrod straight as I feel Tucker loop his pinkie finger over mine.

I want to look. I want to see what our nearly intertwined fingers look like together, but I'm scared that if I even breathe, he'll move.

Kyle takes the coffee-table stage, kicking his mom's basket of potpourri to the side, and breaks into a very passionate rendition of Taylor Swift's "You Need to Calm Down," which is honestly pretty edgy for him and I'm a little bit impressed.

Before long, the living room is shouting along with him, and when the song ends, he lets himself free-fall onto the couch, where Clem and Alex catch him. And all the while, Tucker's pinkie finger stays right where it is.

"Who's next?" Alex asks from underneath Kyle.

"Pumpkin!" screams Kyle.

Immediately, I want to duck into his mom's silk robe like a turtle, and on top of that I don't want this moment with Tucker to be over.

"Yes!" chimes in Clem.

Tucker nudges me, his pinkie leaving mine. "Say yes."

I shake my head.

"You could get up there and sing 'Jesus Loves Me' right

now and this whole house would go nuts. That's how drunk everyone is," he says.

"Yeah, everyone else is drunk," I say. "The problem is I'm not."

"It's perfect," he says. "You'll be epic to everyone either way."

I look at him, the word on the tip of my tongue.

"Say it," he urges.

"Yes," I blurt before I can change my mind.

Kyle howls and throws the mic at me, which I catch, but barely. I check the songbook and go with a song I feel deep down in my bones.

I hike one foot up on the coffee table, testing its stability. It's solid, but it's also probably never had to hold a six-foot-three, three-hundred-plus-pound person before.

There's a moment of quiet while I'm waiting for the song to start and I'm forced to look at everyone staring back up at me. I don't have the benefit of being under a spotlight in a dark bar.

"I want you to know that I'm happy for you. I wish nothing but the best for you both," I sing.

A few people cheer with recognition. This is the one and only Alanis Morissette song I know, which I was exposed to on our way home from a choir competition in ninth grade when Ms. Jennings played us her personal playlist on the way home. I immediately went home and listened to the song on repeat while I sang/screamed along, feeling all the anger of a woman scorned. Unlike the song, I'd never been left for another woman, but something about the pain and anger made me feel validated and invigorated.

Clem holds her lit phone up, and a few people, including Tucker, follow suit as we reach the buildup for the chorus.

"And I'm here to remind you of the mess that you left when you went away."

I guess I'm not the only one who feels this song so deeply, because the whole living room is singing along. More phones pop into the air. Some people from the backyard fill in.

Suddenly, I'm untying my robe and whirling it around me as I pace back and forth on the coffee table.

"You better work!" shouts Kyle.

It doesn't matter that I'm in old sweatpants and a T-shirt and Kyle's mom's robe. I'm in drag. Because drag is more than makeup and gowns and bodysuits and tucking and sequins and wigs. Drag is about what you exude. Drag is a choice. And in this moment, in front of almost the entire senior class, my choice is to fully embrace Pumpkin. Embracing Pumpkin doesn't mean leaving Waylon behind, because there's no Pumpkin without Waylon.

The entire house is screaming along with me. There are no spotlights, because this song is a solo that belongs to each and every one of us.

The end of the song is coming and I have a choice to make. A choice that rides on a gamble and a little bit of faith.

"You, you, you oughta know!" I sing into the microphone just before I make my best attempt at a death drop, my body slamming down with one leg shooting out and the other awkwardly bent to the side, and sweet Jesus, I should probably stretch before I do that again. It's not perfect or pretty, but I let my body hit the coffee table with enough force that after a brief second, the wooden legs collapse beneath me.

Panic stops my heart. This is every fat kid's worst nightmare. I didn't just break a chair. I broke a damn coffee table. But I knew what I was doing when I went for that death drop. In fact, I'd bet that almost anyone's death drop would kill this coffee table. And even if that's not true, I don't care, because that might have just been the most monumental moment of my life. Sometimes you just have to break a damn coffee table.

I close my eyes and clutch the microphone to my chest. I'm not ready to see anyone else's reactions yet. I still want this moment to be only mine.

"Pump-kin, Pump-kin, Pump-kin!" It starts out slow and quiet, but by the time I open my eyes, tons of faces— many familiar and others not—are looking back down at me. And they're chanting. They're chanting for me.

"Pump-kin, Pump-kin, Pump-kin!"

I sit up as though their cheers are resuscitating me. As though they're giving me life.

Tucker reaches out his hand for me and helps me to my feet.

The crowd quiets, and I hold my arms out as I take a deep curtsy, causing them to erupt in cheers all over again.

TWENTY-SIX

The next morning when I wake up, I find a garment bag hanging over my door.

As I'm still rubbing the sleep out of my eyes, Mom knocks and peeps her head inside. "I thought you could use something for Saturday."

"Oh." I sit up in bed and slide on my bear-claw slippers, every muscle in my body groaning. "Thanks." I check under the sheets for any potential morning embarrassment. Last night I dreamed that Tucker picked me up for prom in the pumpkin carriage from Cinderella.

She takes a sip of her coffee, standing there in the doorway in a fuzzy robe with her hair swirled into a bun. "You hadn't said anything about it, and I figured I should pick something up before it was too late. You know Regina at Levine's is always letting me know when they get your size in, so she was able to get me something ordered. We can bring it in to get it tailored or Grammy could always do it, too."

I rub my knuckles into my eyes and stand. "That was thoughtful." I'm trying my best not to sound disappointed.

I don't know what I expected to wear to prom. I unzip the garment bag down the center to find a black tuxedo with a white tux shirt and pants on a separate hanger. It's nice. But plain.

"Grammy has all those bow ties of Grampy's. I thought you could go over there and see what you could find."

I pull the jacket out to try it on.

"I even thought about getting you a top hat, but if we're lucky you'll be wearing a crown."

"Lord willing and the creek don't rise," I tell her, quoting one of Grammy's favorite old-timey Southernisms.

She laughs while I check myself out. The jacket fits, but it's boxy and is definitely the kind of thing specifically constructed to hide a body instead of display it.

"Is it a rental?" I ask.

"All yours. I always say tux rentals are a scam. Do you like it?" she asks, her voice slightly eager.

I nod. It feels nice, but it doesn't feel like enough. It doesn't feel like the version of Waylon I'm ready for the world to see.

"What's wrong?" she asks. "I saved all the receipts. Honestly, I bought it on a whim. You've been so busy, and I didn't want you fighting half your senior class for whatever's left this week. You know most of those boys haven't given a single thought to what they'll wear to prom."

"No, no," I tell her. "It's really nice. I think I need to find the right bow tie." I remember Kyle and Alex's matching bow ties, and I can't help but wonder how Tucker and I would look in matching bow ties.

"All right, baby, I'm going to do my hair and then we've got family dinner at Grammy's later. Bring the suit."

"Yes, ma'am . . . and thank you, Mom." I step forward and give her a tight hug, last night's discussion with Tucker still fresh on my mind. I'll take all the boring clothes in the world if it means I get to have her around.

"Real proud of you. Always have been." On her tiptoes, she gives me a kiss on the cheek. "Take a shower and brush your damn teeth."

I definitely pulled a muscle. Or ten. Note to self: future death drops will require extensive stretching prior to execution.

"Moving a little slow there, son?" Dad asks as he reaches a hand out to me and hoists me from Grammy's couch.

"Waylon really left it all out on the dance floor at Kyle's party last night," says Clem while she helps Mom set the table.

"Well, I think it's nice y'all had a little end-of-the-year get-together for your club," Mom says.

"It was very quiet and intimate," I say. "Truly a restorative evening."

Clem's eyes bug out, telling me to shut up.

For some reason, I think Mom and Dad wouldn't actually flip out too much if they knew about last night's party, but I guess I'd rather not have to find out. Honestly, we're so close to full-fledged adulthood that it feels like we're going through the parent/child motions.

"Waylon, let me see this suit of yours," Grammy says.

I whimper. "Do I have to try it on?"

"I'll pin you in it later this week, but at least come show me what I'm working with."

I follow Grammy to the end of the hallway where she, Bernadette, and Cleo share a crafting room.

After I unzip the garment bag, Grammy's brow furrows and she holds her chin in her hand.

"Boring," she declares, diagnosing the tux.

I sigh, and shut the door so Mom won't hear. "Thank you."

"Do you even want to wear a suit?" she asks.

I think about that for a moment. I think I might really love being Pumpkin, but for prom night, I really just want to be me. With a sprinkle of Pumpkin. "I think so. But I guess I pictured . . . have you ever had this idea of something in your head and you want to make the thing in real life match the idea in your head so badly?"

"Pumpkin, I've never worn a piece of clothing straight from the rack in my life. What you're talking about is my calling."

"I don't know what exactly it should look like, but right now it feels like I'm wearing a curtain. A drab curtain. I want this suit to speak for me. I want people to see this suit and know exactly what I'm about."

She throws an arm around my shoulder. "Well, baby, that's a tall order, but Grammy is on the case."

She lays the suit out on her sewing table and begins to inspect every seam and stitch.

The doorbell rings and in unison from half a house apart, Grammy and Mom call, "Can someone get that?"

"On it," I say, leaving Grammy with my suit.

I limp over to the front door, and open it to find—

"Tucker," I say breathlessly. "Is everything okay? What are you doing here?"

Tucker holds a store-bought pound cake in one hand and pushes his hair back with the other. "Uh . . ."

Last night, soon after my death drop, Tucker went home to check on his dad, and every other thought since then has been dedicated to trying to decide if I should text him. (The other thoughts were primarily about my groin muscles and disappointing tuxedo.)

"You made it!" Mom says as she rushes me from behind and pulls Tucker inside. She takes the pound cake from his hand. "Oh, now this will be lovely with some fresh berries and cream. Come, come, come. We were just about to eat."

"Your mom wasn't kidding about not letting me skip out on another invitation," he whispers. "She blew up my phone all morning."

I follow the two of them through the kitchen into the dining room, where we all sit down. I motion to the chair beside me for Tucker to sit in. Meanwhile, actual fireworks are going off in my stomach. Tucker is here. At family dinner. By invitation of my mother!

"Grammy, this is Tucker," I tell her.

She grins. Today she's wearing a red-and-white ging- ham romper that comes down to her knees. The collar is lined in rhinestones and she wears matching sparkly red sneakers.

"I can see where Waylon gets his good taste from," Tucker says. "Thank you for your help with our coveralls."

Grammy lets out a girlish giggle. "Oh, now, Waylon, this boy is good. A real charmer. You should—"

And right as she's about to say something I'm sure will embarrass me, Dad comes in with a tray of burgers and hot dogs. "Tuck!" he says. "So glad you could make it."

"I'm glad too, for the record," Clem says. "Though I would have invited Hannah had I known that we were inviting . . . people."

"Hannah is always welcome, dear," Mom says. "But I wanted to invite Tucker since he and Waylon are working so closely together on prom court and as a thank-you for working on my car."

I want to tell her she could have at least told me, but I don't want to risk Tucker feeling awkward.

"Well, you're welcome," Tucker says quietly, blush creeping up his neck.

The burgers and hot dogs are overdone, which is pretty on par for Dad's lackluster grilling skills, but Mom's mac and cheese is good enough to elicit an audible groan from Tucker.

"Secret's in the mustard powder," she says before he can even manage to compliment her.

"So, dear boy," Grammy says while everyone either finishes up or decides to abandon ship on their plates, "where do you see life taking you after graduation?"

"Ugh." Clem flops in her seat. "Grammy, you know that's the actual worst question you can ask a high school senior, right?"

"I'm trying to get to know our mysterious guest," Grammy says defensively.

Tucker waves his hands. "It's fine, it's fine. I, uh, don't have much of a plan beyond taking care of my dad and taking care of his shop."

The thought of him rotting in that dingy little garage makes me feel hopeless. I want to live in a world where Tucker can dream as big and ridiculously as he wants.

Grammy's expression softens. "Is he ill?"

Dad clears his throat. "Mom, don't pry."

"He's got a drinking problem, ma'am," Tucker says as simply as he would say his dad has brown hair or is short or any other fact you can discern from a quick look at someone.

We all fall quiet. And it's not because what Tucker has said is embarrassing or uncomfortable, but he says it in such a matter-of-fact, immovable way. Like it's a thing that could never possibly change.

"My mother did as well," Grammy says.

I perk up at that. I never knew that. I never met my great-grandmother, but I've heard so much about her that she's always felt real and tangible to me, but no one ever told me she was an alcoholic. Judging by the confusion on Clem's face, she didn't know either.

When I look to Dad, he nods.

Grammy and Tucker share a quick look, like they're in some kind of club.

This got heavy. Fast.

"Well," says Clem, trying to change the mood, but she's got nothing.

"I work for your son as well," Tucker adds.

"Yes!" Dad says, charging in with the change-of-subject brigade. "He does indeed. One of my best guys."

"Thank you, sir," Tucker says.

For the rest of dinner, Tucker and I tell everyone all about our experiences on prom court, and everyone is excited, but Grammy glows with pride.

Mom makes fresh whipped cream and serves it with berries over the pound cake Tucker brought. When Cleo and Bernadette get home from bingo, they join us and tell us all about their latest adventures and even a few dirty jokes, until it's getting dark enough that Grammy has to turn on the lights.

Tucker glances at his phone. "I better get going."

"Prom court panel tomorrow," I remind him. "Dress code is—"

"Sunday best," he finishes, like the very detailed email from Mrs. Leonard said. Tomorrow, the entire prom court will sit on a panel in front of the whole senior class in an effort to make the voting process more than a popularity contest.

"I'll walk you out," I say.

After he says some quick goodbyes to my family, I lead Tucker outside to where he's parked on the street.

I lean against the tailgate of his truck with my arms

crossed. "Thanks for the pound cake?" It comes out more like a question.

"Are you sure about that?" He laughs, and then swallows. "You were pretty incredible last night."

"Thanks for the nudge," I say, feeling suddenly shy as I remember his lips on my neck.

He steps toward me and pushes the toe of his boot between my two feet. "I guess I'm a really, really efficient nudger."

Overhead, the streetlights flicker to life. I can hear the blood rushing in my ears. I've spent the last few weeks explaining away every little touch or sign, but there's only one explanation left.

Tucker snakes an arm around my waist and presses his hand flat against my back, pulling me to him.

I let out a short gasp, and run the tip of my fingers along the line of his jaw, something I've wanted to do for a very long time, I think. His lower lip is full and tempting.

"I need to talk to you," he says, and his voice is husky.

"I don't feel like talking right now." I kiss him, my lips parted, before he can say another word. Whatever he needs to say can wait. His hand against my back is unmoving as our bodies press so close together we could melt into one. My hands race up and down his arms as his tongue deepens our kiss. Nothing about this first kiss is gentle or patient.

I open my eyes for only a second, but it's long enough to see one of Grammy's curtains shift, and I'm quickly reminded that we're standing in the middle of a street making out like we're starved for it.

I tilt my head back so that I'm barely out of his reach, and he leans forward still searching for me. It takes his body a moment to catch up, his lips still nipping at the air between us. It's maybe the sexiest thing I've ever seen.

"I'll see you tomorrow," I say breathlessly. "Sunday best."

He nods, finally taking a step back.

I feel all the blood rushing back to my brain and away from my pants.

"Monday morning," he says from the driver's side of his truck. "Sunday best."

TWENTY-SEVEN

I find Hannah pacing the backstage of the auditorium on Monday morning. She's wearing black jeans, combat boots, a white button-up shirt, and a WORLD'S #1 DAD tie.

The minute she sees me, she says, "I'm kind of freaking out. Like, to the point I'm wondering if I should lie and say my 'lita died to get out of this."

"Excuse me?" I ask. "The ever-cool-as-a-cucumber Hannah Perez is fuh-reaking out?"

"Maybe not the time to rub it in, okay?"

I shake my head. "You're right. Sorry." I'm still completely buzzing from my mini make-out session with Tucker—who, by the way, I haven't seen all morning, but who I did text with until I fell asleep. "What's got you so nervous?"

"I don't—" She shakes her head furiously. "I don't know. I feel like I have gnats in my stomach."

"You mean butterflies?" I ask.

She shrugs and slumps against an empty prop table. "That's a little less gross, I guess."

"You'll be fine," I say.

"Prom court!" calls Mrs. Leonard. "We're on in one minute!"

"Shit, shit, shit, shit," Hannah mutters.

I've never seen her so panicked, which is, by extension, making me feel panicked. I didn't realize that Hannah's indifference to everything had this calming effect. She can't lose it, because if she does, we both will. "You did that whole pageant a couple years ago, and you were fine then," I say as casually as I can even though I can feel sweat gathering in places where I don't want sweat to gather.

"But this is different," she whines as she paces in a circle.

"How is this different? It's a bunch of people competing for something that doesn't actually matter and being judged by standards that don't mean anything in the real world."

"I didn't care about *that*," she blurts.

"But you care about this?" I ask.

She stands up and begins to pace again. "Think about it. What an epic way to end my time in this hole of a place. Prom king. Dancing with the girl I love—"

"Love?" I knew they were serious, but love is such a big, permanent word.

Hannah nods.

"Does Clementine know that?"

"No, but she will." She begins to chew on her cuticles, and I pull her hand away.

"I want to tell her," she continues, "on the dance floor. I want to give her one magically stereotypical high school moment. Is that so weird? I never did homecoming or sports or plays or anything, but I feel like I'm owed at least one moment. *We're* owed. And I hate wanting it, because I'm close enough to get it, ya know?"

I nod. "We're flying close to the sun here." I understand completely. Being this close to accomplishing the high school dream is intoxicating.

"But it's ridiculous to even think about saying out loud. Small-town stud wins homecoming king and dances into the night with her perfect girlfriend. That's not real. But it could be. And now I want it and when I don't get it, it'll hurt. The disappointment will sting." She inhales sharply, and her faint smile looks like it could devolve into tears at any moment.

I shake my head. What would Clem do? She would give a pep talk. "You are smart and funny and you've got this style that's all your own. The crown can't be your prize. Don't make it your goal. You can't control that outcome, but what you can control is telling Clem you love her. That's the prize. That's the magically stereotypical moment for you to share with her. The crown? That piece of plastic is just the cherry on top of your queer sundae."

"Let's go, people!" calls Mrs. Leonard.

I pull Hannah by the wrist. "Come on, Romeo, let's do this."

"Speaking of queer sundaes," she says, "I like the outfit."

I do a twirl. "Oh, this little thing?"

My mom had so kindly ironed the khaki pants I've worn to weddings, funerals, church. But after a quick skim through Grammy's closet last night, I opted for leggings and a knit rainbow poncho. Grammy called it the statement of all statement pieces. Nothing says fat gay guy running for prom queen like a rainbow poncho, and after that kiss last night, no one can tell me a damn thing.

We all line up, and that's when I see Tucker three people down, next to Hannah and the other king nominees. He wears black jeans with brown boots and a black-and-white check shirt rolled up to the elbows. So basically, he looks like a hot lumberjack. Wow, I didn't know I had a type, but apparently I do, and the category is: hot lumberjack.

I catch his eye, and he leans out of line to give me a wave.

Beside me Melissa waves at him as well, but then notices that his gaze reaches over her head to me. She shakes her hand out, like she was shaking it awake after falling asleep instead of waving at her ex-boyfriend.

"Blood circulation is a bitch," I say.

She laughs. "So you saw that?"

I wink down at her. "Secret's safe with me."

She sighs, and it's the kind of sigh only induced by hot lumberjacks. "Thanks."

Onstage, Millie Michalchuk wears a sharp black skirt suit with a baby-pink blouse and a bow tie that looks like cat whiskers. It's the kind of outfit that says *I am very serious about everything including looking cute.*

She announces us one by one, reciting a brief bio she must have written for each of us, because I have no memory of writing one myself. Everyone else's bios are lists of extracurriculars and academic achievements while mine mentions choir and my "tight-knit" relationship with my twin sister. Even Hannah surprises me with the fact that she's in the top 5 percent of our class, but—maybe it's my imagination—I swear that after I'm announced, the cheers from the audience are louder and more enthusiastic than they are for the rest of the queen nominees. I can't help but wonder if my performance on Saturday night was memorable for others too.

The queen nominees sit in a row in chairs while the king nominees sit staggered behind us on stools.

Tucker leans forward and says, "Can we talk after this? About prom?"

I smile and nod wordlessly. Is Tucker Watson going to ask me to prom? It takes every ounce of self-control for me not to whirl around and demand he spit it out right this moment.

Millie asks us each a few basic questions, like our favorite classes and who our heroes are. (My answer, Ursula the sea witch, is met with applause and whoops of delight.)

"Okay," says Millie, "Waylon, I'm going to let you start us off with this one. What's your favorite memory from your time at Clover City High?"

I laugh, momentarily forgetting that I'm onstage in front of the entire senior class. "Nothing."

The air is sucked out of the auditorium and it's so quiet I can hear my heart thumping in my chest.

"And everything," I quickly add. Because I have absolutely nothing to lose right now, I decide the only way I can answer this question is to be honest. "I'm only eighteen, ya know? I can't tell you yet if these will be the best or the worst years of my life. What I can tell you is that I love my friends—some of whom I've only made in the last few weeks." I search for Willowdean and Ellen and Amanda, who are giving me their most encouraging smiles from the second row. Ms. Laverne stands at the back of the auditorium in her white scrubs and cardigan, waving frantically, while Corey and a few of the Prism kids are watching me intently. "I think one day it will be easy to look back on this time and see that I was this gay kid trapped in a small town. And yeah, sometimes I feel like that. But sometimes I'm with all of you and I see that we all feel trapped and the only thing stopping us from feeling free is our fear of what others will think."

In the last row, Patrick Thomas snickers with Aaron and some other guys.

I feel myself recoiling away from the microphone in my hand, but I grip it tighter and continue on, my voice unwavering. "But for us seniors, we have barely two weeks left of school. This whole chapter of our lives is about to end! Some of us might not ever see each other again. Some of us will get married. Some of us might only be friends for now and others friends for life. What's holding us back from falling wholly into the people we want to be? Why are we waiting to spread our wings when, if we could leave behind all that fear, the next two weeks could be our greatest memories of this place?"

The second I'm done I look at the microphone in my

hand like it's possessed me.

And then, slowly, everyone begins to clap. Willowdean stands, followed by Amanda and Ellen. A few others do too. Callie and Melissa, on either side of me, join in.

Blush heats my cheeks and I nod once before passing the microphone.

The rest of the panel is sort of a blur. I say things. People even laugh at my stupid jokes sometimes. Hannah doesn't completely croak when all eyes are on her, and the whole thing ends up being pretty not bad.

"Final question," Millie says, "and perhaps the one your peers are most curious about. Who are you taking to prom?"

The crowd lets out an *ooooooh* and a few wolf whistles. My stomach sinks. Millie, I love you, but this question! Is! The! Worst!

Hannah goes first, biting her lip as she takes the microphone. "The most beautiful girl in the world and my girlfriend," she says, a shyness in her voice I've never heard before. "Clementine Brewer."

On the front row, Clem buries her face into the collar of her shirt for a moment, so that all you can see is a forehead and two braids with two little clear bauble hair ties at the end. She peeks her head back up, like a very cute turtle, and blows Hannah a kiss.

The auditorium eats it up.

Hannah passes the mic to Callie, who looks over her shoulder to Mitch. "Mitch, will you go to prom with me?"

"I thought you'd never ask," he says with a drawl.

"Oh, hell," I mutter, because that's when I know exactly what I have to do. I have to put my money where my mouth is. I have to make these last two weeks of high school the best weeks of high school, and that starts now. I'm going to ask Tucker Watson to prom the moment we get off this stage. I'm not waiting for him to ask me. I'm taking the plunge. I'll show up in my own damn pumpkin carriage and pick *him* up. Honestly, I'd do it now with a full audience, but I don't know who Tucker is out to or if he is at all, so my grand gesture will just have to be 10 percent less grand.

Next is Bekah Cotter, and with a giggle, she says, "I'm going with the best dates a girl could ask for—my best friends, Lilly, Bethany, and Mia."

"We love you, Bekah!" a small chorus of girls sings from the center of the auditorium.

Beside me Melissa takes the mic as she wipes a sweaty palm down the front of her skirt. "I, uh, wanted to take someone who I'm close with and means a lot to me, so my date for prom is . . ." She gulps so loudly you can hear it in the mic. "Tucker Watson."

There are a few gasps and *aww*s, but mostly all I can hear is a sudden ringing in my ears.

"I knew it! I knew they would get back together," someone seated near the stage says.

"That's what I'm talking about, Tuck!" some guy shouts.

I breathe in. I breathe out. You're on a stage in front of tons of classmates. This is not the time to freak out. This is not the time to panic. Even though you just found out that the stupid, cute, smart lumberjack boy who's been leading you on for weeks is going to prom with his ex-girlfriend. Delightful, really.

I allow myself a brief glance over my shoulder, expecting to find Tucker giving me some kind of sign that Melissa has it wrong and that he meant to ask me to prom. He hadn't gotten around to it yet. There has to be an explanation.

But instead Tucker is looking at Melissa and Melissa is looking at Tucker. He gives her the boyish grin I've come to fall so hard for, except this time it's not meant for me. This time I'm on the outside looking in.

TWENTY-EIGHT

The moment Principal Armstrong takes the stage to dismiss us, I push past the other contestants to get the hell out of there. I had managed to give a quick answer to Millie's question, saying that I planned to be free and single at prom. Woot.

I feel so stupid. Ridiculous, actually. Three weeks ago, I didn't even care about prom. Hell, I wasn't even planning on going. But now every time I've pictured myself at prom, I can't imagine the evening without Tucker.

I push the bar on the emergency exit door and am immediately blinded with sunlight. As my eyes adjust, I find myself at the edge of the school's property with only an overgrown field and an abandoned dumpster in sight. Before the door behind me can fully shut, it swings open again.

"There you are," Tucker says. He kicks a crumbling brick into the doorway to keep it cracked open. "You could have locked yourself out."

"As long as I don't get locked out with you," I spit back at him.

He reaches for my hand, and I flinch, stepping away from him.

"Melissa and I go way back," he says. "We promised to go to prom together after the breakup."

"So you're telling me not to be weird about you going to prom with your ex when you kissed me yesterday?"

"When I said I'd go with her, it seemed like a good idea at the time. I didn't think I'd meet anyone—I never thought I'd have a chance with you, Waylon."

"Well, you did and you blew it," I say through gritted teeth. *Stay calm*, I beg myself. *Stay calm. Don't let him see how much you care.*

Easier said than done. "You've dragged me along for the last two weeks and you never once thought to tell me that you already had a date for prom?" I let out a growl as my eyes begin to burn with tears. "I hate that I even care about this! This is so ridiculous! I hate you for making me like you. I hate you for making me care about something as sucky as prom. I hate you. I really, really do."

"Waylon, come on. You don't mean that," he says weakly.

"Maybe I don't, but I wish I did." I shake my head in frustration. "What the hell do you expect me to think, Tucker? You let me find out onstage in front of the whole damn senior class. And God forbid *I* want to be your date to prom!"

"You do?"

"Are you really that big of an idiot?" I don't give him time to answer. "Most of all, I hate you for making me doubt myself. Because deep down, I know that if you really wanted to go with me, you would have talked to Melissa. You would have figured it out. And whether that's because you don't want the whole school to know you like guys or because you don't want the whole school to know that you"—I motion down the length of my body and with the flick of my hand, I picture every stretch mark and roll—"like this guy . . ."

"What is that supposed to mean?" he asks.

"I'm a fat, femme gay guy with drag-queen aspirations," I say plainly, almost defeated. "The person who decides they want to be by my side has to do it with their head held high. I'm done being with people who are embarrassed by me or ashamed of me. I'm too good to keep secret." I say the words, but I don't know if I mean them. I don't know how I ever possibly could. But I have to, and maybe if I say it enough, I'll believe it too.

"I'm sorry." He holds his hands around his head, like he's in excruciating pain.

I want him to tell me I'm wrong and that he'd be proud to be with me, but he doesn't. Tears begin to spill down my cheeks as his silence grows. I step past him. "Excuse me."

He grasps my hand, but my fingers slip through his as I walk back inside.

I follow a hallway to the auditorium exit where Hannah and Clementine are eagerly waiting for me as teachers do their best to disperse us all and send us back to class.

"Where is he?" Clem demands. "I'm going to kill him. I'm going to kill that shithead jock."

I shake my head. "You don't have to kill him. I already did."

"I'm sorry." Hannah frowns as she touches my forearm gently. "I was starting to think he was an all-right guy."

"Yeah, well, an all-right guy doesn't make out with you in front of your grammy's house and then take someone else to prom."

"You were brilliant, though," Clementine says, throwing her arms around my neck. "I mean, Waylon, you stand a real shot at winning this thing."

"You have to say that," I drone. "You're my sister."

"Uh, no, sir. When's the last time I said anything just because you were my brother?"

"I guess I shouldn't bring up the time you legit didn't tell me about your life plans because you didn't want to hurt my feelings?"

"Low blow," she says.

I shrug.

"She's right, though," Hannah chimes in. "People are talking. Between your outstanding karaoke performance over the weekend and your really freaking smart and relatable answer today, people are talking."

After another hug from Clem and one last death threat for Tucker, I wave them both off and head to class. Despite the growing pit in my stomach over Tucker, I can't help but feel a little bit of electricity with every step.

I don't know if Clem's right. But she's not totally wrong. People are waving. They're smiling. They're saying hi. They know my name. Both of them, in fact.

TWENTY-NINE

After the last bell, I head over to Mrs. Leonard's classroom for our final Monday afternoon prom court meeting before prom this weekend. I've managed to avoid Tucker all day, but I can't ignore the dread settling in my chest as I turn the corner into the home ec classroom.

But Tucker isn't here yet.

"I was so proud of y'all this morning," says Mrs. Leonard once we're all settled. "About half of you still have at least one of your projects to complete, which must be done by the end of the school day on Friday for you to remain eligible."

She passes out a schedule for Saturday night, and explains how we will all need to check in with her once we arrive and how voting will go down that evening. But I can barely make myself pay attention. Part of me is praying Tucker shows up and the other part is clammy at the thought.

But he never shows.

After Mrs. Leonard dismisses us, she calls me over to

talk to her. "Tucker came to see me this afternoon," she says.

"Um, okay." I can't imagine what him going to prom with Melissa has anything to do with Mrs. Leonard.

"He's decided to step out of the running for prom king."

"What? Are you serious?" There's a twinge in my stomach, and I didn't think I could be any more disappointed by him. But of course, he's going with Melissa. Why am I even surprised?

"He did, however, get approval for your legacy project if you'd like to go through with it. He said it was your idea, anyway."

I dig my toe into the linoleum floor and nod.

"I also want to give you the option of joining forces with another group in case it's too much for you to take on by yourself." She bites down on her lip for a moment. "But I have to be honest and say that with a grand gesture, I think you could really turn this whole thing on its head."

"You think I could win?" It's one thing for my sister to say it. Or even Bekah. But Mrs. Leonard, the woman who's been heading up prom court for years? She knows her stuff.

"I think it's worth throwing your weight behind."

I nod. "I'm good on my own then."

"Good," she says. "Good."

Walking out to my car, I think about the plans we'd discussed for our legacy project. We didn't talk too much about it, but we knew what we wanted to do. Just not—

"Waylon!" calls Kyle as he steps out from an intersecting

hallway. "I've been looking everywhere for you."

"Lucky me," I say.

He throws up his hands. "I can hear you."

"What?"

"All the little things you say about me under your breath. I. Can. Hear. You."

I shrink back, feeling immediately like a shit human being. "I . . ."

"It's fine," he says with a sigh. "I was wanting to tell you that Friday night is amateur night at the Hideaway. I'm a little fuzzy on all the details of my party over the weekend, but I remember you absolutely bringing the house down, so I thought maybe you should go for it."

"Oh."

"You know, you're basically a rock star to the younger students in Prism. The freshmen think you walk on air. I know you feel uncomfortable sometimes. Like, with yourself and your body, but—"

"Stop. I know I'm an asshole sometimes, okay? But that's why."

Confusion furrows his brow. "What's why? I was only trying to encourage you."

"You weren't, though. Whether you mean to or not, you go out of your way to tell me that I'm something to be ashamed of. You've been doing it ever since you lost weight. Well, good for you! You're not fat anymore. But some of us are and some of us are okay with it! My body contains me and that's what makes my body good. That's enough."

"Waylon, I know it's really hard to see people lose weight when you struggle with weight yourself, but you have to know—"

"Did you ever stop to think about how all those times you talked about your former fat self, you were talking about me too? Every time you called yourself sad or in need of a lifestyle makeover, you weren't only talking about yourself. You were talking about everyone who looked like you. So, yeah, I'm not going to lie. You do things I think are annoying and silly, but the reason I cringe every time I see you is because when I look at you, I see the person the world thinks I should be . . . the person you think I should be."

Kyle's eyes are watering and the color is lost from his skin. "Waylon, you . . . I'm sorry. I've admired you for as long as I've known you. Your confidence . . . I just. I never meant for you to feel that way."

I can feel my own tears building. "I'm sorry. I have to go."

"Waylon?" Clem asks through my door. "Mom called. She's helping Dad out at the office. She said we're on our own for dinner."

"Fine," I say, facedown in my sheets.

The door creaks open. "Waylon?"

"What?" I moan.

My mattress sinks a little as she plops down next to me. "Is it that boy? If he hurt you even more, I'll make his life hell."

I turn my face to the side, a tear streaming down my cheek. "Don't hurt him. He's not worth the energy. I don't even think he's why I'm upset."

"Who dares to make my perfect specimen of a brother cry? I'll break their face."

"Kyle."

Her jaw drops. "You and Kyle . . . ?"

I roll over. "Oh God, no. I . . . I'm always shitty to him and so he said something about how he notices. And then he said he was only trying to get me to go out for amateur night this Friday night, but then I ended up totally unloading on him about how awful he's been since he lost weight."

She leans over to push a curl off my forehead.

"I don't care that he lost weight. That's not the problem. He should be able to do whatever he wants with his body, but it's the way he talks about it."

"Flaunts it is more like it," she says.

I sigh. "Yeah, sort of. I've never even said anything about it to him after all this time, because he would assume I'm jealous. And that's not what this is about. This is about him making it perfectly clear that people in bodies like mine are failures."

Clem nods sympathetically. This—fatness—has always been the one frontier where we have trouble connecting, but she's always been here to listen and always stands up for my body—even when I'm the one bashing it.

"I know being fat wasn't easy for him. It's not easy for anyone, but the difference is that I think I'd enjoy my life a hell of a lot more if I didn't spend every ounce of energy trying to starve myself. Even now, you've seen the way he is with food and how intense he is about working out. He's terrified of ever looking like me again. There's nothing wrong about thinking about what you eat or working out. I love dancing!"

"I know you do," says Clem. "And singing. And lip-synching. Which is exactly why you should take a chance and sign up for amateur night."

"I don't have time for that, and even if I did . . . there's no way."

She pushes at my shoulder. "Stop it! You were amazing at that party. Now's the time!"

I shake my head. But then I remember the sheer joy I felt performing on that coffee table. "I would only do it if you were there with me the whole time."

She's not so quick to answer. "I have something on Friday, but maybe I can make it work."

I scoff playfully. "I'm sorry to interrupt your super-busy schedule."

"It's not that. It's just that there's a meetup happening in Odessa for University of Georgia incoming first-years. It's like a chill coffee-shop thing and there aren't even that many of us, but I should totally be back in time. I'll have to meet you there, but I promise I'll be there, okay?"

"How are you even getting there?"

"I thought I could take Beulah?"

I scoff. "You're scared of driving outside of parking lots."

She shrugs. "Time to face my fears."

Soon Clem and I won't have to deal with who needs the car to go where, and I'm going to miss every second of it. I haven't done a very good job of supporting her and her big move, but it's time I do. "I should drive you. There will be more amateur nights."

She shakes my shoulders. "No! Heck no. This is way too big to miss. We're going to be doing lots of things apart from each other pretty soon. Think of this as practice."

"I don't wanna," I half joke.

She takes my hand and runs her finger over the silver polish on my nails. "I'll get Hannah to drive you and I'll meet y'all there. I promise.

"You promise-promise?"

"Promise-promise."

THIRTY

After giving myself a full day to mope, I wake up on Wednesday morning ready to make something happen.

Yesterday after first period, Tucker handed me a note. I waited until last night to read it, and after a good angry cry, I fell asleep with it balled up in my fist.

> *Waylon—*
> *By now I guess you've heard that I dropped out of prom court. I was only in it for you, honestly, and I'd rather people vote for Hannah instead of me, anyway. Before I quit, I talked to Principal A and got the OK for us to paint a wall in the 300s hall. I marked it with an X. I can still help you with the project, though. All you have to do is ask.*
> *—Tucker*

Ask Tucker Watson for anything? Fat chance.

The real problem is that I need something from Kyle, and in order to talk to Kyle, I have to *talk* to Kyle.

I stay behind after choir is dismissed, shooing both Clem

and Hannah ahead of me, and catch him on the way out the door. "I think we should talk," I tell him.

Alex looks to Kyle, who nods.

Kyle leads me back into the choir room, which is empty since Ms. Jennings left for lunch.

We sit on the bleachers, and at the same time, we both blurt, "I'm sorry."

"Let me go first," I say.

"No, no, please. Let me," Kyle says. "I need to say something."

I nod. "Go ahead."

"I . . . when you said all those things you said the other day, my first instinct was that you were wrong and that you couldn't see past yourself. So that's why I apologized, because I figured I would say sorry and it would be over and we could graduate in two weeks and move on. But then everything you said started to really fester inside of me, you know? It's hard for me to even think about what my life was like when I was still . . . bigger. And I'm starting to think that maybe that has less to do with how I looked and more to do with how I felt about it."

He takes a deep breath and shakes his head, like he's trying to clear his thoughts. "What I'm saying is I guess I have a lot more things to sort through than I realized, and what you said brought up a lot of things that I'd pushed to the side . . . things that I thought I was magically cured of after I lost weight."

"I'm sorry," I say quietly. "That's a lot to have to deal with."

"No, no," he says quickly. "Those are my issues to work out. I'm the one who's sorry for the way I've made you feel and that this has apparently been going on for so long."

"Well, that's a little bit my fault too. I could have said something instead of being all passive-aggressive."

He laughs. "I do thrive on clear and direct communication."

"Yeah. Not exactly a strong suit of mine. I'm doing amateur night, by the way. Or at least I'm going to attempt to, so thanks."

"Yes!" Kyle clenches both his fists. "Me and Alex are totally going. We can say we knew you when."

I take a deep breath. "But Kyle?"

"Yeah?"

"I need a favor."

The Prism Club is bigger than I'd imagined. There are thirty-six members in total. Clem's jaw drops when Hannah and I walk in, signing our names to the clipboard.

"Welcome," Kyle says with a smile. "We have one—no, two!—new members with us today."

You better believe I coerced Hannah into coming to this with me.

Behind Kyle, a few ninth graders who I vaguely recognize give each other brief excited glances before feigning indifference, and beside them Corey from choir gives me a small wave.

Even though I say I'm not one for organized groups, it hits me that I've never actually put myself out there enough to be considered part of a group and I feel a little regretful that my beef with Kyle held me back from this one. Except it wasn't just Kyle. It was me and my fears and anxieties, too, that I wouldn't be the right kind of gay and that I would be alienated by the one group where I should belong.

I feel like a real tool for only showing up here when I need something, but—"I need your help with something," I say, and look to Kyle for his express approval before I continue.

He bows his head solemnly. "Anything we can do for our once and future queen."

I laugh. "Okay, well, it's not that serious. Actually, nothing is ever that serious. But this is time-sensitive. Like, tomorrow time-sensitive."

"Well, consider our schedules cleared," says Alex.

THIRTY-ONE

When I filled everyone in Prism in on my plan, they were completely on board. We would paint the wall outside of the cafeteria in the 300s hall. Corey had the idea that we should paint the wall the colors of the Pride flag.

Dad helped me source the paint and supplies, so on Thursday, after school, I showed up prepared.

Thirteen members of Prism, including Clem, Alex, Hannah, and Kyle, volunteered to come help me, which was way more than I expected on such short notice.

Like Tucker promised in his note, he marked the wall with an X.

"You're a genius!" Kyle calls to me as I carry the paint down the hallway with Clem and Hannah.

"Well, yes, of course," I say. "But why exactly?"

He gently knocks his fist against the wall. "For priming this thing last night."

"Um, that wasn't me."

Clem and Hannah look at each other knowingly.

"My heart is not the gates of heaven or something," I say to them. "He can't get back in with a prayer and a few good deeds. It's going to take a lot more than paint primer."

"Everything has a price," Hannah says ominously as she pulls her hair back into a floppy bun.

"I don't want to think about it anymore," I say. "Can we get to work?"

The three of us set our buckets of paint down, and Alex is already hard at work taping off the wall for each color.

On top of a plastic tarp, we lay out small rollers and brushes alongside trays of paint. As people file in, Kyle assigns jobs. Some of us do edges while others take on the work of filling in the larger spaces. The wall Tucker secured for us is so big, I almost second-guess that we got approval for the whole thing. But Tucker did prime all of it, so I guess this is right.

Around six o'clock, Mom shows up with take-out boxes full of tacos.

"Wow," she says. "You can't miss this wall. That's for sure."

"Is it cheesy?" I ask her. Originally, I assumed we'd paint the wall white, or maybe even yellow if I was feeling a little wild, but the rainbow really screams *we're here and we're queer!* I've spent so long wearing fugly cargo shorts and boring polos that rainbows are really speaking to me lately. It's more than a flag or a symbol to me now. It's a message. One that says I'm unafraid.

She leans against my shoulder and pulls me to her. "You say cheesy like it's a bad thing."

"So it's cheesy." I let out a full-body groan.

"It's earnest," she says. "Not everything has to be

sarcastic or edgy. It's okay to be vulnerable and sincere."

It is viciously unfair how easy it is for parents to read their kids sometimes. There are days when I think my mom is clueless. Like she's from another planet. But then she goes and says the kind of thing that strikes me right down to the core, reminding me that she's not so unaware after all.

"Vulnerable-shmulnerable," I say. "I'm working on it." I say it as a joke, but the thing is, I don't think I'm joking. Maybe it's why finding out Tucker was going to prom with Melissa cut so deep. Before him, the only person I'd ever let in close enough to hurt me was Clem . . . and maybe Lucas, too. Until this whole nomination thing, I would have laughed in the face of anyone who told me I was even *going* to prom. The fact that I'd be so invested in who Tucker Watson was taking as a date? Perhaps the funniest joke of all time.

But here I am. Painting a wall that I hope will inspire someone—anyone—and feeling so raw that my whole body seems to be on the constant verge of a breakdown.

"Will y'all be much longer?" Mom asks.

"We've got to be out of here by eight o'clock," I tell her.

She taps my nose with her index finger. "I'll see you at home. Check your shoes for paint. Lord knows you won't be tracking that stuff into my house."

After a brief taco break, we attack the wall once more to cover up any spots we might have missed, and when we're done, Kyle sends a few freshmen to recycle the take-out containers while the rest of us clean paintbrushes and gather up the remaining supplies. Once we're finished, Corey raises their hand.

"What's up?" I ask.

"Maybe we should get here early to write out truths? To show everyone else how it's done before the whole student body gets here."

I look to Kyle, who shrugs.

I turn back to the wall, which is definitely still wet. Too wet to use the paint markers we put in the small mesh cup holder Clem bolted to the wall. "Yeah, let's shoot for seven thirty."

"And I'll text everyone else who couldn't make it," Kyle adds.

For a moment, it's silent. "Oh!" I hold a hand up. "Thank y'all. I just—this would not be this"—I gesture to the wall—"without your help. To be honest, I probably would have tacked some butcher paper to the wall and called it a day."

Simone says, "Honestly, it's pretty cool to be a part of this."

Beside her, Corey nods with a smile. "Yeah, just do us a favor and win. You too, Hannah."

I let out a dry chuckle. "You got it."

THIRTY-TWO

The next morning, I am absolutely buzzing with nerves. Clem rides to school with Hannah, so I decide to stop and get everyone doughnuts as a final thank-you for all their help.

When I get to school, there are about a dozen cars already in the parking lot, and when I get inside and make it to the 300s hall, I find well over half of Prism is there waiting for me.

A sigh of relief puffs out the minute I see our wall and that it's intact. Even though I had no reason to believe so, a small part of me expected to find our work vandalized this morning.

I pass out the doughnuts, and while everyone mulls over the wall with paint pens in hand, I admire our work.

The wall stretches out about seven yards, and there are horizontal stripes painted every color of the flag. Directly in the middle, overlapping through the yellow, green, and blue, giant white letters read WE ARE . . . On the far right side is a laminated poster that reads:

Welcome to Clover City High School's WE ARE wall.

This wall is a safe place to write your truth. It can be serious or fun or a secret or not. As long as it's true.

This wall will be repainted and maintained by the Prism Club.

Bullying and harassment will not be tolerated. Any and all names used will be immediately painted over.

This wall is not a bathroom stall. Don't treat it like one.

WE ARE CLOVER CITY HIGH SCHOOL.

This legacy project was created by prom queen nominee Waylon Brewer and prom king nominee Tucker Watson.

Even though I'm not feeling even a little bit generous toward Tucker, I decided to include his name. He primed the whole wall and got permission for the project, so while he's a jerky hot lumberjack who I definitely hate and he's out of the running for prom king, he deserves to have his name up there.

Armed with paint pens, the members of Prism don't hold back. There are all sorts of things written on the wall.

PIZZA ENTHUSIASTS!
Nonbinary
Super, super gay!!!!
Asian American
She/Her/They/Them
TOTAL nerds

Survivors

JEDIS

TROMBONE PLAYERS

Plant-loving vegans!

Ace for days!

Seniors!!!!!!

"Your turn," Clem says, passing me a pen.

I tap the pen against my lips for a moment before writing: QUEENS.

"Nice," Hannah says. And with a pen of her own, she writes: KINGS.

"Mind if I add something?" asks Corey as they step in between us.

"Please," I tell them.

In big block letters, they write: ROYALTY.

"Perfect," I say, nodding at their handiwork.

Slowly all around us, students begin to fill in. Some read the wall and move on. Others don't even stop to look. But a lot of them—more than I expected—are lining up for a chance at the wall. Some of them aren't even bothering to wait for paint pens, and instead opt to dig permanent markers out of their backpacks.

Kyle even runs down to the art room to see what other supplies he can scour.

There are so many people that we're causing a traffic jam. Teachers are trying to weasel their way through, urging students to head to class and telling them that they can visit the wall during their off periods.

Amid all the chaos across the influx of people, I see Tucker.

He looks over the wall, one side of his lips lifting in a crooked smile. And then he sees me, looking at him, and his whole expression sinks.

My fingers tingle, begging me to wave. To call him over. But instead I let the crowd stand between us.

During each passing period, I make a point to walk through the 300s hall, and every time the wall is more and more full. I even see a few faculty members jotting down confessions of their own, including Ms. Jennings, who waves from the other end of the hall.

Just before I'm about to go to choir, I watch as Willowdean writes something on the wall in tiny little letters that are impossible to read. From the other side of the hallway, Bo sidles up next to her and writes something below her words.

She looks up at him with a pained smile, and it's something that feels so familiar to me. Slowly, she writes something in response to him. They go back and forth like that for a few moments, and I can see them slowly gravitating closer to each other, like it's inevitable.

"What's going on?" a deep voice whispers in my ear.

I jump back and spin around directly into Hannah. "Way to scare the shit out of me!"

"Did you like my voice?" she asks. "That's the voice I use when a number I don't know calls."

"And how's that working out for you?"

She smiles sheepishly. "It was actually very awkward when my admissions counselor called and I had to pretend to be my uncle."

"That is a gripping story, but I'm sort of eavesdropping on—" I turn back around and they're gone. "Wait. Where'd they go?"

"Where'd who go where?" Hannah asks as she smiles down into her phone.

I catch a glimpse of who she's texting and the top of the screen reads *my sweet clementine*. I swear to God, I will never escape couples for as long as I live. "Willowdean and that Bo guy. They were right over there writing secret messages to each other."

Hannah shrugs. "On that wall?"

I nod.

"So go read it and find out," she says in a matter-of-fact way.

"That's like their personal correspondence," I say.

"Yeah, on a very public wall."

She takes my hand. "Come on."

We wade through the thinning crowd as the last bell for the period rings. The writing is so small that I have to squint to read it, but scrawled there for everyone to see is a private conversation.

alone
YOU DON'T HAVE TO BE
being together takes two
I'VE BEEN DISTRACTED

by who
NOT BY WHO, BY WHAT
?
CAN WE TALK
are you ready to tell me the truth
ARE YOU READY TO LISTEN

Hannah lets out a low whistle.

"What do you think it is?" I ask eagerly. "This is juicy. What if he has some kind of weird secret like he's actually a flat earther?"

"Well," says Hannah with a soft chuckle, "then I guess Will is better off alone."

I decide to stay on campus for lunch so I can keep an eye on things, and honestly revel a little bit in how cool this is.

As I'm walking down the hallway with Clem, Hannah, Alex, and Kyle on our way to the cafeteria, my stomach drops.

I knew it was only a matter of time before Patrick Thomas discovered the wall, and I know that there will always be Patrick Thomases. It's the exact reason the wall was left to a group like Prism.

"Ignore him," says Clementine.

"When I'm dead."

Patrick holds a permanent marker in his hand, and he makes his way across the wall, adding vulgar notes and slurs to places where he's clever enough to think of one.

And when he's stumped, he writes something like *slut* or *assface*.

I storm toward him and yank the marker out of his hand as swarms of students circulate in and out of the cafeteria.

"What the—" He whirls around, ready for a fight. "Oh, it's just the homo pumpkin princess."

Hannah tugs at my arm. "Come on. Let's let the office know what he's doing and then we can touch up the wall after school."

"Uh-oh," says Patrick. "Somebody call the PC police. I pissed off an ugly lesbian."

And that's when Clem pushes past the both of us. "Oh, hell no!" she says, and before any of us can stop her, my sister, who has been known to humanely catch and release spiders—SPIDERS!—winds her arm back and punches Patrick Thomas in the face.

"Hell yeah!" a girl shouts. I follow the voice to see Willowdean, Millie, Ellen, Amanda, and Callie all staring wide-eyed.

Immediately, blood begins to pour down his face and neck. "You—you broke my nose!" He screams, his voice cracking. "You dumb lesbo bitch!"

"What's going on here?" asks Mr. Higgins. He groans the moment he sees Patrick, and I can't tell if it's because of the blood or the fact that it's Patrick.

"That stupid lesbo broke my nose!" he says, his eyes wild, and if we weren't in a crowded hallway, I would actually fear for our safety. Still, I put my body between him and my sister just in case. If he's going to get to her, he's got to get through me. Well, and then Hannah, who is holding Clementine protectively, and shielding her from Mr. Higgins's view.

Getting in trouble like this so close to graduation and prom is the kind of thing that really throws a wrench in shit. Clem could easily get banned from prom and graduation for this. Hell, they could expel her and then all her big plans would be totally screwed.

"Enough with the slurs, son. We don't tolerate that kind of language," Mr. Higgins says in a firm, even voice. "Someone get this boy to the nurse."

Patrick uses the hem of his shirt to soak up the blood as Aaron and Bryce part a path for him toward Ms. Laverne's office.

"Now, who's responsible for throwing the first punch?" asks Mr. Higgins, his hands on his hips and his keys jingling from his belt loop.

"I don't want anyone else to get in trouble," I hear Clem say quietly.

I turn as fast as I can to stop her from coming forward, but she steps past me in the opposite direction.

"It was me." Her voice is soft. "I punched Patrick Thomas. And I'd do it again."

Mr. Higgins nods once. "You'll have to come with me, Ms. Brewer."

Clem steps in line behind him, her hands gathered in front of her, like she's marching to her execution.

But then someone steps out in front of Mr. Higgins,

stopping him in his tracks. "It was me. I punched Patrick Thomas."

Mr. Higgins lets out a grumbling sigh. "Move aside, Ms. Dickson," he says to Willowdean.

She shakes her head furiously. "Clementine was covering for me. You know how much Patrick has taunted me since we were kids. This isn't our first physical confrontation. I thought I'd give him one last parting gift."

"Well, I guess you can come to the office too and we'll let Principal Armstrong sort it out."

"I punched Patrick Thomas!" says Ellen, stepping out in front of Willowdean.

Whispers begin to circulate through the crowd.

"I punched Patrick Thomas," says Millie, her hands fixed on her hips.

"I punched Patrick Thomas," Hannah calls from beside me.

"I punched Patrick Thomas."

"I punched Patrick Thomas."

Tucker steps forward, and I feel a tingle in my chest.

"I punched Patrick Thomas."

"I punched Patrick Thomas."

So many people are coming forward that I can barely keep up.

"Oh, hell," I hear Mr. Higgins say.

"I punched Patrick Thomas."

"I punched Patrick Thomas."

"I punched Patrick Thomas."

It feels like a chant. A rallying cry. Not only against

283

Patrick Thomas. But against anyone who would dare stifle us or silence us. I've never felt a part of this school. For so long, this place was something to just survive, and everyone I went to school with was one more thing to endure. But it turns out that all that's divided us is what unites us in the end.

"I punched Patrick Thomas." My voice rings loud and clear.

THIRTY-THREE

That night, Clem takes the truck like she said she would. I stand in the driveway and watch her drive away like a nervous mother. "Don't forget to use your blinker and check your mirrors!" I shout.

When Hannah shows up to pick me up, though, Millie is behind the wheel with Amanda in the passenger seat. The side door slides open and Willowdean pats the seat beside her. "Your chariot awaits."

If I didn't feel the intense claws of peer pressure sinking into my flesh, I would backpedal right into the safety of my house.

Hannah leans forward from the third row. "Time's a-wastin'!"

I hoist my duffel bag over my shoulder and hop in next to Willowdean, and I literally have to bite my tongue to stop myself from nosing in on her boy drama. Behind me, Callie, Ellen, and Hannah are all squished into the third row.

"Hannah told us you were performing tonight," says Millie as she speeds off out of my neighborhood, through residential streets. "And we had to be there!"

"That's so nice of y'all," I say, the words forming a rash in my throat. Great. More people I know watching me perform. I would have preferred to spend this drive in the silence I know Hannah would have gladly afforded me, because hell yes, I am definitely freaking out about what I'm going to do. But alas, I have no truck, and either I take this ride or I stay my ass at home.

"Besides," adds Willowdean, "we had to celebrate Patrick Thomas getting banned from prom."

I gasp. "What?" Now, that is worth celebrating.

"According to my mama," Callie says.

I'm shocked. Patrick never got in trouble growing up. Somehow, it was always the person he taunted who managed to carry the punishment. "Wow. Kill me now. My work here is done." Clementine had been sent home early from school because they couldn't definitively pin the punch on her and they counted it as a one-day suspension. Which is why I'm surprised Patrick's punishment was more severe—but after all these years and all the students he's tortured, it was about time.

"Buckle up!" Millie calls to me as she absolutely floors it past the NOW LEAVING CLOVER CITY sign. She honks her horn and throws her arms up briefly. "Woo! Jesus, take the wheel!"

Everyone shrieks.

"Millie, he can't literally take the wheel!" Ellen yells from behind me.

Amanda leans over, placing a hand on the wheel. "I'm not Jesus, but I've got the wheel!"

Millie laughs, taking the wheel again. "Sorry, y'all. I'm just so dang pumped to graduate." She shakes the steering wheel. "University of Texas, here I come!"

Behind me, Callie groans. "Well, I'm glad someone knows where they're going."

"Everyone gets wait-listed," Millie says. "You'll have answers by the end of the month, without a doubt. And even if those don't pan out, you've already gotten into Stephen F. Austin."

"I was originally wait-listed at University of Kansas," Ellen says.

Willowdean hisses as she turns around. "Can we not say the K word? What am I going to do without you?"

"What are you going to do without me?" Ellen asks. "What am I going to do without you on your Euro adventure?"

"Wait, wait," I say. "What? You're going to Europe?"

"No! I mean, maybe. Nothing's decided. And my mama would kill me if I did."

"That's so cool. I don't even know anyone who's been to Europe, but my grammy says she's taking me and Clem for our twenty-first birthday," I say, sounding 100 percent like the country bumpkin I am. "But why are you going to Europe?"

"Bo asked me to go with him," she says quietly.

"I'm sorry, but is this the boy who ghosted you?" I ask,

trying not to let on at all that I was snooping on her earlier today.

"He wasn't cheating on her," Ellen chimes in. "He was working out with old teammates and getting back into basketball after an injury."

"And this leads to Europe how?" Based on the interaction I witnessed today, I did not see this coming.

"He was scouted by a European basketball team from Sweden," Willowdean says like it's the most normal thing in the world. "They want him to play in their junior league and then maybe they'll move him up to their regular league."

I hold my hands to my head and make an exploding noise. "They have basketball in Europe? I thought they only had soccer."

"That's actually football," Callie says.

"Okay, wow, I didn't know I could care even less about an organized sports thing," I say, glad for a distraction from my very imminent in-real-life drag debut. "But let me get this right: your super-hunky boyfriend is going to Sweden to play basketball and he wants you to go with him and you're considering staying here?"

"Thank you!" says Ellen, throwing up her hands. "I keep telling her that she can always go for a few months and then come back and go to school, but when else will she get a chance to live in Sweden of all places?"

"He's not technically my boyfriend again," Willowdean tells us. "And I'm still upset that he couldn't just come out and tell me what was going on."

288

"He was probably scared of going after it and not making the team," Millie says. "It feels like you fall twice as far when there's an audience."

"Would going to Europe interrupt any big plans you have?" I ask.

Willowdean frowns. "Honestly, the only thing I had planned for next year was going full time at work and taking classes at Clover City Community College. I thought maybe I could transfer somewhere else and learn about working on the business side of the music industry . . . but no, I guess I don't have any big immediate plans."

"So what's holding you back?" I ask.

She shrugs. "I'm scared that he'll be busy all the time and I'll be alone a lot—"

"But that might be good for you!" Ellen says gently. "Getting out there and exploring on your own."

"And I picture everyone in Sweden looking like living, breathing Barbie dolls," she says.

"Sounds like some beauty pageants I know," Callie says with a smile.

Ellen leans forward. "I don't know what the right answer is, but it's usually the thing that scares you most."

"So all of you at least have a sort of plan set in place?" I ask everyone else.

"I wouldn't call my life planned," says Callie.

"I haven't decided which school I'm going to yet," Amanda says with a shrug.

"I thought you settled on San Antonio," says Millie. "They have a great physical therapy program."

"*You* settled on San Antonio," Amanda reminds her.

And even though the thought of life after high school makes me ill at the moment, it's nice to see that other people are total codependent messes.

"So, are you going to Sweden or not?" I ask Willowdean.

She shakes her head. "Oh, Lord, I don't know. I love him a lot. I'm scared to go and I'm scared to stay." She sighs. "Can we please talk about someone else's mess of a life?" Willowdean asks.

"Not it," I mumble.

At the Hideaway, all seven of us file in with big black Xs on the tops of our hands. Tonight's event is more of an open mic, which means I'm not actually competing for anything. It's one of the only things keeping my nerves at bay.

"This is where we leave you," Hannah says, after making a quick run to the bar to sign me up.

Behind her, Alex and Kyle wave at me, flashing me their thumbs-ups.

I must look helpless to Hannah, because she touches my arm and says, "She'll be here."

"I know." Clem hasn't texted or called yet, but I don't want to nag her. I want to show her that I can be totally chill and that she can trust me not to freak out every time she does something without me. I'm a whole new Waylon. Sort of.

"Thanks," I tell Hannah. "Text me if you hear from her."

Behind me, I step through a parted curtain into a small

open-air backstage that has been set up for anyone who needs to prep their hair and makeup. There are a few folding chairs and a table with a mirror tilted against the wall and a few floor lamps without shades. I plop my bag down on the table and unravel my headphones to plug into my phone, so I can listen to my song over and over and over again.

I brought Clementine's Merle Norman makeup kit, which I plan on replacing with much better products the moment I have actual money that belongs to me.

As I'm plastering my eyebrows to my forehead with a stick of glue, an older man with a potbelly and olive-toned skin sits down beside me with a dress bag in one hand and a makeup-stained lavender Caboodle in the other.

He smiles at me in our reflection, and I yank the headphones from my ears.

"First time onstage?" he asks over the tempo of the music.

"Yes," I say. "No, well, yes, formally."

He opens his Caboodle to reveal stacks of makeup palettes and piles of lip liners and lipsticks. "My kit is your kit."

"Thanks," I say, my face nearly turning into the heart-eyes emoji at the sight of his stash.

I continue to do my makeup, but now that I have company, I hesitate with every stroke. My new friend is doing everything he can not to stare at me, but we can't really avoid each other, and it turns out that painting your face with an audience is actually awful.

As I'm reaching for my lip liner, he passes me a sleek metallic tube. "Try this one." He motions to my bag, where my brand-new wig from Party Zone is still in the wrapper. "It'll complement the hair. And you might want to let that girl air out."

I fumble for the wig and pull it out of the bag, but it might as well be a ball of static.

"Do you mind?" he asks.

Shaking my head, I hand over my dumpster fire of a wig. I ran out after school to get one once I realized I only had the one from my video at home.

"I'm Nick, by the way."

"Waylon."

He reaches under the table and comes up with a wig stand. "Or first name: Peppa; middle name: Roni; last name: Way."

"You're Peppa Roni!" There was something about him I thought was familiar. "But last name: Way?"

"My drag mother. Surely, you've seen Lee up there."

"Ohhhhh," I say. "I just thought . . . you're . . ."

"Older," he says with a smile. "Lee used to deliver pizza for me when he was still pulling weekend bartending shifts here."

"So Lee is Lee . . . that's their drag name and their real name?"

He nods as he attacks my wig with a pick comb and hairspray. "Lee is Lee. In or out of drag. So you go to school in Odessa or something? A college kid?"

I shake my head. "Clover City born and bred." It takes

everything in me to not ask him a zillion questions, from best tucking practices to where I can buy shoes to fit my ginormous feet.

"A true West Texas queen."

"We'll see. I'm two weeks from high school graduation and have zero plans other than possibly going to community college. Not exactly glamorous." I uncap the lip liner Nick shared with me. It's a bright, fiery orange.

"Well, if you ever feel like making pizzas, I've employed my fair share of up-and-coming queens." He sets out a lipstick for me to try. "Pair it with that."

I begin to follow the line of my lips and he laughs, but not in a mean way.

"No, no," he says. "Draw the lips—what's your drag name?"

"Pumpkin Patch," I tell him.

"Now, that's a good one. Draw Pumpkin's lips. Not Waylon's. Overline those babies. They won't be perfect, but one day you'll find the right shape. You gotta get it wrong before you can get it right."

I do as he says, and he's right. They are definitely not perfect, but once I fill them in with the lipstick, which is more red than orange, they sort of look good. If I squint.

My phone buzzes. Clementine!

Hannah: Nothing yet.

I hit Clem's name in my phonebook, but my call goes straight to voice mail. I normally never leave voice mails, but tonight calls for a voice mail. "Clem, I, uh, wanted to see where you are." And then quietly, so that hopefully

Nick can't hear me over the music, "I'm really nervous. It would mean a lot to have you here. But also, please be careful. Call me."

"Here," says Nick after rooting through his bag. "Take this. It's always good to have a prop. There's nothing worse than not knowing what to do with your hands."

He hands me a pink fan with scalloped edges. I open it to look it over carefully. "I'll give it back as soon as I'm done."

"Nah," he says. "Keep it. You know how to snap one of these things open?"

I laugh nervously.

Nick leans over and positions my thumb along the stem of the fan. "There ya go. Now flick your wrist, and voilà."

I do as he says and the fan spreads, making a satisfying noise. "So dramatic," I say. "You didn't have to do all this for me."

"Nah, I'm on last tonight. I've got time to kill. Knock 'em dead," he says.

A girl with a buzzed head and a cat-ear headband pokes in through the curtain. "Pumpkin?"

I raise my fan in the air.

"Two more ahead of you and then you're on," she says.

I nod and attempt to swallow, but my throat is too dry. At least I'm lip-synching tonight.

It's nice to have Nick here. But I don't know Nick. And Nick isn't Clementine . . . or Tucker.

Filling my lungs, I take a deep breath in and remind myself that for some ridiculous reason, this is something I want. Something I think I might love, actually. I love drag. I love doing drag—what little I've done so far, at least. Admitting that, even to myself, is terrifying and exhilarating all at once. I remember what Willowdean said in the car about being scared to go and scared to stay. I feel that to my bones.

Clem, I type, **are you almost here? I go on in a few minutes. Please say you're on your way.**

Or that this is just bad cell service and you're actually parking right this minute.

And please don't be dead. Because if you're dead and I'm freaking out because you're not here to see me perform, I'll feel like a real asshole.

You'd tell me if you were dead, right?

I'd know because the whole twin thing, right?

I'm trying so hard not to freak out right now.

"You're up!" says the hairless cat girl.

"Break a leg!" calls Nick, who is halfway through his Peppa Roni transformation in his wig cap and half-baked face.

I step through the curtain and immediately see all of my friends clustered together, chanting, "Pumpkin, Pumpkin, Pumpkin!"

"People, folks, y'all," says Lee from her barstool perch on the far end of the stage, "it is my great pleasure to welcome to the stage for her Hideaway debut, Miss Pumpkin Patch!"

My heart beats through my chest, and I wobble on my heels, steadying myself on a stranger's chair. Well, I wouldn't call them heels. They're sandals with a kitten heel that I found at the thrift store, and my toes hang out of the front. Surely all baby drag queens are as big of a mess as I am.

I allow myself a quick glance across the room, and sitting there at the bar is Tucker.

He smiles, and I don't have the mental capacity to play games or pretend I'm not happy to see him. My lips twitch into a brief smile back at him, and I take the stage.

Lee holds her hand out for me as I take the last step. She pulls the microphone down and says, "The heels get easier, I swear. You got this, baby."

She takes her seat like she is *the* queen and I'm performing for her court, which I guess is the case. I feel suddenly shy, waiting for my music to begin.

And then my song begins, the iconic intro immediately recognizable to the entire audience.

I snap my fan open like Nick taught me and hold it in front of my chest. "At first, I was afraid. I was petrified," Gloria Gaynor sings as I mouth along. "Kept thinking I could never live without you by my side."

I look out to the audience for a face, anyone I know. But the lights are blinding.

Up on this stage, all I have is myself. Waylon Russell Brewer, aka Miss Pumpkin Patch.

It doesn't matter who's in the audience or what they're thinking or what they're doing, because for these three minutes and eighteen seconds, the world revolves around me.

Soon, I'm stomping across the stage lip-synching "I

Will Survive" while the entire club sings along. And I feel the words all the way down to my toes. I will survive.

I wish Clem could see this, but right now, this isn't for the people watching me. This moment is for me. It's all for me. *I've got all my life to live. I've got all my love to give. I will survive.*

THIRTY-FOUR

"Clementine didn't die. Her phone did." I roll over onto my stomach and rest my chin in my hands as I finish telling Grammy about my very dramatic evening.

"Well," Grammy says, "I'm determined to come see you at one of these drag night shows." She looks down to Clementine, who is lying with her head in Grammy's lap. "And I'm glad you're alive."

The phone charger in my truck wasn't working, so once Clem left her meetup, she had two options: One, try to figure out how to get to the Hideaway without navigation, or two, drive home, charge her phone, and try to meet up with me from there.

When Clem finally got through to us on our way home, I was sure she was dead in a ditch. Hannah not so helpfully pointed out that Clem could have bought a new charger at a gas station, and I could practically see Clem's fingers slither out from inside the phone and choke Hannah to death.

Once we got home, Clem groveled, but I was too happy

she was alive and too exhilarated from my performance to even pretend to be mad.

"Big night tonight," Grammy says.

Clementine sighs. "That's why we're here."

"Ahhh. The tux." She gently moves Clementine's head from her lap and stands. Her purple polka-dot leggings and matching tentlike tunic perfectly coordinate with her purple headband and purple reading glasses hanging from a chain around her neck. "It's not quite done."

"You mean we've been lounging around here in your living room all morning and my tux isn't even ready?"

"Well, y'all better scoot so I can finish up." She takes my hands and pulls me to my feet. "Have a little faith in your dear old grammy. Y'all go do what you gotta do, and I'll bring it by the house later today."

Clem glances down at her phone. "I gotta go if I'm going to make it to this hair appointment Mom set."

Grammy shoos us both away. "You take your sister, and"—she digs through her purse on the coffee table before handing me a crisp fifty-dollar bill—"y'all go get your nails done. Ask for my lady, Rita. Give me until about half past six."

I nod, but she must see the anxiety in my wrinkled brow. "You're going to look smashing," she says, setting her hands on my shoulders. "Now, y'all run along and get pampered. Let me take care of the rest."

Clem and I park at Mom's hairdresser's house. She's a woman named Carla who converted a corner of her garage into her own little beauty shop. If you don't mind getting your hair done alongside her husband's work desk and riding lawn mower, she's a steal.

While Carla fusses with Clementine's hair, giving her a hard time about never coming in and split ends, I sit in a lawn chair next to the window AC unit and scroll through photos on my phone. After my performance, I clustered together with Alex and Kyle and everyone else for various selfies. It might be the flash or it might be the fact that my foundation is three shades too light, but all I can see are lips, eyes, and my wig. I don't care though, because I can practically hear the joyous laughter just looking at these pictures.

Tucker: You were great last night.

My whole body tenses into a knot as the message lights up my screen. My thumb hovers over the alert as I contemplate swiping it away.

Thank you, I finally type back. **Still mad at you.**

Tucker: I still want to kiss you.

My jaw drops, and I can feel myself getting flustered.

"Are you okay?" Clementine asks over the blow-dryer. "You look like someone poured bleach on all your favorite clothes that you never wear."

"I'm fine," I shout back, and shove my phone into my messenger bag.

Clem discreetly points up to her head and makes an *eek* face.

"Hey, Carla," I call. "Maybe we could scale back on the volume. I think Clementine might like something a little more . . . sleek."

"Sneak? She wants to look sneaky?" Carla shouts.

Clem shakes her head, telling me to give up before I make it worse.

I'll fix it later, I mouth to her.

She flashes me a thumbs-up.

Clem and I go get our nails done, and I guess Grammy must have called ahead, because her nail tech, a young Black girl who is constantly talking to someone on her Bluetooth headset but is also somehow incredibly meticulous, is ready and waiting for us. Clem gets her nails done in lavender, which is boring, but it matches her dress and she'll probably chew off all the polish by tomorrow morning anyway.

I show Rita a picture on my phone of a black manicure that fades into gold at the tips. She wordlessly nods and begins to work her magic, which makes my nails so pretty, I swear I could work my own magic with these fingers.

Back at home, I take a quick shower and put a little bit of oil in my curls before letting them air-dry while Clem gets dressed.

The doorbell rings, and I race to answer it. I swing open the door, and—"It's only Hannah!" I call.

"Wow. Thanks," she says.

"Sorry. I thought you were my tux delivery. But oh my God! Your hair!"

Her brows pop up expectantly. "You like?"

"I love!" Hannah has chopped her shaggy, coarse waves into a chic look that perfectly embodies her. She has an undercut with the rest of her hair tamed into curls and cut into a short bob, all nested over to one side. "Gorge," I declare, and twirl my finger for her to give me a spin.

Hannah holds her arms out and obliges before posing with one side of her jacket collar popped up and the kind of smooth grin that could make a whole town lock up their daughters. She wears a navy-blue tux with a matte black vest and a lavender velvet bow tie. Her pocket square is a black-and-lavender floral print, and I have to admit, I'm very proud. "Very nice," I say. "Very dapper. Now, sit," I command before racing back to Clem's room.

"Let's see this hair," I tell my sister, who is wearing the dress she bought online from the Forever 21 clearance section. It's a black mod-looking number with a giant lavender bow that hangs from the collar down the length of the dress. She's also traded her glasses for contacts, which she's always too lazy to do in the mornings.

"Did you and Hannah match on purpose?"

She swivels around in her desk chair. "What? No. I just told her my dress was lavender and black."

"Well, she must really like you. A very chic color combo, by the way."

She smiles, and I think she might actually melt at the thought of Hannah matching her outfit to her dress.

"Hair time," I say.

Clem had shown Carla a picture of Adele, but all Carla saw was BIG HAIR and she sort of ignored the whole sixties vibe of it all. I'm not necessarily good with hair, but I still do my best to tame it all into a ponytail at the nape of her neck with a good bit of volume left on top.

"The tux has arrived."

I turn around to find Grammy framed in the doorway. "Yes! Thank you!"

She hands the garment bag over. "Now, I just went with my grandmotherly intuition here."

"I'm sure it's perfect," I tell her, and run into my room.

"Wait a minute," she says, following me down the hall. "I've got one more thing." She pulls a shoebox from her giant tote bag. "I should have given these to you the other day before your big show, but they just came in the mail this morning."

I lay my tux on the bed and open the box to find bright-red patent leather heels. "Oh my God, how did you find these in my size?" The heel isn't too tall, and it's thick, so I think I might actually be able to walk in these. Tonight!

"Would you believe me if I told you the girl at the library reference desk helped me find them? Turns out there's whole internet stores just for drag queens."

I drop them on my bed and throw my arms around her. "Thank you, thank you, thank you." I'm so lucky to have someone who believes in me this much. It makes me not only want to do drag, but do it and be tremendously good at doing it.

"Well, you know your grammy had to be the one to buy you your first real pair of high heels. Honestly, it's a shame we don't wear the same size. Now, go get dressed."

I unzip the bag and try my best not to look at anything too closely. I want to have a big reveal moment in the mirror, so I put it on as fast as I can and highlight my cheeks with a little bit of shimmery eyeshadow before adding clear lip gloss. And then I step into my shoes, balancing myself on my bedpost. I let go and—okay, okay. This isn't so bad. I'll probably bring a spare pair of shoes in the truck, but I think this is going to work.

I step in front of the mirror hanging from the back of my door and let myself take it all in.

I run my fingers down the front of my suit jacket. It nips in at all the right places. The pants are cut close to my thighs and are hemmed short enough to show off my heels. My black bow tie is sharp, but the real showstoppers are the rainbow lining of my suit jacket and the rainbow cummerbund draped around my belly like a victory banner. For as long as I can remember, my clothing has never felt like me, but this outfit doesn't sacrifice a thing. It shows me off. Not just my body. But *me*.

Grammy outdid herself.

There's a quiet knock on the door, and I open it to see Grammy waiting for me.

"Well?" she asks.

"It's perfect. It's everything I wanted," I tell her.

"I tailored the pants a little, like you kids like to wear them. Skinny pants."

I reach for her hand and squeeze it.

"Did you see inside the lapel?" she asks.

I open my jacket to see a small, slightly lopsided pumpkin stitched into the black fabric right before the lining begins.

My eyes begin to water and she waves a finger in my

face. "No puffy eyes for this queen."

I nod with fervor.

She takes a step back to admire her handiwork. "When the world isn't selling what you're looking to buy, you just have to take it upon yourself to cut your own pattern."

THIRTY-FIVE

The three of us take every possible combination of pictures you can assemble with three people before prom.

Hannah's grandmother is even there with her cell phone snapping pictures.

While Hannah is running back to her car for the matching corsages she bought for her and Clem, Hannah's grandmother nudges me with her elbow. "Clementine talks about you nonstop. I'm always telling her to bring you over."

"I'm a recluse, Ms. Perez," I whisper.

"Call me Grandma Camile or 'Lita. And from the way my Hannah tells it, you're the life of the party."

"Oh, is that true?" Has Hannah told Grandma Camile about my drag queen aspirations?

Her eyes sparkle a little as she watches Clementine pin the corsage to Hannah's jacket. "You interested in keeping an old lady with an empty nest company? I'm sure you're busy with plenty, but—"

"Actually," I tell her, "old ladies are right on brand for

me." I could hang with Grandma Camile every once in a while. She's got good energy.

She pats me on the chest and needlessly straightens my bow tie. "It's a date. Now get over there so I can get some more pictures."

The three of us assemble again, and my mother poses us like bendable Barbies until my jaw aches and the smile has melted off my face.

"Tío Braulio says to knock 'em dead tonight!" Grandma Camile tells Hannah with a thumbs-up.

"Tell him I said thanks and to stop sending me envelopes full of pennies for my birthday. It's not funny and I only accept payment in gift cards now that I'm a grown-ass adult."

Grandma Camile tsks at her. "Enough with the mouth, mija. My Facebook audience is family friendly."

Hannah's jaw drops open. "Are you livestreaming this?" She breaks her pose with Clem and begins to stomp forward, reaching for her grandmother's phone.

"Aaaaand that's a wrap on prom pictures," I say as Clementine laughs so hard she's got tears streaming down her face.

We drive in my truck to the Clover City Country Club and Dance Hall, where nearly every wedding and special event in town is held. Last year, the club supposedly told the school district that they'd have to find a new place to host prom after some students drove a couple of golf carts into a pond, but I guess someone's parents stepped in with a threat, money, or both, because they let us back in.

"I think that's the line for valet," says Clem, pointing to a line of flashy cars.

"Is that free?" I ask. "Does that come with the ticket?"

"Shouldn't there be some kind of nominee perk?" Hannah asks.

As we walk in, I call over my shoulder, "You live in Clover City! You are not too fancy to park your own car!"

This year's theme is Hollywood Nights, and there is an actual red carpet rolled out for us. At the start of the carpet is a sign that reads THANK YOU TO OUR SPONSOR, JED'S CARPET! Inside, we hand over our tickets, which were actually the perk of being a nominee. Everyone else had to cough up eighty bucks for this evening of elegance. There are balloon arches and cardboard cutouts of Hollywood stars like Robert Pattinson, The Rock, Beyoncé, Jennifer Aniston, Cardi B, and Homer Simpson, which I'm guessing generated a heated discussion among the decoration committee.

While we wait in line for pictures, more people than I've ever met in my life come up to say hi to me and Hannah.

"I feel like I'm at my own funeral," Hannah says between hellos.

"Or wedding," Clem offers. "Less morbid."

Tucker and Melissa are three groups ahead of them, and being a tall, fat ginger in heels makes hiding from them impossible, so instead I turn my back.

"Is he looking?" I ask Clem.

"That depends. Do you want him to be looking?"

"Clem, just answer me." My stomach flip-flops.

She cranes her neck around me. "It's hard to say. He's definitely looking . . . around."

A group of girls in what appears to be different variations of the same dress wave as they pass us. A shorter girl with narrow shoulders and heavy hips doubles back to whisper, "We totally voted for y'all!"

"Eeee!" Clementine claps and lets out a little shriek as Hannah and I eye each other with hesitant excitement.

"Okay, y'all, listen up. Pep-talk time." Clementine claps her hands atop each of our shoulders, like we're huddling up at the big game or whatever. "You're both my favorite people. Shhh. Don't tell Mom and Dad."

"Or Grammy," I add.

Clem shakes her head. "Grammy doesn't count. She's a deity. Grandma Camile, too."

Hannah nods. "Fair."

"Now, listen up, team, you're both already royalty, and if you don't win, it will be the injustice of the decade, but the ones losing out will be them, not you. Because this is only one night in a long line of great ones for both of y'all, but for some of these people, seeing y'all win might be the most epic thing they ever see. Tonight is just our warm-up, babes."

"Okay." I let myself believe her completely. It's terrifying.

We're a tangle of limbs as the three of us squeeze in for a hug. Maybe being the third wheel isn't so bad after all.

The photographer directs Hannah and Clementine to

step in front of the backdrop under a gold-and-silver balloon arch.

"Wait a minute!" Clem says as she reaches for my hand.
"I need both my dates in this picture."

"Clem, it's fine. Really."

"Waylon, get in here," Hannah demands with a lopsided smile. "Please. I've never been on a date with a dude.
I gotta commemorate my one and only."

We do our best Charlie's Angels pose and a few others
before the photographer informs us that there is indeed a
line of people waiting. And the whole time I have to force
myself not to check and see if Tucker is watching.

Hannah and I track down Mrs. Leonard, who is doing
laps around the ballroom in a shiny burgundy pantsuit that
screams *mother of the bride* with a clipboard in her hand and
her sparkly pants swishing around her ankles.

"Mrs. Leonard!" I call. "We're here!"

She spins in a circle, following my voice until she sees
me. "Ah, yes!" She gives Hannah and me a once-over.
"And don't you both look . . . handsome."

I'll take it.

"Thanks," Hannah says over the music. "So we check
in with you and then what?"

"Enjoy prom! We'll be crowning king and queen in forty-
five minutes." And then she floats away into the crowd.

"What's longer?" Hannah asks. "Forty-five minutes or
forty-five years? Asking for a friend."

I feel like I might puke if I even open my mouth right
now, so I just shrug.

On one side of us, the dance floor is flush with people grinding on each other who greatly outnumber the teachers trying to pry them apart before anyone gets pregnant.

I turn back to Hannah and Clem. "Can we please find a dark corner where we can count down the next forty-five minutes in peace?"

Clementine sighs and stares at the dance floor with a forlorn look on her face. "But afterward we dance? Win or lose?"

Hannah takes her hand and kisses each of her knuckles. "Win or lose."

Clementine holds her other hand out for me, and we find a table at the back of the room, near a large bay window overlooking the golf course.

I watch as friendly faces trickle in. Millie is in a striking hot-pink tea-length dress with light pink polka dots. She's draped on the arm of her boyfriend, Malik, who's wearing a vintage-looking tux with black pants, a baby-blue jacket, and a matching ruffled tux shirt. On Millie's other arm is Amanda, in a black jumpsuit that dips down low in the back. Close behind them are Ellen, who wears a vibrant yellow gown that perfectly drapes her frame, and Tim. He pulls her through the crowd with their pinkies interlocked in what might possibly be the cutest public display of affection. Rounding out the group is Willowdean, her curls tamed into finger waves and a green velvet gown hugging every curve. She stands by herself, glancing around the room.

A hand reaches out from the crowd behind her, and Bo

steps forward in a well-fitted tux. With his free hand, he yanks at his collar and Willowdean laughs as she reaches up for a kiss and then wipes away the smudge of lipstick she left with her thumb.

I shrink back and concentrate on my phone. I like all of those people—a lot, in fact. But I don't have the bandwidth right now.

While the DJ (who I'm pretty sure is just someone's brother with a Spotify Premium account) cycles through a few slow songs, the three of us sit there scrolling through our phones when Kyle and Alex saunter up hand in hand in their matching teal bow ties.

"Wow, so this is where the party's at," says Alex.

"Do y'all even know how hard we worked on these decorations?" asks Kyle as he plops down beside me. "And you're over here on your phones."

I look up from my phone, where my thumb was hovering over Tucker's contact information. (Would it be so weird to text him even though we're in the same room?)

"The decorations are perfect, Kyle," Clem kindly tells him on behalf of the three of us.

Kyle bows his head solemnly. "Thank you."

And admittedly, the balloon columns and arches are pretty epic. String lights drape from corner to light fixture to corner again, weaving a glittering web all over the ceiling. And every table is ornately decorated with tall centerpieces of vases full of branches dripping with crystals and strips of film. Along the side of the room is a nacho bar and a punch bowl, which is well guarded by various faculty members.

"Kyle," I say, "this is the shit."

He perks up, his eyes wide with surprise. "You really think so? Last night, after your performance, Alex and I came straight here so we could get a head start on the twinkle lights. You would not believe how many yards of lights this took. It means a lot to know that you like it."

"Totally. I especially love the collection of Cullen family cutouts over by the voting booth." I point over to a couple of well-loved Twilight cutouts that are held together with packing tape and a prayer, including Edward, whose hair is bending forward.

"Alex's older sister is a former Twihard," he says over the music.

"Hey," says Hannah, "once a Twihard, always a Twihard."

Clementine's jaw drops. "I'm sorry. What?!"

Hannah shrugs and pulls Clem down into her lap. "I loved those movies when I was a kid."

Clem crosses her arms over her chest. "Fine. Jacob or Edward?"

"Neither. Team Jessica Stanley."

"I don't even know who that is!" Clem cries.

"Guess we're due for a *Twilight* marathon then," Hannah says with satisfaction.

"Count me in!" I say. "I'm pro anything that sparkles in the sun."

Kyle laughs and leans toward me. "You were really awesome last night. Are you—"

I don't hear whatever he says next, because right behind him, in the distance, Tucker Watson is storming out of prom, his head bowed down as he shoulders his way through the crowd.

I stand up without even realizing it. "I have to go," I say.

Behind me, Clementine says something, or maybe it's Hannah, but I don't turn around to see. Instead, I push past the mass of people still filtering in through the door, many of them standing and waiting. Waiting for someone to take their ticket. To take their picture. To get to the taco bar. And some of them waiting for nothing at all as they awkwardly mill about, trying to recognize the people they see in class every day who normally wear pajama pants and flip-flops but are tonight dressed in the Clover City mall's finest offerings.

I try to keep track of Tucker's head as it bobs through the crowd, but I lose him in the balloon arches. "Tucker!" I call. I can't imagine getting on that stage without him in the audience. The memory of his smile last night before I performed flashes through my head.

Soon, I'm outside, standing in the valet carport, looking for the back of Tucker's head. I reach down to take off my heels and search the parking lot barefoot.

"You got your ticket?" a short valet with a buzz cut asks me.

I shake my head and stumble past him.

An engine rumbles to life. Tucker's truck. I recognize

the taillights as it backs out. I remember making out with my back pressed against that tailgate.

"Wait!" I say, even though no one can hear me and it doesn't matter.

Tucker's tires squeal as he hooks a turn right past me with Melissa in the front seat.

He's gone. He left. Without me. But of course he did. He came here with someone else, so of course he left with someone else.

"Waylon!"

I spin around.

Hannah stands with her hands braced on her thighs, panting. "It's time."

THIRTY-SIX

I let myself take one deep inhalation of fresh air. "Let's do this."

Inside, Hannah pulls me by the hand through the crowd. Being smaller and shorter, she has an easier time navigating than I do. Not to mention the heels.

At the front of the dance floor is a small stage, where all the other contestants except Melissa are lined up with Mrs. Leonard.

"Have y'all seen Melissa?" Bekah asks when we file in behind her.

"She just left with Tucker," I say.

Hannah turns to me with wide eyes, and I nod solemnly.

"You said what now?" Mrs. Leonard asks. "Melissa left? Why, she just got here!"

"Are you okay?" Hannah asks quietly.

I exhale and nod. I don't know if I'm okay now, but I will be. I have to be.

Behind her, Callie—her long, silky red dress perfectly matched to her red lips—shrugs. "I knew her and Tucker would get back together."

And even though Callie is probably not even an authority on these things, my heart sinks a little lower.

Mitch tilts his chin toward me. "I like the look."

I tug down on my jacket, adjusting it. "Thanks."

Bryce grunts. "You look like a gay magician."

Everyone glares at him, burning him with their silence.

Finally, Callie snorts. "You would be so lucky."

I grin. "Hocus-pocus, asshole."

"Whatever," he says, and turns his attention back to the stage, where Principal Armstrong is giving a very long and very detailed speech about what happens when you drive drunk. Spoiler: everyone dies.

Hannah leans over to me. "I think gay magician might be my new aesthetic."

"What if we win?" I ask her in a panic.

Hannah takes a deep breath. "If you tell anyone I said this I'll kill you, but I think we might. At least one of us."

I take her hand and squeeze tight. "You'll always be my king."

"And you, my queen," she says.

Principal Armstrong drones on for a whole ten minutes while Mrs. Leonard organizes us into two lines, one for king nominees and the other for queen nominees.

"So, be smart tonight, CCHS, and whatever you do . . ." Principal Armstrong holds the mic out to the crowd and everyone drones, "Don't drink and drive."

"That's your cue!" Mrs. Leonard says, urging us up the steps of the stage.

Nerves suck the air out of my lungs, and the only thing

getting me through this moment is that I'm mere minutes away from knowing my fate.

"Now, it's with great pleasure that I give you your senior prom court nominees!" Principal Armstrong says.

Like last night, the lights onstage are bright, but I can still see everyone out there on the dance floor, and the sight of all their eager faces makes my guts cringe.

Clem waves to me and then blows a kiss to Hannah. She stands with Alex right in front of Millie, Malik, Ellen, Tim, Amanda, Willowdean, and Bo, with his arms draped over Will's shoulders.

Once all of us nominees have shuffled into our places, Principal Armstrong says, "To crown your king and queen, I'd like to invite Kyle Meeks and Miranda Garcia to join us onstage."

Kyle and Miranda take the stage, each with a sash draped over their arms and a pillow in their hands with a crown on top. Both crowns are huge and ornate, trimmed in gold with rhinestones, and definitely not the cheap-looking plastic kind that I'd imagined in my head.

Kyle glances at me, and instead of his usual eager smile, his lips are pressed into a firm, thin line, and he won't even make eye contact with me.

My breath hitches. *Oh God. How could I be so stupid?*

That's when I know. I didn't win. Hannah probably didn't either. I want to kick my own ass for being foolish enough to believe that either of us could win.

Principal Armstrong steps back from the microphone and Miranda steps forward. "Good evening, juniors and seniors!" she says. "Kyle and I would like to take a moment to thank the accounting club and Mr. Copeland for tabulating voting results all week including this evening. The numbers have been checked, double-checked, and triple-checked. We would also like to thank Wilson and Meyer Accounting Firm for sponsoring the prom court crowns and sashes and for checking our final count, which was our closest prom court vote on record."

"Nerds!" someone shouts from the crowd.

Miranda laughs. "Yeah, nerds with 401(k)s and savings accounts. Sign me up."

A few teachers throughout the room snicker.

Enough already! I nearly scream. Just get it over with.

"Come on!" a girl shouts.

"Crown someone already!"

I hate a heckler, but they're not wrong.

Miranda sighs into the microphone. "Without further ado . . ."

The DJ plays a drumroll sound clip, and on either side of me Bekah and Callie take my hands, which are slick with sweat. The warmth radiating from their palms spreads up my arms and into my chest, and I decide it's okay. It's all okay. I don't have all the answers. I don't know where I'll be at this time next year. I don't even know who I'll be. But I know that I love the people in my life, no matter where they are.

I've made plenty of mistakes, but I can't bring myself to regret any of it. The video. The makeup. The lip-synching. The push and pull with Clem. Hell, even Lucas in the back of a grimy gas station. And Tucker. Tucker was definitely not a mistake. My wounds are so fresh they sting, but I'm grateful for him and the person he believed I could be, because it turns out, I am that person. I always have been deep down. I was waiting for my moment. But there is no moment. The only moment we have is now.

I let out a shaky sigh and squeeze both Bekah's and Callie's hands. It doesn't matter which of them wins. They're both good down to their bones.

I shut my eyes tight since these lights aren't bright enough to block the audience from my line of sight.

Miranda continues, "We are pleased to announce your prom queen and king are"—Kyle leans into the microphone to join her, and they say in unison—"WAYLON BREWER AND HANNAH PEREZ!"

There are shrieks, cheers, and a few faint boos. Bekah and Callie crowd me in a tight hug. "I'm so happy for you!" one of them says.

"Oh my God, oh my God, oh my God, oh my God," I say over and over again. I might be crying. Or sweating. I can't tell.

Someone takes my hand and pulls me forward. It's Hannah. King Hannah. I might have a broken heart and a sister moving halfway across the country, but I think that one of the best things to come out of all of this is . . . Hannah. My friend. Perhaps my best friend outside of Clementine.

Kyle places the sash over my head, and it reads CCHS PROM QUEEN. He lets out a shriek. "They told us the results right before we took the stage. I couldn't even look at you without giving it away."

Well, that explains his somber look. I give him a quick hug, because even if Kyle and I are only starting to find our footing, this whole road began with him and his dumb Facebook post.

I turn to Hannah, the crown glittering above her brow and the CCHS PROM KING sash proudly displayed across her chest. "Can you believe this?" I whisper to her.

She lets out a wild giggle. "No. Yes. Yes. No. I don't even know! I can't wait to tell my 'lita." Her eyes begin to water.

I pull her to me in a tight hug. "Stop-stop-stop! You're going to make me cry."

Her fingers dig into my sides, squeezing me as hard as she can.

"Hannah?" I say. "Thank you." For pushing me to do this. For being my friend. For so much. But if I say much more than a brief thanks, I think my guts will spill out of my mouth.

"Let's welcome our king and queen to the dance floor," says Miranda, "as they share their first dance as Clover City High royalty."

I hadn't even thought about the fact that I'd have to dance with someone, but there's no time to hesitate. We exit off the stage, and the DJ asks, "Any requests?"

Hannah shrugs, so I cycle through my mental playlist and say, "'Dancing Queen'!"

The DJ gives us a thumbs-up. "Good choice, my queen."

The music starts, and I immediately take Hannah's hand, spinning her across the floor. We have no idea what we're doing, but we skip around each other, dancing close and then far, spinning each other around and under, screaming the lyrics at the top of our lungs. "Dancing queen, young and sweet! Only seventeen!" My open tuxedo jacket flashes colors of the rainbow as I spin.

After the chorus, I pull Hannah to me and we hold each other as we dance.

"Are you ready for your big moment with Clem?" I ask her.

"We can dance for the whole song. I don't want you to have to give up your spotlight."

I shake my head. "No way. This is too perfect. You have to tell her now."

We stop right in front of Clementine, who's beaming with pride, her hands clenched together. I take her hand and join it with Hannah's. "Go. Dance," I say to my sister.

Clementine's blue eyes sparkle, and she kisses my cheek before taking the floor with Hannah, neither of them really leading and neither of them really following.

I stand near Alex and Kyle, watching them dance, the two of their foreheads pressed together, and I hope this moment is as perfect as Hannah dreamed it would be.

The DJ lets this song play out and then leads us right into another Abba classic, "The Winner Takes It All."

Someone taps my shoulder.

I turn as everyone around me works their way back onto the dance floor, until everyone around me is slow dancing.

"Tucker," I say breathlessly. "What are you doing here?"

His hair is messy and pushed to the side, like he'd been

running his hands through it, and he's dressed like a cow-boy going to church in a dark-charcoal three-piece suit with a bolo tie and well-loved but freshly shined camel-brown cowboy boots. "It's prom," he says, like even he's a little bit lost in the magic of it all. "I couldn't miss seeing you get crowned."

"You left," I say, frantically searching his face for any kind of answer. "You left with Melissa."

He slowly shakes his head, lines forming between his furrowed dark brows. "She asked me to take her home. I had to tell her. I couldn't let her think we were here . . . together, and that I wasn't thinking about someone else the whole time."

"You were thinking about someone else?" I ask, hope brimming inside of me.

He nods. "Constantly. Waylon, I was an idiot. I felt like I owed something to Melissa after we'd promised to go to prom. I was wrong for thinking it wouldn't be a big deal to you. I was wrong for not just telling you that I like you. A lot. I just—you're going places. And I might be stuck here, taking care of my dad."

"I have no idea where I'm going! I'm eighteen years old and I have an awful sense of direction!" I shout over the swelling music. "And the thought of falling even harder for you and us having to go in different directions scares the shit out of me! But I like you too much. And yes! This is important to me. This stupid crown matters to me. And so does drag. And so do you." I can feel my throat closing up, trying to trap the words in my chest. But I have to admit it.

I have to say it out loud. I care. I care if I win. Or if I lose. Or if I even get to participate at all. And I care for Tucker. I care for him so much. And maybe I'll leave Clover City. Maybe I won't. But it turns out that dreams and hopes and wishes can come true anywhere. Even here.

I take a step closer to him, and he nods as my lips crush against his, my fingers lacing around the back of his neck.

Around us, I hear a few whistles, but I let myself sink against him, as "I Gotta Feeling" by the Black Eyed Peas begins to play. I hate that we missed the slow song, but it doesn't matter, because as we lay our heads against each other's shoulders, we dance at our own pace while everyone else jumps and flails around us.

Just behind Tucker, I spy another couple with their lips locked together. Bo and Willowdean. Once they come up for air, I wave to Willowdean and she waves back before nuzzling into Bo's neck. The four of us circle the dance floor until we're back to back.

I call over my shoulder to Willowdean. "Any big plans for next year?" I ask.

"Do you think they have Mexican food in Sweden?" she yells over the music.

"The burritos will be here when you get back!" I call, but Bo spins her farther into the crowd so that all I can hear is her delighted giggle.

We dance for a while longer, until our feet hurt—well, my feet hurt. A whole bunch of us, Clem and Hannah and all of my new friends—Callie, Mitch, Bo, Willowdean, Amanda, Ellen, Tim, Millie, and Malik—sneak out to the golf course, kicking our shoes off and leaving them at the door.

Everyone plays a game of tag, racing all over the course, while Tucker tries to teach me to two-step, the both of us barefoot on the lush green.

"Where'd you learn how to do this?" I ask, tripping over his feet for the millionth time.

"My mom and dad," he says. "They used to dance in the garage."

"Yeah?" I want him to feel like he can talk, but I don't want to force it, especially tonight, when everything feels just right.

"I used to always wonder if I'd find someone to dance with me."

I look down at our feet. "I think that might be TBD. I can't figure out who leads and who follows."

"We can take turns," he says before leaning down, our noses brushing and our lips nearly touching. Goose bumps skip up my spine as he wraps both his arms around me. I gasp a little and that's when he kisses me, like he's sucking the air right out of my lungs as the golf course lights illuminate us for the entire senior prom to see. I hook one arm around the back of his neck, my other hand splayed out over his chest, as he dips me back and deepens the kiss. I kick one leg in the air, because when someone goes to the trouble of dipping you, you're legally obligated to make the most of the moment.

Once he brings me back up, we sway to the music faintly playing from inside until we settle in a pocket of darkness, away from the bright lights, and collapse onto the green, which is softer than any carpet I've ever felt.

"My queen," Tucker says as he rolls toward me on his side, his grayish-blue eyes sparkling as he twirls a finger through one of my curls. "I have a very important question to ask you about our future together."

I turn to him and run a finger along his jaw. It feels just as perfect as it looks. "I . . . you know that basically everything is a giant TBD right now for me."

He nods. "I know, and I get that we're both living with a bunch of unknowns, but this is something I need to know before we can move forward. It's a very important question."

He's going to ask me to be his boyfriend. Oh. My. God. I, Waylon Brewer, am going to be someone's boyfriend. I solemnly swear to be the best arm candy his arm or any arm has ever seen. "Okay, go ahead."

He swallows and closes his eyes for a moment before opening them again. "Can we get pancakes in the morning?"

I swat at his chest, feeling a little awkward for thinking he was actually about to ask me something that monumental.

He laughs deviously and grins. "And if the answer is yes, will you be my boyfriend?"

My heart flutters in my rib cage. "Yes. To both, but especially the pancakes."

ACKNOWLEDGMENTS

There's no manual on how to publish a book during a global pandemic, but the people I'm fortunate enough to work with have found ways to innovate and push forward with creativity and compassion. They have made this process one of joy during one of the most tumultuous times I've witnessed in my lifetime.

First and foremost, to my editor, Alessandra Balzer, I'm so grateful for our working relationship and the friendship we have built over the years. Thank you for seeing the potential in *Dumplin'* from the beginning (and in me even before then!) and for allowing me to grow and explore this universe. Working with you is one of the greatest honors of my career.

John Cusick, thank you so much for answering every call, text, and email with calm and enthusiasm. You are such a rock in my life, and we have too much fun together to even call it work at this point. Thank you also to Molly Cusick, who started it all and to the entire team at Folio Literary Management.

Thank you to Dana Spector. You are one of the fiercest

women in Hollywood, and I'm thankful to have you in my court.

I'm deeply grateful to Jackie Burke and Anna Bernard, my two publicists, for keeping so many balls spinning—even when I've neglected my inbox. (Which is more often than I'd like to admit.)

My family at Harper has been the best team a girl could ask for, especially Suzanne Murphy, Donna Bray, Caitlin Johnson, Ebony LaDelle, Shannon Cox, Audrey Diestelkamp, Ann Dye, Lindsey Karl, Patty Rosati, Almeda Beynon, Sarah Kaufman, Alison Donalty, Kathryn Silsand, Kristen Eckhardt, Andrea Pappenheimer, Kerry Moynagh, Kathy Faber, and Nellie Kurtzman. Thank you as well to everyone at Epic Reads, HCCFrenzy, and HarperCollins360. So many people carry the torch of bringing a book to readers. I know I'm certainly missing someone, but I'm not any less thankful for those who I have.

This incredible cover would not exist without Jenna Stempel-Lobell and this divine art by Josh McKenna. I also owe a great deal of gratitude to Aurora Parlagreco for setting such a fantastic tone with that first *Dumplin'* cover.

Thank you to Chad Burris for lending your incredible vocal talents to the audiobook and for bringing Waylon to life so vividly.

Many people played a role in making this book the best it could be and I would be lost without their thoughtful guidance. Thank you specifically to Bethany Hagen, Jeramey Kraatz, Phil Stamper, and D. Ann Williams.

Whether it was a Zoom game night, a perfectly timed

meme via text, or a very socially distant hangout session, my friends have kept me sane through this year. Natalie C. Parker, Tessa Gratton, the Taylor family, John Stickney, Hayley Harris, Deanna Green, Ashley Meredith, Luke and Lauren Brewer, Tara Hudson, Adib Khorram, Corey Whaley, and Ashley Lindemann. I love you each so, so much. Thank you also to Bob, Liz, Emma, Roger, Vivienne, Aurelia, Pam, and Frank. I'm so grateful to call you family and always be able to count on your love.

I owe a great deal of gratitude to my *Dumplin'* movie team. You all have brought me so much happiness and I'm so proud of all that we've created. Thank you especially to Kristin Hahn, Jennifer Aniston, Mohamed AlRafi, Trish Hoffman, Kelly Todd, Danny Nozell, Danielle Macdonald, Maddie Baillio, Bex Taylor-Klaus, Odeya Rush, Luke Benward, Hillary Begley, and Georgie Flores.

Thank you especially to Ginger Minj, who spurred me on to write Waylon's story.

And of course, the one and only Dolly Parton. Dolly, you shine light on everything you touch. Never in my wildest dreams did I imagine that my little books would bring us together, but they have and it's turned out to be one of the most incredible things that's ever happened to me. Thank you for your friendship and support.

Mom and Dad, thank you for always allowing me to be too weird and too loud and too much. You never said no. (Actually, sometimes you might have, but it was probably for good reason, and I ignored you anyway.)

Dexter, Rufus, and Opie . . . yes, I am thanking my dog

and two cats. Thank you for the cuddles and for all the joy you bring me.

Ian, our love is my favorite inspiration. Thank you for believing in me even when you have absolutely no reason to and for always letting me sleep in.

Lastly, to my readers . . . there is not enough gratitude in the world to properly express how much your support and enthusiasm means to me. When *Dumplin'*, the first book in this series, released in 2015, we lived in a different world. I didn't know how a book about a fat person who just wanted to take up space and find love might be received. I didn't know if there was an audience for the kind of stories I wanted to tell. But it turned out that I wasn't alone. Since then, and thanks to the work of so many artists and activists, the conversations around bodies have changed astronomically. We still have such a long way to go, but I'm eagerly looking forward to every step of that journey. Thank you for being part of this moment with me and for proving that good stories come in all shapes and sizes.

Creating and living in the world of Clover City has been an honor and I've been able to do so for three books because of you, my dear readers. Thank you for finding a place in your heart for Willowdean, Millie, Waylon, and the whole gang. From the bottom of my heart, thank you. I love you. Go big or go home.

**TURN THE PAGE TO START READING
THE FIRST BOOK IN
JULIE MURPHY'S FAITH SERIES**

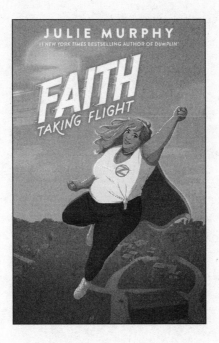

 *PROLOGUE*

THREE MONTHS AGO

It was supposed to be an epic summer. It would be my last summer with Matt and Ches before our senior year and we had big plans—the kinds of plans that involved a whole lot of nothing. Like racing to eat snow cones before they melted down our arms and floating in Matt's neighborhood pool until our skin wrinkled and curling up together by night to watch every episode of *Battlestar Galactica* followed by a marathon of our favorite episodes of *The Grove* (selected by yours truly).

All of that changed the day Matt and Ches showed up at my house during our first full week of summer break and broke the news that Matt would be spending most of the summer with his grandmother in Georgia. Not only that, but Ches would be joining him.

"I won't go if you don't want me to," Ches had said to me apologetically.

But I couldn't blame her. Matt's grandma had a soft spot for Ches, who'd never even left the state of Minnesota. I was sad and felt left out, but I couldn't blame her. Matt felt bad too, but his grandmother's retirement community only allowed her to host two people at once.

The first few weeks without them were fine. I'd fallen deep down the rabbit hole of *Kingdom Keeper*, a new multiplayer online role-playing game. I'd tried but failed to get Matt and Ches into it, so that we could play from afar, but they were busy exploring Atlanta. At least they sent me selfies from their adventures at the aquarium and the Coca-Cola museum. Besides, there were plenty of other people to play with in *Kingdom Keeper*, and putting yourself out there is a heck of a lot easier when you're an avatar.

One night, a private message popped up on my screen from an orc who went by Sting.

STING: Hey, you're in the Midwest, right?

A few of us had organized into different regional groups with the hopes of doing some meet-ups. Sting knowing I was from the Midwest was the least alarming thing about him. (Trust me. You should have seen his victory dance. It involved thrusting. Lots of thrusting.)

YOUGOTTAHAVEFAITH: Yeah. The land of cheese and malls.

STING: Cool. A bunch of us are meeting up at Mall of America on Friday. You should go!

I wish I could say I took the time to consider all the reasons why meeting a stranger from the internet was a less-than-stellar idea, but I missed my best friends desperately. Besides, we were meeting at a mall. What could possibly go wrong?

YOUGOTTAHAVEFAITH: Count me in!

Grandma Lou dropped me off since she needed the car, and I headed straight to Nickelodeon Universe, where I was supposed to meet the whole group. Sting said he expected at least fifteen or twenty people. I loved Matt and Ches, but the idea that I could make my own friends separate from them excited me in a way that now riddles me with guilt. What if I'd just stayed home? But I was so lonely without them.

There was only one person waiting for me that day. Sting. A white guy with mussed brown hair and a square jaw. Jeans, a black T-shirt, and a black baseball cap. He was definitely too old to be in high school, but I could imagine him in college. Okay, well, maybe grad school.

"YouGottaHaveFaith?" he asked, a charming smile playing on his lips. "I thought it might be only me."

"No one else came?" I asked, my stomach plummeting. I was basically one second away from starring in an episode of *To Catch a Predator.*

He smirked, appearing suddenly boyish. "Just me and you. I guess that's what I get for trying to make new friends."

I could kick myself for how gullible I was, but that little

response set me at ease. "I know the feeling." Extending my hand, I added, "You can call me Faith."

He chuckled. "Pleased to make your acquaintance, Faith. It's Sting . . . from *Kingdom Keeper*. You can call me Peter."

Peter and I spent the whole day together, riding roller coasters, eating pretzels, and playing with all the different gadgets in the types of stores people rush to for Father's Day. At the end of the day, when it was nearly time for Grandma Lou to pick me up, Peter and I took one last turn at the pretzel place.

"I think you might be special, Faith," he said. "Have you ever felt like you were special?"

I snorted. "Uh, definitely not."

He shook his head, and I could swear he blushed a little. "No, I mean, don't you ever wonder if your whole life is a TV show and you're the star?"

I gulped down my orange soda, not sure how to respond, because, yes, of course, I'd had that very same thought, but how could I even admit to that? I'd sound nuts, plus this was quite possibly the cutest guy who'd ever given me the time of day. But there he was, putting himself out there. It only felt fair to do the same.

"I know exactly what you mean. Do you want to hear something really weird, though?"

He tore off a piece of the cinnamon sugar pretzel we were sharing. "Oh, yeah. Lay it on me. I'm the king of weird."

"So my parents died when I was a kid. Both of them. In the same car accident."

"Oh, Faith—"

"It's okay, it's okay. That's not what this is about. Well, it is. Kind of. Anyway, sometimes I wonder if them dying was part of some bigger thing. Every superhero and character I've ever loved had to go through some awful thing to achieve greatness. What if that was my awful thing?" I sighed, feeling guilty about how self-centered I knew I sounded. My parents didn't live and die just so I could be a superhero or something ridiculous like that. "Some days," I say, "that was the only way I could get past it all, pretending that their death was part of some bigger picture. But it wasn't. They're just dead. Gone. Forever. No higher—"

"Faith." He looked straight at me, unflinching. In a matter of moments, he'd become someone or something else completely. There was nothing boyish about him anymore. "What if I told you there was a way to find out? A way to get the answer to every question you'd ever asked? Maybe your parents' death was for a higher purpose."

"But—how could—"

"There's only one way to find out. I've been through some shit, Faith, okay? I'm not perfect." He zoned out for a second, concentrating on his hands before shaking his head. "Hell, I don't even know that I'm good, but sometimes the only way I can cope with it all is to know that everything I've done and everything that's happened to me has brought me to this point." He shook his head, and for the first time I felt like maybe I was getting a glimpse of the real Peter and not the guy who was trying to be on his best behavior or feeding me some line I'd want to hear.

After a moment, Peter looked me right in the eye. "I know I haven't given you a lot of reasons to trust me. As far as you know, I'm just some rando from the internet, but Faith, I need you to know that I've felt lost like you do and sometimes I still feel lost. What I'm offering isn't a magic pill. But I think there's something special about you, and I think you might have the kind of potential you can't even begin to imagine."

I felt like he was dancing around the real question here. "I don't quite understand what exactly it is you're saying."

He must have seen the skepticism on my face, because he added, "Your parents were great people, Faith. I believe that every moment in our lives serves a purpose, and maybe everything in your life has led you here to this moment. I don't know for sure, but I bet Jack and Caroline would agree."

"How do you—"

"We know everything about you, Faith. We've chosen you for a reason," he said with absolute certainty.

Part of me was unnerved by him knowing my parents' names, and the other part of me just wanted to know how.

"Just say it. Just tell me what exactly it is you're talking about."

He scooted to the edge of his chair, so that his voice could be the quietest whisper in the midst of the chaotic food court. "Superhuman abilities, Faith."

Everything around me silenced until there was nothing left in the entire mall except for me and Peter.

I felt like a bird that had just flown straight into a glass window. "Wait. Are you telling me superheroes are . . . real?"

Peter grimaced. "I wouldn't exactly call us superheroes. I don't think you could really use the word 'heroic' to describe the people I work for," he scoffed.

"Wait. Go back. You're saying superheroes are real and you think I might be one?"

He glanced from side to side and then finally shrugged. "Well, sort of. Yeah, I guess that's what I'm saying."

"Sign me the heck up." I didn't know if I could trust him or if I even should, but I knew one thing: I'd do anything for answers. The logical part of my brain told me this guy was a creep and that I should run, but I couldn't help but think back to every movie, television show, and comic book I'd ever loved. Peter could lead me to my Giles or Professor X or Gandalf or Nick Fury or Dumbledore.

"There's no guarantee, Faith, and there are possible side effects. You'd also have to find a way to leave home for the rest of the summer, but we've got a solid cover for you. We do think you have the potential to be someone very special. We think you could be a psiot."

"A psiot?" I asked. "What even is that?"

"Psiots are people gifted with superhuman abilities. We think your abilities are dormant inside of you. Potential waiting to be unlocked, and my organization has the keys."

"Just freaking say superheroes!" Despite his aversion to the superhero label, the flashing neon sign in my head read *SUPERHERO*. You, Faith Herbert, could be a superhero. Grandma Lou says I believe in too many things, but I can't help but think life is a little more fun that way. And if superheroes were real, then maybe my whole life had prepared me for this moment. Maybe the massive collection of comics my parents left behind was more than a reminder of what was. Maybe those comics—some of my most prized possessions—were meant to be the ultimate guidebook.

Peter sent me home with everything I would need. Permission slips, camp brochures, and emergency contact information for Grandma Lou. I'd only be gone for a few weeks, and he swore I'd be perfectly safe. He'd gone through the same program, he said. And look at him! He was fine! Normal even!

"So this is basically like superhero camp?" I asked.

"Sort of. Fewer canoes. Definitely no campfire songs." He dropped a hand on my shoulder. "See you on Monday, kid."

The next Monday, Grandma Lou dropped me off in the school parking lot, where a bus waited for me along with Peter, dark bags under his eyes and much less boyish than I remembered, in a Camp Pleasant Oaks Staff T-shirt. Grandma Lou stuffed some cash into my pockets and gave me a tight hug before sending me on my way.

"You're sure about this?" Peter asked quietly as I boarded the bus, his easy confidence from just days ago beginning to waver.

I nodded with absolute certainty.

As I sat on the bus, with a handful of other kids my age who I didn't recognize, eager nerves ate away at me. The small Asian girl who sat beside me, freckles spread across the bridge of her nose, leaned in and whispered, "Can you believe how lucky we are? I always knew there was something different about me. My name's Lucia, by the way."

I smiled, too nervous to remember my own name, let alone introduce myself.

After hours on the bus, we drove into the heart of Chicago. I'd never been to Chicago, and if my nerves weren't eating me up, I'd have taken in the sights a little bit more. As the sun set across the glistening skyline, the bus turned down into a parking garage and into a giant freight elevator that took us deep underground, and my stomach immediately sank as dread slowly crept over me. This wasn't the camp of burgeoning superheroes I'd expected.

As we plummeted down, a few kids around me screamed, and beside me Lucia began to cry. Whatever we'd each been sold, this wasn't it.

When the elevator finally stopped and the door to the bus opened, a tall blond white guy who looked like an evil Ken doll on steroids trotted up the steps. "Everybody off the bus," he barked. "Line up in a single file. Welcome to the Harbinger Foundation."

Peter sneered at the man. "Better keep a lid on all that charisma. The new recruits might actually start to like you, Edward."

Outside the bus, Peter leaned against a headlight, while the evil Ken doll, Edward, paced back and forth. "You're here thanks to the goodwill of Toyo Harada. Follow me to your rooms, where you'll find your uniforms. Please leave your personal belongings here, to be collected and tagged," said Edward.

I had hope that this could still be a good thing. Maybe these people were just really serious about what they were doing. And shouldn't they be?

Edward led us down a long cement corridor through a door that required his thumbprint to open and into a hallway of rooms made entirely of glass, leaving very little privacy, with Peter on our heels. One by one we were assigned rooms with a bed, sink, and toilet behind a small partition.

"Faith Herbert?" Edward called. "Until further notice,

you will be referred to as the number embroidered on your uniform."

I walked into my room and the glass door slid shut behind me. I pressed my palms against the glass, trying to push it back, but I was locked in.

As Peter walked past me, he kept his gaze focused on the ground.

"Peter," I said, but he didn't look up. "Peter, I need to talk to you." I knocked on the glass, trying to get his attention, but he was gone and the group was on to the next room. I told myself that the rooms were soundproof and he probably didn't hear me, but I had a feeling that wasn't true.

Waiting for me on my bed was a pair of white pants and a white shirt with a *6-973* stitched to the front. I wasn't Faith Herbert. I was 6-973. I created a million different reasons for why anyone would treat us all like this, but every show, movie, and comic I'd ever read told me everything I needed to know. I'd been assigned a number. I'd been labeled. I was an experiment.

FROM *NEW YORK TIMES* BESTSELLING AUTHOR JULIE MURPHY!

Meet FAITH,
the fan-favorite superhero
from Valiant Comics

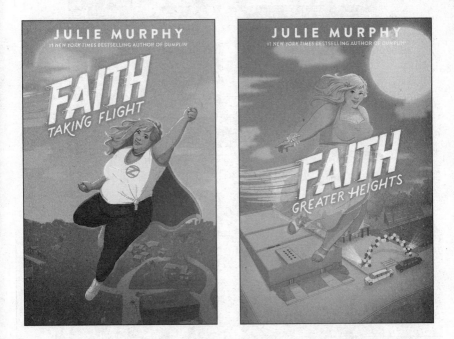

An origin story like you've never read before!

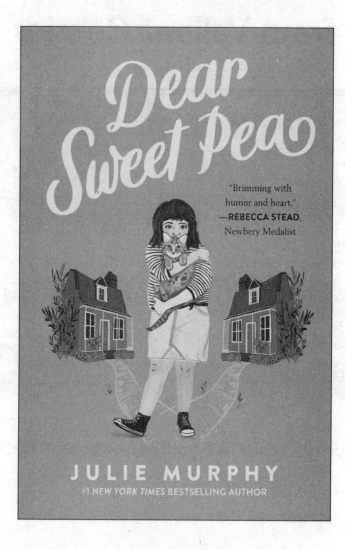